Also by Nicole Helm

Cowboy SEAL Redemption

NICOLE HELM

sourcebooks
casablanca

Published by Sourcebooks Casablanca, an imprint of Sourcebooks, Inc.
P.O. Box 4410, Naperville, Illinois 60567-4410
(630) 961-3900
Fax: (630) 961-2168
sourcebooks.com

Printed and bound in the United States of America.
OPM 10 9 8 7 6 5 4 3 2 1

*For Megan & Maisey and farmhouses
in the middle of nowhere.*

Chapter 1

JACK ARMSTRONG STOOD OUTSIDE THE STABLES OF Revival Ranch almost wishing he were back in a war zone. He knew how to go about completing a mission.

He didn't know anything about talking to a therapist.

He didn't *have* to talk to her, of course. Gabe had reminded him of that at least ten times today. No one was pressuring him to take this step.

But here he was, and he couldn't even pinpoint a reason. Maybe it had something to do with the way his nightmares had started to include people from his civilian life—Mom and Dad, Becca and her goat. Those definitely ate at him more than nightmares that were distorted memories of a day over a year ago, and the friend he'd actually lost.

Maybe it was watching Alex, his former SEAL brother, put weight back on, come back into himself after making regular appointments with Monica. Alex had gotten together with Becca, the co-owner of their ranch and partner in their foundation, and infused a lightness into their little world that hadn't been there for a very long time.

Or maybe he was just in a rut. Summer equaled plenty of work around the ranch in general. Plus, they were putting the finishing touches on the bunkhouse that Alex, Gabe, and he would move into. At the end of the day, he was bone-deep weary and his injuries ached and ached.

But he couldn't sleep, and when he did, the nightmares often plagued him. He was tired. Exhausted. And if this was going to help…

Hell.

"If you're waiting for a welcome dance, I'm afraid I don't know the steps."

Jack tried to smile at Monica, Revival's on-site therapist. She'd appeared at the stable door, that kind smile on her face. Jack liked her enough as a person, and he really enjoyed her ten-year-old son, who helped around the ranch sometimes. But he'd been irritated this spring when Becca had announced she wanted an on-site therapist for their foundation. He wasn't sure he'd gotten over that irritation, but he'd learned to deal with Monica the person.

Neither of them were here as regular people right now though.

"What am I supposed to do, just…walk in?"

Monica made a grand gesture. "Simple as that. Walk in. Grab a brush. I told Becca and Alex we'd handle the horse grooming this afternoon."

Even though Alex had told Jack a little about how his sessions went, Jack still had this prevalent idea in his head of a couch in a corner and a shrink with a notebook. But Monica went straight to the horses they'd all used out on the ranch earlier in the day and got to work with grooming.

Jack could only follow suit. He grabbed the bucket of tools for his horse and started the tasks he'd learned only this spring. He may have grown up on a farm, but they'd never had horses.

Jack eyed Monica suspiciously, but she didn't talk. She didn't study him. She was doing nothing he expected a therapist to do. Her focus was all on grooming Becca's horse, Pal.

"So, aren't you going to ask me questions?"

"What kind of questions?"

Jack frowned. "I don't know. About whatever we're supposed to talk about."

"Well, what would you like to talk about?"

"I don't know," he replied, wholly baffled. "Whatever I'm supposed to talk about."

"There aren't any supposed-tos, Jack."

"Then how are you going to fix me?"

She raised her eyebrows at him over the back of the horse. "I can't fix your PTSD."

"Then why am I here?" he demanded, exasperation winning out over his confusion.

Monica took a few seconds of silence, as though she was considering the answer, but shouldn't she have known? Wasn't it her job to know?

"My job isn't to be your life coach. It's to listen to whatever you want to say or have to say. It's to offer coping mechanisms if you're having a particular issue, and it's to maybe try to guide you a bit to your own epiphanies. But they have to be yours—your choices, your feelings. I can't map them out for you."

"That's crap."

She laughed good-naturedly. "Perhaps. But it's working for Alex. So why don't you tell me what changed your mind about this?" She waved a hand to encompass the stables. "You didn't want me here."

Jack scowled and focused on his horse. He hadn't wanted Monica, or any therapist, here. Hadn't thought it necessary. Sometimes, he still didn't.

Then he remembered the bone-deep fear of watching Alex fall apart. Alex, their leader, a guy Jack had hero-worshipped in the beginning of his SEAL career, who'd devised this plan for them after the attack that had gotten them all removed from military life.

Even though the past few months had shown Alex getting better, Jack was still haunted by how gaunt and lost Alex had been.

Jack didn't feel that bad off, but he knew he wasn't right. He knew at some point he needed to find a purpose because, with each passing day, he felt like he had less and less of one.

"Alex is better," Jack said, staring hard at the horse's flank.

"He is. And you'd like to be?"

Jack ran the brush over his horse, focusing on the animal's hair. "Yes." He'd like to be, though he wasn't sure he was ready for the work it would take to become better. Didn't that take a certain amount of acceptance? He didn't think he had acceptance in him. Not the driving force kind that Alex had found anyway.

"The first step is realizing it's not a fix or a switch I can flip. Getting better is a process, and it's not going to be comfortable or happen overnight. It's hard, grueling work."

"I was a Navy SEAL."

"You were, and now you're not."

———

After a few weeks of sessions, no matter that they'd touched on a great many things—his military service, his childhood, his hopes for Revival—the words "you were, and now you're not" repeated over and over in his head like a loop.

He felt worse after having talked to Monica a few times now, and that pissed him off, because he was supposed to be better.

He stalked across the yard from stables to house after another session, grumpy as hell and not in any mood to talk to Alex or Gabe, but they were both on the porch as if waiting for him.

"How's it going?" Alex asked, leaning against the railing, failing at casual.

Jack merely grunted and shrugged. He hated that they both waited after every session and asked if he was okay, if things were okay. He wanted to pretend he'd never been so stupid as to think therapy could fix him.

But he still went to every session, and he still went to where Alex and Gabe were waiting after each one.

"It's not easy. Nothing important ever is. Think of it like BUD/S training," Alex offered with the kind of straightforward pragmatism Jack couldn't help but appreciate, said in a sympathetic tone Jack wanted to burn to the ground.

Jack grimaced. "I hated BUD/S training."

"Exactly."

Jack didn't know why that soothed some of the jagged edges, but it did. Not all of them certainly, but at least some. "Pioneer Spirit?"

"Uh, well, Becca's mom is coming over for dinner."

"Say no more. We're out of here," Gabe said, jumping to his feet from his seat on a porch chair, at least in part for comic effect.

"And I wanted to let you guys know, whenever you're ready, you can move into the bunkhouse."

Gabe raised an eyebrow at Alex. "We? As in not you."

"I'm staying put," Alex said in that tone that brooked no argument.

Not that Jack or Gabe would argue, and Jack supposed it wasn't a surprise. Alex and Becca had been hot and heavy for a while, even more so since Alex had gotten some help. It made sense.

It still felt…weird.

"We'll meet you at Pioneer Spirit later though. Becca and I." Alex shoved his hands in his pockets, rocking back on his heels. "So don't get drunk before we get there, huh? It wouldn't kill either of you to lighten up on that score."

Gabe gave him a mock salute, and Jack tried to smile. He and Gabe had been spending a lot of time at the bar in town lately, but…well, Alex didn't get to boss them around anymore. Especially if he was staying in the main house, while Jack and Gabe moved out to the bunkhouse.

"I better help Becca with dinner," Alex said absently. "See you guys later." He disappeared inside.

"He seem weird to you?" Gabe asked, frowning at the door.

Jack shrugged. "Not particularly. You ready?"

Gabe slung his arm over Jack's shoulders. "I am always, always ready to drink my troubles away."

"And I will always, always drink to that."

Rose Rogers surveyed her kingdom: a dimly lit bar sparsely populated by old ranchers and young drunks with Hank Williams Jr. rasping from the jukebox that played mainly country classics.

For three years, Pioneer Spirit had been all hers, and it had yet to get old. For a little girl who'd grown up like she had, owning something, running something, was quite the coup, no matter that it was a run-down townie bar in the middle of nowhere Montana.

She didn't dare take any of it for granted, because it was miles better than anything that had come before.

Which was why she needed to figure something out to protect this. Her father being out of jail put too many question marks in the air. He'd always been a cruel man, but would he be a vindictive one? Would he have the opportunity?

She scowled. She wouldn't give him the opportunity to hurt what or who she loved again. So she needed to find a way to neutralize the potential threat and not wince every time her bar door swung open.

But wince she did, every single time. This time, as every other time before, it wasn't her father. Instead, Jack So-and-So and Gabe Such-and-Such marched in. The two men had become something like fixtures in her bar this summer, and she'd gleaned a thing or two about both from serving them and maybe, on one or two occasions, being a little charmed by them.

Hard not to be charmed, since she didn't know men like them. Their little trio, because Alex Maguire often joined their group as well, had never once sexually harassed her or any of her waitresses, and they'd never gotten in a fight or damaged property.

Not once. They seemed to live up to the fictional idea of honorable military men, and on top of all that, they were building some charitable foundation at the Maguire ranch.

Rose kept waiting for one of them to turn out to be a turd, but they were unfailingly polite, excellent tippers, and sometimes even made her laugh or become interested in their stories—very much against her will.

Gabe was a flirt, but it wasn't that kind of persistent attention she usually nipped in the bud. It was friendlier, somehow. Maybe because he was never handsy, never pushy. Just flirtatious comments whenever she came around. He was also a very equal-opportunity flirt. Any woman who'd ever been in her bar had been charmed by Gabe Cortez, including a few elderly ladies who'd been left blushing.

God help the woman who fell for that mess. Either mess, really. Because both Jack and Gabe clearly had a whole lot of mess underneath their polite, friendly facades. Gabe masked it with smiles and flirtation, and Jack masked it with…well, a stoicism Rose admired.

Until he got drunk. Then she'd catch little glimpses of a guy with a sense of humor. Honestly, if she hadn't spent the past few years watching her sister's husband prove to be an upstanding guy, she'd think they were both serial killers, but she'd finally accepted that not all men were her father.

Even if most were rotten.

Still, Rose couldn't say she minded these two decorating her bar stools. Handsome to a T, the lot of them. Jack and Gabe were like two sides of the same Navy SEAL coin. One tall, dark, and too handsome for his own good, the other Mr. All-American fair-haired fighter for justice. With a limp.

She wasn't sure if it was the limp or the stoicism that got to her the most, but Jack was a bit of a problem. In that, if he didn't show up on his normal nights, she wondered why. In that she often caught herself watching him when he was in the bar.

One time, he'd gotten really drunk and told her an elaborate story about cow tipping. She'd believed it, hook, line, and sinker, and she never believed liars. But he'd laughed hysterically when he'd realized he'd fooled her.

She'd been pissed for weeks, but ever since, she'd known there was just something different about Jack whatever his last name was.

Someone like her had no business finding him intriguing. She was rotten to the core, snarky and mean at whim, and he was the kind of guy who said *please* and *thank you* and had sacrificed life and limb for his country.

Maybe that's why she was fascinated. Besides, it was a nice little fantasy. The big, strong military man who would protect her from any harm.

Silly, foolish, and utterly untrue, but irresistible nonetheless considering, a few years ago, she wouldn't have even been able to fantasize about such a thing.

"You want those two?" Tonya asked, nodding toward Jack and Gabe as she poured cheap whiskey for a group of ranch hands.

She wanted one of them anyway. "You take them." Rose put two bottles of beer onto a tray and nudged it toward her waitress.

Tonya slid the whiskeys to the man waiting to take them to his friends. "I'm just going to put their tips in the tip jar, so if you're doing that out of charity—"

"Charity doesn't exist here," Rose replied, flashing a menacing smile. Tonya's husband had been hurt in a ranching accident, and they were struggling to make ends meet. She was a good bartender, would make a good manager if Rose could ever back off a little without feeling panicked. Rose would make sure Tonya took all the tips at the end of the night regardless.

Tonya grumbled, but she hefted the tray to take to Gabe and Jack. Rose watched her go. Gabe and Jack smiled politely at Tonya, and she laughed at something Gabe said. Rose couldn't hear it from where she stood, but it was likely a marriage proposal. Gabe threw those out like candy.

Her gaze fell to Jack, and for a second, she allowed herself the happy pleasure of just staring at his face. A classic handsome, really—what might have been wholesomeness if not for the beard and the haunted blue eyes.

Blue eyes that were now staring straight at her. She flashed him a grin, and he lifted his bottle in a little salute.

Sometimes she really considering corrupting Jack the Navy SEAL—at least a little bit.

The sound of the door opening, just a faint squeak under the din of the bar, eradicated that consideration in an instant. She flinched, her gaze immediately moving from Jack to the door.

But it wasn't her father standing there. And what would she do if it turned out to be? She rubbed the knife she carried in a little hidden holster on her belt. She kept a revolver behind the bar in case of emergencies. She could protect herself against her father.

And still fear had sprouted like a weed since hearing

he'd been released. That old, shaky fear, those old, defeatist thoughts.

She took a deep breath. She'd gotten this far. Nothing would get in her way again. She'd protect everything she held dear no matter the cost, and she wouldn't allow herself the luxury of falling for any fantasies.

Girls like her didn't get the happy ending, but she'd make sure she was safeguarding her sisters one way or another.

She glanced back at Jack, who was still staring at her, a puzzled frown on his face.

"Not for you," she muttered to herself, and got back to work.

Chapter 2

JACK HAD DOWNED HIS THIRD BEER BEFORE HE considered the fact that Alex had asked them not to get drunk before he and Becca showed. Gabe was two ahead of him, and Jack had no doubt Alex's comment about laying off had only spurred Gabe to do the opposite.

Contrary asshole. Jack nearly smiled.

"Another round of Buds for you gentlemen," Rose Rogers said, setting two bottles in front of Jack and Gabe.

"Marry me," Gabe said, clasping his hands together in a pleading gesture.

"Sorry. I only entertain marriage proposals before the first drink. Stay sober next time, cowboy."

Gabe settled his Stetson on his head with a grin. "I really do look the part, don't I?"

Rose rolled her eyes and moved her shrewd gaze to Jack. He only knew a few things about Rose Rogers: she owned Pioneer Spirit, never seemed to be anywhere but behind the gleaming slab of wood, and kept him and Gabe well served because they were good tippers.

But there was something about her dark eyes that always tempted him to wonder about the smart-mouthed, tattooed bar owner.

And he'd always remind himself what *wondering* about the opposite sex got a guy and move on.

Except tonight she was different. She was on edge, maybe even a little… *Afraid* wasn't the right word. Jack couldn't imagine Rose *afraid*, but there was definitely a worry written all over her face for about a second every time the door opened.

"You boys got a sober driver?"

"Alex and Becca are meeting us here later."

Rose nodded. "Then I'll keep them coming."

"No more for me," Jack said, trying for offhanded. Both Gabe and Rose looked at him with a kind of wide-eyed surprise. While he was also an asshole, he wasn't a contrary one like Gabe. More, Gabe's drinking was starting to concern him, and Jack knew the only way he had a leg to stand on when it came to helping his friend was to get his own crap under control first.

His phone chose that moment to chime, the tone he'd set for his mother, and he stopped caring about anyone's drinking. "On second thought, bring me two next time."

Rose nodded and sauntered down the bar to her next customer, and Jack stared at his phone.

"Your mom again?"

"Yup."

"She's not giving up."

"Nope." Jack sighed as the chiming stopped. No doubt Mom would leave a message. Again.

When his phone rang again rather than making the voicemail sound, Jack downed his beer. He knew his mother well enough to know, if she wasn't leaving messages anymore, she'd just keep calling until he gave in. Might as well take the call here and now. "I'll be back," he said, sliding off the barstool.

"You sure you want to talk to your mom when you're drunk?"

Jack grabbed Gabe's fresh beer and downed that too.

"Only half-drunk and wishing I was a hell of a lot further gone for this conversation." He slapped the bottle down and hit Accept on his phone, moving through the back hallway so he could get away from the noise of the jukebox.

"Hey, Mom."

"Well, *finally*. Do I have to full name you, young man?"

Jack smiled as he stepped out of the back door of the bar. The parking lot was lit only by a small light above the door. Otherwise, the summer night was dark.

In the dark, with a couple of beers in his system, he could miss his mother and hate that this was the way things were.

"Maybe. How are you, Mom?"

"Angry with my oldest son."

"So same old, same old."

Mom chuckled. "Now, if you had answered on my first call, I would have phrased this as a very polite question, but as you've been avoiding my calls for a *week*—"

"I texted."

"Coward that you are," Mom joked, and then there was that horrible, awkward silence where he knew she regretted her choice of words. Because Mom or not, you didn't call a former Navy SEAL who'd survived a close-range grenade blast a coward.

"We're coming to visit," Mom said firmly. "Which you'll note is not a question but a point of fact," she added, her tone back to the breezy, take-no-lip tone he remembered from his childhood. A million years ago, when he'd been young and dumb and so ridiculously sheltered from the cruelties of people. He'd been well acquainted with the cruelties of Mother Nature, of banks, even of God. But never people.

"Jack?"

He walked farther into the dark, cool Montana night and tried to anchor himself in the present. Even if it was a present he didn't know how to navigate, it was better than the past he didn't know how to leave behind. "I'd love for you and Dad to visit," Jack forced himself to say. "Montana is beautiful. I'm sure you'll love it. But who'll watch the farm?"

"You let us worry about that. We all miss you. Sarah can't come, but the rest of us all are."

"The rest of you," Jack echoed, the effect those words had reminding him a little too much of that grenade blast over a year ago. The landing, the horrible second of stillness before everything exploded into excruciating pain and the certainty he was dead.

Well, it wasn't that bad. Nothing was that bad. And he'd survived that, hadn't he?

"Yes!" Mom said overly brightly. As if she could simply *will* the rift in their family back together. "Your dad rented one of those RVs, and it'll be a nice trip. You haven't met your nephew yet."

His nephew. Yeah. He hadn't. Nor did he want to. It wasn't the kid's fault how he'd gotten here, but that didn't mean Jack felt anything other than...

Well.

"It's been so long, Jack," Mom said, her voice getting that scratchy quality that always got the guilt pooling in his gut. The situation wasn't Mom or Dad's fault, but...

"Mom." He didn't know how to respond. Breathe.

This was too much. All of them coming here to his sanctuary, invading it as if they *all* were welcome. He clutched the cell in his hand a little too tight—so tight he wasn't sure he'd be able to unclench it once this nightmare conversation was over.

"Yo, Jack. I need your help."

Jack looked in confusion at the woman calling his name from across the parking lot. Rose was standing by the door in the little pool of light, hands on her hips, looking badass and hell bound as always.

He couldn't fathom why Rose would need his help.

"Who's that? Was that a woman?" Mom asked.

"Um. That was Rose."

"Rose. Who's Rose?"

"Well, no—"

"Madison was so worried you hadn't moved on yet and that this trip would be too difficult for you, but you have a Rose!"

Jack scowled. Madison thought he hadn't moved on? All that confusion and pain swirled into something much darker. Anger. Fury. Revenge.

"Yeah. I have a Rose. She's great, and she needs my help. I'll call you later to work out the details." With that, he hit End and stared at the woman who'd just unknowingly saved him.

—◊◊◊—

Rose surveyed the somewhat drunk and very angry man in her parking lot. She supposed some women would be scared in this position, but some women didn't carry weapons concealed in their clothes, and some women hadn't grown up like she had.

Jack might be drunk and angry, but compared to some, he was a pussycat.

A really hot pussycat. She sighed. He was standing out there, somehow looking like a broken heart in human form. The kind of frozen horror she knew too well. Just like she knew she shouldn't get involved but had opened her big mouth anyway.

"What'd you need help with?" he asked, his voice a dark, delicious rasp.

You are not looking for delicious, Rose Rogers. Not from Mr. Boy Scout. "Looked like a shitty phone call," she offered with a shrug. "And I'm a Good Samaritan. At least to customers who tip as well as you do."

He crossed the lot then, mostly shrouded in dark until he got a few feet from the door. "Thanks," he offered.

Which should have been the end of it. "Well, I was taking the trash out if you want to give me a hand." *Why are you helping him? You do not help.*

"Sure."

Which was not the answer she'd expected. In her experience, men were quite happy to take favors and not so happy to offer them. But she was hardly one to look a gift man in the mouth.

She pulled the two bags of trash to the door. He didn't hesitate or even only take one—he grabbed both heavy bags and walked to the Dumpster out back.

With that limp.

Operating a townie bar in the middle of Montana ranching country meant she'd learned a lot about the fragility of the male ego. And since not every guy fixed a bruised ego by beating the shit out of his kids, she'd learned to have a little empathy.

She didn't need to be a mind reader to know a man like Jack wouldn't want anyone rushing over to grab the trash from him because he had a limp. A limp he'd probably earned doing something suitably badass and Navy SEAL-y, saving the country for good and right.

But that didn't mean she could just *let* him heft her trash either. She did her best to follow Jack at a leisurely pace, to act like it was no big deal to grab one of the bags to heft into the Dumpster before he did both. And she quickly focused the subject on something that wouldn't have a thing to do with his limp.

"So, what kind of phone call does a guy take in the back parking lot of a bar?"

Jack dropped his bag and the Dumpster lid. "The kind you've been avoiding for a week."

"Paternity test gone wrong?"

He gave her an odd look, because of course this guy wouldn't be on the receiving end of a surprise paternity test or any other seedy thing. Of the three former SEALs, Jack was the least likely to do any sort of line crossing. Alex was quite the do-gooder leader of the group, but he had an edge to him. Gabe flirted with anything that moved, but Jack…

Jack was polite, respectful. A lot stoic, which only faded occasionally when he was very drunk. He didn't flirt, and he was kind.

She didn't understand kindness. Some stupid part of her wanted to.

"My mother," he offered in that same gravelly tone that had her mind drifting to a slew of seedy things she could show him.

Except he'd been talking to his *mother*. "Oh, well, sure. That's something I'd just keep avoiding too."

"She's coming to visit. Well, my family is."

"And that's bad?" Which was not only not her business, but she also didn't care. In the wide, crazy world of family troubles, things didn't get much worse than what she'd survived. Still, she'd asked, and she needed to get ahold of that stupid instinct to want to help.

An upstanding, strong, stoic man like Jack hardly needed help from *her*.

"It's complicated." He studied her, closing one eye and then the other in that way he always did when he was drunk enough to be philosophical but not drunk enough to turn into Mr. Comedian. The cool, pale blue of his eyes popped even in the dark of a summer night. "How would you feel about pretending to be my girlfriend when my family comes to visit?"

Rose threw her head back and laughed. As if the word *girlfriend* would ever adequately apply to someone as rough and damaged as her, pretend or otherwise. Especially when family was involved. But Jack wasn't laughing at her. He was studying her.

She stopped laughing. "Oh my God, you're serious."

Jack shrugged. "It's either that or I ask my therapist, and I have a feeling she'd find that problematic."

Rose blinked at him. Therapist. Fake girlfriend. Likely a little drunk.

Yeah, Jack wasn't a threatening or mean guy, but he was also a *large* guy. Strong. Intimidating if he wanted to be. She'd heard Gabe brag to one of her other bartenders about their days as SEALs. Even if most of Gabe's talk was crap, you couldn't get by in the Navy SEALs being a wuss.

And she very much needed a little show of power

with everything going on right now. This…well, this was the opportunity to employ a little of that without having to be beholden to anyone, and that was something to consider.

"What do you need a fake girlfriend for?" she asked, walking with him to the back entrance of her bar. She watched his profile harden until he no longer looked like just any drunk, angry guy.

She didn't know the first thing about military stuff, but she could see the soldier in him now, all ramrod tension and a kind of focused fury.

"I need to prove a point," he said, his voice devoid of any emotion, keeping that intense gaze of his on the door.

She pulled the door open, the dim hallway light spilling over his face. He'd been coming to her bar for a few months now, and he'd gotten shaggier and a little hollowed out as time went on. But his already-golden hair—a pinch too long for a military man—had lightened in the sun, the same way the sickly pallor she'd first seen on him had warmed into a sun-kissed glow. He clearly hadn't shaved in a few weeks.

There was something about all of that, added to his troubled blue eyes and the smile that never seemed to reach them that had Rose far too interested in what point Mr. Soldier might need to prove.

But this wasn't about *him*. It was about her. From here on out, her life was supposed to be about *her*. "I've got one condition for you, soldier."

"Technically, I was a Navy SEAL, so it'd be sailor."

She would not let those little flashes of humor get to her. This was no great favor. She was going to use

Jack for her own purposes, and because she was a decent human being, she'd give him something in return.

Tit for tat. Minus anything to do with her tits. *Remember that.*

"Sailor. I like that even better. Okay, so here's the deal. I'll play whatever little game you've got going on, and you do me a favor a few nights a week at the bar."

"What kind of favor?"

"You play bouncer for me. There's been a guy…" She had to figure out a way to frame her request so it didn't seem like it had something to do with her. Luckily, Rose had always been quick on her feet. "He's harassing one of my bartenders, and she doesn't want to get the police involved, but she's jumpy. All I need is for you to watch the door for the guy on Friday and Saturday nights when I can't keep an eye on it myself."

"And for something as simple as that, you'll pretend to be my girlfriend?"

"Oh, Jacky boy, nothing's ever as simple as that." Nothing. Ever. She held out her hand. "Do we have a deal?"

He stared at her outstretched hand for a long time before he finally reached out and shook it. His hand was large and his palm rough as it slid against hers. He gripped her hand tight.

"Deal," he said firmly. It seemed as though everything about him was firm. Strong. Endlessly fascinating.

Rose grinned and pretended the flutters in her stomach didn't exist.

Chapter 3

JACK RETURNED TO HIS STOOL AT THE BAR, BUT HE didn't touch another beer. As much as he *wanted* to get blackout drunk and forget the conversation he'd had with his mother, it wouldn't change what awaited him.

He watched Rose while he pretended to listen to Gabe try to make some case for the Yankees' crap bullpen. What he thought he'd known about Rose didn't seem to fit into the interaction they'd had outside.

She ran her bar like an old, snarly navy captain might run a ship. She was quick, efficient, and mostly mean. Her smile had always reminded him of a blade, and that was something he'd never seen in a woman.

She hadn't been all sharp outside in the dark though. And while she'd only agreed to his plan in return for a favor of her own, it wasn't actually *for* her. It was for the safety of one of her bartenders instead.

There was a lot he didn't understand about life since he'd returned to the civilian side of things, so he supposed Rose Rogers was just another thing to add to the list.

"Finally," Gabe muttered, gesturing toward the door. "The dynamic duo has appeared. Looking happy enough to make me puke, per usual."

Jack glanced at the front doors. Alex and Becca walked toward them, Becca's arm wrapped around Alex's waist and Alex's arm slung across her shoulders.

Usually if Becca and Alex were around each other, they were grinning—or trying hard not to grin. There was something a little different about the jovial looks on their faces this evening though.

"Hey, guys," Becca greeted, her cheeks pink and her eyes a little red as if she'd been crying. Which was weird.

"What's up with the two of you?" Gabe asked, studying them suspiciously.

Becca looked up at Alex, who gave her a little nod, and then she was waving her hand in front of both his and Gabe's faces.

Jack was a little too well acquainted with this whole process. Even though it had been years ago—years and years ago—he could remember Madison doing the same thing when he'd awkwardly shoved a ring on her finger.

She'd waved that sad, little stone in all their friends' faces as if it were something meaningful and important instead of a promise she'd inevitably smash to bits.

"We're getting married!" Becca said excitedly.

Jack *knew* he was supposed to be happy for them, but there was something dark and sharp in his chest that hadn't yet allowed that knowledge to move on to become actual feeling.

Jealousy, if he had to name it. That was supposed to have been *his* life. With Madison. And she was living it with his brother, working on the family farm and everything. Their kid. His family.

And he was here. Half a country away from home. Stuck in this empty, blank space.

"Are you going to congratulate us?" Becca asked, her eyebrows furrowing, that little dent of worry settling itself in her forehead.

It was a look Jack never wanted to be on the receiving end of, especially not *now*. So he moved first, which was a bit of a surprise to him and probably everyone involved.

"Congratulations," Jack said sincerely. Because he did mean it. He shook Alex's hand and gave Becca an awkward hug. Gabe followed suit, the congratulations and jokes about giving Becca a good-luck kiss paving over that long, uncomfortable silence that had come directly after their announcement.

"Let's get a drink. What would you consider celebratory, Bec?" Alex asked.

"Whiskey," she said. Alex and Becca exchanged some secret smile, and Alex went to the bar to order their whiskeys. Gabe pulled a chair over for Becca, smiling broadly and talking in that overly cheerful way he had when he was the opposite of cheerful.

Jack plastered the best smile he could manage on his face.

"So that's why you had your mother over for dinner and we weren't required to be there," Gabe said, taking a very, very long drink from his bottle directly after.

Becca smiled, a little blush in her cheeks. "Yeah, that was pretty much the thought behind it."

"How'd your mom take it?"

"She cried. I cried. In a good way, I think. I hope. It was mostly good." She glanced over at Alex, balancing four tumblers in his hands as he walked toward them. "I'm happy. That's what matters."

Alex put the glasses down and they each took one.

"How about a toast to the happy couple?" Gabe asked, lifting his glass in the air.

Becca held up her glass and smiled. "I think a toast to being happy would work."

"I'll drink to that," Alex said, clinking his glass to hers.

They all brought their glasses together, but it didn't escape Jack's notice that neither he nor Gabe echoed Becca's toast about happiness. Luckily, Alex and Becca were too lost in each other and the moment to catch on.

Which was for the best. Alex had found someone to bring him out of the dark place he'd been in since the accident, and *that* was worthy of celebration.

Rose approached and slid another round of whiskeys onto the table. "I hear congratulations are in order, so here's a round on the house. And a little goodwill to you all bringing more heavy tippers to Blue Valley in the near future," she said, referring to their plan to bring in more injured soldiers to work on Revival Ranch.

"Thanks, Rose," Becca said with a big grin.

"And for you." Rose turned to Jack and fished something out of her pocket. "My number," Rose said, slapping a Post-it into his palm. "You let anyone else see that and I'll personally make you wish you'd never been born." She trailed her fingers up his arm, while Gabe, Alex, and Becca stared at them openmouthed.

"See you later, sweetheart," she murmured, brushing her bright-red lips across Jack's cheek before sauntering away.

Jack stared down at the Post-it and then turned to watch her disappearing form.

What had that been about? Maybe she thought the point he needed to prove was to his friends, or maybe she just wanted to mess with Gabe or make Jack uncomfortable. With Rose, there was just no way to tell.

But no one had touched him like that in a very long time. Something intimate. Her lips brushing against the whiskers of his cheek. That had to be the cause of the vibration that ricocheted through him. Not necessarily Rose herself, but the absence of such a physical contact suddenly interrupted.

"You care to explain that one to us, buddy?" Gabe demanded, staring after Rose as well.

Jack cleared his throat and shoved the Post-it in his pocket. "It's nothing."

"She kissed you!" Becca said, her voice high pitched and maybe a little too delighted.

"She's just messing around," Jack grumbled, uncomfortable with all three of his friends' attention.

"I saw her almost break a guy's hand for trying to grab her *elbow*," Alex pointed out. "Whatever that was, it was a little more involved than messing around."

Jack took a long drink of his whiskey, not bothering to look at any of them. He focused on the sticky table underneath the glasses. "I just agreed to do her a favor is all."

"What kind of favor?" Becca asked. Her curiosity did nothing to ease the uncomfortable weight deep in his gut, nothing to erase the feeling that Rose's brief kiss had left a brand.

"She needs some help for the bar. Security. Just Friday and Saturday nights. She figured I'd be a good candidate. Former military and all."

"So why didn't she ask me?" Gabe demanded.

"I don't flirt with all her bartenders."

"Who knew it paid to be a humorless motherfucker?" Gabe grumbled.

Jack raised his glass and smiled. "Oh, it always pays to be a humorless motherfucker, my friend."

Gabe laughed and chucked a crumpled-up napkin at him. The subject change worked, and they spent the rest of the evening celebrating Alex and Becca.

If Jack caught himself following Rose's trajectory around the bar or reliving that short, inconsequential brush of her lips…well, no one had to know about it but him.

Rose had always loved summer. It had been the most freedom a girl like her had been allowed. She could escape. She could disappear. She could spend days outside, and no one would ever find her. Summer was a blessing even these days when she had nothing but freedom and power.

She drove her coughing and wheezing car up the slope to the Shaw ranch. It was gratifying to see the beautiful place slowly come to life, even though she had next to nothing to do with it.

In the two years since her sister had moved in and married Caleb Shaw, the pair of them had put their hearts and souls into transforming the place. Rose had watched it go from something hardscrabble and dreary to something bright and welcoming.

Which never failed to set Rose a little bit on edge. Bright and welcoming was something she still didn't know how to settle into.

The only comfort in that was that her sister had never known it either and was still thriving in this bright and welcoming life. Delia had always been the source of Rose's hope, even in those dark, dark years.

She swallowed. She would not allow those dark years to come back. Not under any circumstances. Which was why she needed to let Delia and Caleb know about what was going on, no matter how much she didn't want to. Them being blindsided would be worse.

So she was going to spend a nice evening with her sister and niece and the Shaws, and then talk to Caleb and Delia after Sunny had gone to bed. She was going to make sure they protected themselves. It wasn't a failure on her part that she couldn't protect them too.

It wasn't.

Rose drove the remainder of the path up to the Shaw house. Delia was sitting on the porch, the fading sunlight glinting against her dark hair. There was such a marked difference in her sister these days. No longer the sharp, fierce protector. She'd gotten a chance to settle in and build a family and a life that included plenty of food and shelter and love.

There was a deep, sharp pang Rose was beginning to have trouble fighting away. Jealousy, plain and simple, though Rose had no right to be jealous considering everything she'd done.

Rose forced herself to smile and look at this as what it was—visiting her niece, a girl who Rose loved with a fierceness only matched by the love she had for her sisters.

She'd made a lot of mistakes in her life, and she would never be the type of person her niece could want to be *like*. But she still wanted to be the kind of person that her niece could be proud of. She wanted Sunny to always know you could have nothing, you could be nothing, and you could still find strength and power.

Rose slid out of the car and waved, walking toward the porch stairs. Caleb stood in the yard, urging Sunny to let go of the toy horse she was holding on to and take a few steps toward him.

Rose opened her mouth to say something about putting too much pressure on a not-yet-one-year-old. Before Rose could get any words out, Sunny let go. A hush fell, as though everyone in the yard held their breath.

Rose was not an emotional person. She didn't cry ever.

So why watching her brother-in-law joyfully coach his little girl into her first steps made her eyes burn, Rose didn't know. But it was there, some horrible tide inside her that she couldn't fight or ignore. Her niece was taking her first steps, and her brother-in-law was the kind of man who would hold out his arms and scoop her up when she fell and kiss her face as though she was the most precious thing in the world to him.

Rose glanced at Delia and saw the same emotion she felt. The kind of raw feeling only little girls who'd grown up with cold, violent fathers and then somehow witnessed amazing ones could truly appreciate.

Rose did her best to swallow down the lump in her throat and get ahold of it all before she walked up the stairs to where Delia was sitting on the rocking chair on the porch, watching.

Apparently Delia had no compunction about showing her emotion, because the tears were trickling down her face. She sniffled and glanced at Rose with a rueful smile. "You came at the wrong moment if you want to avoid emotional crap."

"Damn."

Caleb was still in the yard, eagerly trying to get Sunny to walk a few more steps. His smile was so big, it nearly split his face and Rose didn't know what to say.

So instead of saying anything, she took a seat on the porch next to her sister, watched a really good guy be a really good dad, and tried to ignore any pangs that provided.

"I haven't told the other girls yet," Delia said quietly. "Girls" in this case meaning their three other sisters who didn't live in Blue Valley.

"Told them what?" Rose asked, shading her eyes against the setting sun.

"I'm pregnant."

Rose whipped her head to face Delia. "Again? After being so sick with Sunny?"

"Oh, like I could keep it in my pants with all that going on." She gestured toward Caleb as he walked toward them, Sunny cradled in his arms.

Rose's heart ached in a way she didn't understand. Oh, she'd witnessed plenty of imperfect moments between Caleb and Delia. Arguments and demands, days when the baby was screaming and nobody knew what to do. She'd seen all sorts of versions of the ways families didn't work. Seeing that there could be moments like this almost made it seem worth it.

Rose shook that thought away. Worth it for other people—not for her.

"Congratulations, Sissy," she managed to say, because Delia had been through enough. She was the oldest, the one who'd done everything she could to protect them, save them. Delia was the only one Rose couldn't keep the tough girl act up for. "I hope you know how good a mom you are."

"Damn it. I had just stopped crying."

Rose laughed, but she also realized that her reason for coming over would have to wait. She wasn't going to worry Delia with her news now, when she'd already had such problems during her pregnancy with Sunny.

Rose would have to keep this to herself and far away from the Shaw ranch. Maybe with Jack's help she *could* protect her sister from ever knowing the threat existed. If it kept Delia and Sunny away from the man who'd made all her sisters' childhoods a living hell, she'd ask Jack for a *million* favors.

"I hate to break it to you," Caleb said, stepping onto the porch with Sunny in his arms, "but I'm on dinner duty tonight. I hope you like frozen pizza."

Rose got to her feet, holding her arms out for Sunny. The little girl squealed and launched herself from Caleb's arms to Rose's, making all sorts of babbling noises as if telling Rose all about her great adventure in walking.

"With this company, how can I complain?"

Chapter 4

JACK TRIED NOT TO GRIMACE AS HE MANEUVERED himself off the horse. He'd spent the morning working with Hick to move the cattle from the south to the north pasture on horseback, and now he was going to pay.

The grizzled ranch hand, who didn't say much and therefore was one of Jack's favorite people at Revival Ranch, surveyed him with an eagle eye.

"Seems to be gettin' worse," Hick said, nodding at the leg Jack was trying to surreptitiously massage.

"It isn't," Jack returned. Which was sort of the truth. In the grand scheme of things, his leg was no worse than it had been when he'd arrived. Of course, it wasn't any better either, and the scarring on his leg tended to pull. Especially when getting on and off the horses. It never failed to make him think he should have just gone home to Indiana and lived his life climbing in and out of tractors. But Mike and Madison had ruined that for him. Not his accident or the Navy SEALs. His fiancée and his brother had blown apart that life plan irreparably.

But it had been nearly two years. A long stretch of trying to wrap his mind around what his brother had done to him. He was supposed to be getting over it. Moving on. Forming a new life plan.

Except now his family was coming to *him*, and all he could seem to think about was finally having to face this horrible thing he'd been avoiding and—

"Break wouldn't kill you."

Jack scowled at Hick. Before he could assure the old ranch hand he was fine—at least as fine as he was ever going to be—the sound of a puttering car engine, followed by an impressive backfire, interrupted the pastoral quiet.

They both squinted at the unfamiliar car that clearly needed something like a new transmission and who knew what else. It stopped at the end of the drive and a dark-haired woman stepped out.

Jack inhaled, not quite sure what odd thing shifted in his chest when he recognized the screw-the-world stride coming right for them.

"Is that the girl who runs Pioneer Spirit?" Hick asked, something like awe in his voice.

"Uh, yes." He could feel Hick's eyes on him, but Jack ignored it. Then Becca stepped out of the stables with Monica. Jack and Gabe appeared from the bunkhouse, where they'd been working on some minor repairs.

Rose walked across the yard, making a beeline straight for him, and Jack shoved his hands in his pockets, feeling a little too on display for his tastes.

"This is quite the welcome committee," Rose said as she approached, flashing that sharp-edged smile of hers. The colorful tattoos on her right arm were a bright beacon in the summer afternoon. "I need to talk to you," she said, looking right at Jack. "Privately."

All eyes turned to him. Jack ignored the questioning gazes and nodded toward the bunkhouse. "Follow me." He tried to smooth the more-pronounced-than-usual limp out of his walk, but damn, his leg hurt. If Rose noticed, she said nothing as they stepped into the bunkhouse.

Rose marched into the center of the narrow building, her eyes taking in everything. The two beds on either side, both military spartan. Eventually there'd be more beds. More men. For now, it was just him and Gabe sleeping out here.

"This is where you live?" Rose asked, moving through the room, then back to where he stood at the doorway.

He realized then that she was pacing, no matter how she tried to hide it. An edgy energy pulsed beneath her don't-give-a-shit persona. This was not the in-charge bar owner. This was someone else.

"Yeah. Don't be too jealous," he managed, hoping to see a flash of her usual sarcastic humor.

She didn't crack a smile or give him that smoky laugh. She just looked him in the eye. "I need you to start at the bar tomorrow night."

He wondered if she realized how much emotion swirled in her eyes. Even when she was threatening to kick a rowdy guy out of her bar, she seemed untouchable.

But there was a worry in her dark-brown eyes. Panic.

"Okay," he agreed easily, still studying her, but she looked away.

She grabbed a picture out of her pocket. "This is the guy you're looking for," she said, shoving the picture at him. "He drives a blue 1985 Ford truck. I want you to watch out for that too, even if you're just in town getting a bite at Georgia's or something."

He took the picture and was surprised to find an older-looking guy. Whoever he was, he'd clearly lived hard and mean. Jack was starting to worry that Rose's *concern* was something a little closer to fear.

"You sure you don't want to involve the police? This sounds serious."

"It's complicated." She crossed her arms over her chest, looking at him defiantly. "But your role in this is simple. See him? You tell me. See his truck? You tell me. The end."

Jack frowned down at the picture. There was something about all this that stirred up old gut feelings he'd listened to as a SEAL. The situation reminded him that he'd once protected people and his country and his fellow SEALs.

And for what?

"Are you going to tell me why I'm doing all this?" he asked instead of entertaining the answer to his own question.

"Are you going to tell me what point you have to prove?" she returned archly, as if that would shut him up.

Maybe it should have, but he'd have to explain eventually. Jack was a lot of things, but he was crap for acting. When he was pissed, it showed. Sometimes he could manage to put a blankness over that pissed off, but…he was under no illusions Rose wouldn't figure out what was going on the second his family appeared.

Might as well explain it to her.

"My brother and his wife are coming to visit with my family. Which I suppose would be normal enough if his wife wasn't my ex-fiancée and if she hadn't gotten pregnant by him while we were still engaged."

Her eyebrows rose. "Well."

"And apparently, Madison was worried I haven't *moved on*."

"Oh, so I'm a *fuck you* to your ex." She flashed that smile. "Sounds like fun."

Fun. No, it wouldn't be. Not even a little bit, but at least maybe he could avoid soft-smiled pity and all the shame and fury that went with it. "All I'll need you to show up for is a dinner or two with my family. Maybe popping up unannounced to, I don't know..."

"Bring cookies and blow jobs?"

Jack choked on his own spit. His face heated against his will. "I..." But his voice kind of cracked, and he didn't know what to say when there was an all-too-vivid image of Rose and... Well.

She peered at him. "Are you blushing?"

"No," he replied, trying to scoff as though the suggestion was laughable, not pathetically true.

"You're blushing."

"Men do not blush."

"And yet you're embarrassed." She studied him. "Please tell me you slept through a line of women in eight different countries after you found out."

Jack crossed his arms over his chest, doing his best to look impassive and intimidating. It didn't seem to work, damn it.

"Oh no. No. You *have* slept with other women since then. Please tell me you're not still all hung up on her."

"Well, you know, you find out the woman you love got knocked up by your brother in the morning, get half your lower body blown up by a grenade in the afternoon, and sex doesn't exactly become quite the priority it once was," he said, his voice flat and hard. Because he'd learned that if you said it like that, flat and hard, people were uncomfortable enough to shut up about it.

She blinked at him, but none of the expected pity ever showed up on her face. Something like relief worked through him.

"Pioneer Spirit. Tonight. Seven o'clock."

"What? Why?"

She brushed past him and out the bunkhouse door. "We're going to get you laid, sailor."

"I don't... No. No."

"Don't be late," she returned with a wave as she walked purposefully to her car.

"Rose. Rose!" But she was gone, and she'd never explained why he was on the lookout for some potentially dangerous guy at her bar.

Hell.

Rose surveyed the bar and tried to find the usual feelings that came with the perusal. The power of something of her own. Something only *she* controlled. Finally.

It was hard to find today, and she didn't know why. She only knew it pissed her off.

When Jack walked in through the front door, seven o'clock on the dot, something flipped in her stomach.

She could acknowledge it was attraction. She could acknowledge that after the sob story he'd given her this afternoon, the desire to reach out and help him had nearly swallowed her alive. Mostly because she'd been awfully close to offering herself up to Mr. Navy SEAL.

It had been a *long* time since she'd let a man close enough to see her naked, and mostly she hadn't been too bent out of shape about that. But the way he'd gotten so flustered over blow jobs had made her a little desperate to see all the ways she could make him blush.

She wasn't stupid enough to get mixed up in a guy who made her feel a little off-kilter though. Power was everything in a relationship, and Rose worried he'd have her relinquishing hers before she even realized she had.

Better to help him another way. Better to control the situation than let her errant feelings guide her.

So she watched Jack as he threaded through her sparse, Thursday-night crowd of cowboys, ranchers, drunks, and the sons and daughters of all three as though he were something she couldn't take her eyes off of.

And maybe you can't.

He strode up to her bar and placed his hands flat on the surface, leaning forward. "For the record, I don't *want* to get laid."

Rose had to press her lips together to keep from laughing at the looks *that* earned from the men sitting at the bar.

"In my experience, people usually *want* to get laid—it's the outside factors that make it difficult."

"Amen, sister," said one of the older gentlemen sitting on the line of stools.

Jack's scowl deepened, and Rose couldn't hold back a smile. "You're blushing again, Jack."

He blew out a frustrated breath, and she handed him two bottles of beer. She nodded over to a table where Felicity Bellamy sat alone.

Rose only knew Felicity peripherally, but the woman who ran Blue Valley's little general store seemed like the kind of wholesome, upstanding citizen that former

Navy SEALs who'd been betrayed by their fiancées could find a few hours of comfort with.

"The woman at the table by herself. Her name's Felicity. She runs Felicity's. Offer her a drink. You don't have to sleep with her. Just go talk to her."

"Why are you doing this?" he demanded, those ice-blue eyes of his somehow causing *her* to feel jittery.

Rose Rogers didn't do jittery.

"Just trying to help you." She shrugged, looking away from his gaze and wiping down the bar. "I don't get what the big deal is."

"The big deal is I said I don't want help. The big deal is why you of all people would…" He shook his head and rolled his eyes. "You know what? Never mind." He grabbed the beer and walked over to Felicity's table.

Rose didn't need to watch him walk over there, limp and all. She didn't need to study him sliding into the chair opposite Felicity. And she really didn't need to watch the redhead smile prettily at Jack.

She'd done her good deed, and now the rest had nothing to do with her.

Maybe every once in a while, she glanced over at their table and, yeah, there was this obnoxious sick feeling in her gut every time either of them were laughing or smiling. That was just something else though, like what she'd felt with Caleb and Delia yesterday. It didn't have to do with *Jack*. It was just the feeling that happened when you knew you weren't going to have something. Sometimes it ached a little.

What was wrong with her? She did not moon, and she did not feel *jittery* over watching two of her regulars flirt.

Clearly her father being out of jail was messing with her head and her heart. She was worked up and looking for any kind of excuse not to think about that.

Except she'd taken care of things. She couldn't put the awful man back behind bars, but she could protect herself. On the nights she couldn't watch the bar diligently to see if he showed to enact a revenge he'd promised when she'd gotten him sent to jail in the first place, she had Jack.

She glanced over at the man in question again. Felicity was laughing at something he'd said, and that was great. They both seemed like people who needed to laugh more, and they were laughing together.

Fantastic.

"You okay, boss?"

Rose glanced at Tonya, who was clearly concerned enough over Rose's behavior to brave her temper. Which was the only thing that kept it from boiling over.

"I'm fine. I've got a bit of a headache, and I'm going to go grab some aspirin. Can you watch things for a few minutes?"

"Got it."

Rose forced herself to breathe normally as she left the bar and walked through the back hallway. She glanced around before sliding the panel open and unlocking the hidden door to her apartment and stepping inside. Maybe things were getting a little out of hand. She could admit that much to herself as she crossed the messy, small apartment to her bathroom. She jerked the medicine cabinet open and threw back two aspirin. Then she stood there and looked at herself in the mirror. She did not look like the kick-ass, powerful woman she'd decided to be. She looked scared and stupid.

Rose scowled. Things had been good for about a year and a half now. Really, really *good*. Her sisters were thriving. Her bar was thriving. Life had felt like *life* instead of a prison.

So it should have been no surprise that things were getting complicated again. Sure, her father had gotten out of jail a lot earlier than expected, but at least the others were safe. Three of her sisters were in a different state. Delia had Caleb and a slew of Shaws to protect her. Rose was the only one alone, the only one really at risk.

And didn't she deserve it? After being the favorite for so many years. After courting his favor to avoid the beatings that he'd then pass on to her sisters or mother.

Rose squeezed her eyes shut, clutching the sink. She wasn't going down this road. She had a bar to run. She needed to get ahold of herself and stop acting like a whiny little girl. She had never been that. She was not going to start now.

She inhaled and exhaled slowly, calmly and forced herself to believe the lies she told herself.

Sometimes, lies were all a girl had.

She moved back through her apartment and exited into the back hallway. She paused only to use her key to lock the dead bolt before sliding the panel over to hide the lock.

"You need to—"

She whirled and, in the same movement, pulled out the knife she kept strapped to her belt loop, always hidden under her shirt.

She might have felt embarrassed at her reaction when it wasn't some drunk patron or even her father, but Jack's response was too quick to feel much of anything. His hand clamped onto her wrist, giving her arm a hard jerk that caused her to loosen her grip on the knife against her will.

The knife clattered to the ground, and they both stared at it.

Slowly, his gaze returned to her as hers did to him. He didn't let go of her wrist, and she didn't pull her arm away. She simply stared at him.

"Here's a tip," he said, his voice an awful rasp that made her heart pinch even as it galloped a crazy beat against her chest. "Don't pull a knife on a former Navy SEAL."

"Here's a tip," she returned, surprised and annoyed at how breathless she sounded. "Don't sneak up behind a woman who knows how to protect herself."

He glanced down at the knife he'd so easily knocked out of her grasp. Few things were as horrifically frightening as how easily he'd disarmed her. She had to remind herself he was military, trained to fend off an attack. That didn't mean she was a weakling. She had never, ever been a weakling, and she wouldn't start now.

"Fair enough," he finally said, reaching down and picking up the knife. "I didn't mean to scare you."

"Then don't lurk outside my apartment."

He frowned at the door in the wall that you'd only notice if you were looking for it. "You live here?"

"Yes, I live here. Now, if you'll excuse me, I have a bar to run. And if you're not out there, and I'm not out there, then no one's watching the door." She held out her hand for her knife, but Jack only frowned down at it. "Give me back my knife."

He didn't stop frowning, but he did hand her back

her knife. She placed it in its little holster and started for the bar.

Jack fell into step behind her. "You owe me an explanation."

"If you don't like Felicity, that's fine. Prefer blonds? Rough-and-tumble cowgirls? Glossy city types?"

He cut in front of her, effectively blocking her return to the bar, this big mountain of a man standing in her hallway like he had a right. Before she could give him a piece of her mind for that, or a piece of her fist, he asked the question she didn't want to answer.

"Why are you so afraid of this guy?"

"Don't worry about it."

"I am worrying about it. I'm also worried about you toting around a knife that says *watch your step*."

"I also have a gun that says *come and get it* if that helps."

"It does not."

"I'm not your responsibility, Jack." She gestured toward the door behind him. Any other guy, she'd have the knife back out, but she wasn't so sure she could outmaneuver Jack. How humiliating. Still, she couldn't let that shame show on her face. She looked up at him, employing her most imperious glare.

"And I'm not yours, but you're throwing me at women, trying to get me laid. Why is that?"

"You told me a sob story. I offered a fix. It's what a good bartender does. We want repeat, happy customers. You don't want any help in the female department, that's fine. I'll back off and do my duty as pretend girlfriend, and you'll do your job as bouncer. Now can I go back to my bar?"

He huffed out a breath and stepped out of her way. As she walked the last few yards to the door between the bar and the hall, she paused.

He wasn't following her.

She glanced back and saw that he was leaning against the wall, hands shoved in his pockets, looking up at the ceiling.

"It isn't that simple," he grumbled.

She shouldn't prolong this conversation, but he looked so lost. "What isn't?"

"Women."

"Oh." She glanced down at his general crotch region. He had a limp, so he'd been hurt. "You have an…injury?"

He practically jumped away from the wall. "No!" He stopped himself and cleared his throat. "No," he repeated more calmly. "Everything still *works*. Jeez. I just…"

"You just what?"

"Don't need to have this conversation with you. I don't know why I even opened my mouth."

"I'm a bartender."

He laughed humorlessly.

"A lot of times, people tell me stuff because they need to have the conversation, but they don't have anyone impartial to talk to."

He was quiet for a long time, still not looking at her.

Rose didn't move. She barely breathed. Clearly Jack needed to get something off his chest, and that *was* something she liked about the whole *running a bar* thing. People came to drown their sorrows. They came to feel better about their lives, to celebrate their successes or nurse their hurts. People came to a bar to *deal*. Maybe it was a temporary kind of dealing, but she liked being the one who ran the place they came to cope.

"Maybe it'd be good to get it off your chest." Words she'd never said to anyone. Possibly ever. She did not understand this man's effect on her at all.

"Maybe it would be, but you have a bar to run, remember?"

She glanced at the door. Yeah, she had things to do. Things that were hers to protect. Jack wasn't one of those.

So she nodded and went back to her life before she started believing silly fantasies that whispered *maybe he could be*.

Chapter 5

JACK KNEW HE SHOULD HEAD BACK TO THE RANCH. He definitely shouldn't drink, and he wasn't going to talk to Felicity anymore. She was perfectly nice. Plenty pretty and an easy sense of humor that should have made it all simple.

But he didn't know how to talk to women, and he was tired of all these things that he didn't know how to do. His entire life lately was thing after thing he didn't know how to understand or navigate.

Like why was Rose carrying around a knife? Why did she have a gun? She could be a criminal mastermind for all he knew. And yet he'd seen something in her—the fact that she felt she had to arm herself and the way she'd whirled on him, ready to fight. It all poked and pulled at those instincts that had led him into the navy.

He wanted to help people. He wanted to save people. He wanted to do something important, protect something important. He was strong and he was good and he had wanted to help those who didn't have what he had.

He'd done that, he supposed. He'd served his country for eight years before he'd been injured irreparably. He'd done good. He'd protected important things.

Now? He was a former sailor with a limp and absolutely no game with women. His only saving grace was the fact that he knew a little bit about cattle, thanks to his uncle's farm back in Indiana. Jack might have grown up

with soybeans and corn, but he wasn't completely igno-
rant when it came to this cowboy stuff. So right now, the
only thing he understood was *cows*.

Yeah, he didn't have it in him to resist ordering
another drink—hard liquor this time. Gabe would come
pick him up later, no questions asked.

Well, maybe a few questions about Rose, but the
kind of questions Jack would be able to pawn off. Doing
favors for each other and all that. None of this stuff
about worrying over some woman he didn't know's
well-being.

Nothing about how the whole time he'd spent sitting
at a table fumbling through a conversation with Felicity,
he'd been thinking about Rose—the way she smiled
so sharp and easy. The way she talked as if she never
questioned or worried about anything. She seemed so
infinitely capable and, God, wasn't that what he wanted
right now? To feel capable of anything.

Jack eyed the small group of guys next to him.
Younger. Ranch hands at one of the bigger outfits probably. The asshole next to him had been ranting inces-
santly for who knew how long.

Well, at least Jack wasn't that guy.

"I'm telling you, you gotta be firmer with that woman
of yours. Women need a firm hand to keep them in line."

Jack snorted. *What a moron*.

"You got something to say, buddy?"

It took Jack a few seconds to realize the guy was
talking to him. Jack laughed. The stranger was about
six inches shorter than him, rangy maybe, but Jack was
pretty sure he could have him on the ground in five seconds flat if he felt like fighting.

Lucky for the jerk-off, Jack was too drunk to feel like fighting. "Yeah, maybe I do. If you think a woman needs a 'firm hand,' you probably need your hands broken."

The guy bristled even more, getting to his feet. "Oh, and who's going to stop me? You?"

Jack got to his feet. Slowly, enjoying the way the guy's belligerent stance slumped as Jack stared down at him. "Maybe me. Maybe her. Life is full of surprises that way."

The guy tried to square his shoulders, looked around at his buddies for support, but they were looking anywhere but at him or Jack.

"Which one's the one with the problem?" Jack demanded, pointing his finger at the group.

The men all looked around, clearly no one wanting to volunteer. A few of the guys pointed at a gangly, younger guy in the back though.

"You. What's the deal?"

"N-nothing. Nothing's the deal," he squeaked. "Everything's good."

"He's pissed his baby mama wants him to help out around the house," one of the older men said with a laugh.

Jack shook his head. "What the hell is wrong with you? Do some dishes. Clean a bathroom. Firm hand, please. Put in your fifty-fifty."

The young kid puffed out his chest. "I work all day. Hard."

"Yeah, I'm sure being pregnant's a real walk in the park. You planning on taking care of your kid?"

He bristled, all moral outrage. "Of course I am."

"Then take care of the woman who's doing all the work. Listen to this guy," Jack said, jabbing a thumb toward the original jerk-off. "You'll both get your asses handed to you by somebody one way or another." He turned back to the bar and tapped his glass on the surface. "Another one."

There were mutters from the group, but Jack didn't exactly care. He'd said his piece, and he just hoped that young kid had the good sense to listen to him over the jerk-off leader of his group.

"Last call, gentlemen," Rose said, refilling Jack's glass.

There was a lot of grumbling and tossing bills on the counter before the men headed out.

"Good riddance," Jack muttered.

"That was quite a show," Rose said, leaning her elbows on the bar as she studied him.

Jack shrugged, sipping his drink. "Can't stand that kind of blustering crap. My sister had a boyfriend like that. Firm hand." He made a scoffing noise. "I took him hunting once. Left him in the woods." Jack grinned at the memory. "He suddenly wasn't so keen on being a jerk to my sister."

"Go ahead and head out, Tonya," Rose said without taking her gaze off his. "I've got it from here."

Tonya eyed Jack suspiciously. "You sure about that, boss?"

Rose winked. "Positive. Don't forget to empty the tip jar."

Tonya rolled her eyes. "Half those tips are yours. Rightfully. Pete's doing a lot better. I don't need the extra—"

"Proprietor doesn't get tips, Tonya. If Pete's on the mend, take the money and buy yourself something pretty."

The woman sighed, but she took the entire wad of ones out of the tip jar. "Sometimes I think you're too nice for your own good." Tonya glared at Jack again. "If you lay one hand on her, I'll personally castrate you."

Jack gave the woman a little salute, which only caused Tonya to scowl deeper. But she walked out the front door of the bar, Rose following and locking up behind her.

"How'm I going to get out of here?" Jack asked.

"There's a back way. Which is where my car is. The car I will be driving you home in as soon as I close up."

"Gabe can come get me."

"No worries. I've got somewhere to be that's not too far from your guys' place. What are you calling it now?"

"Revival Ranch." Jack looked bitterly at his new drink. "Some joke."

"You consider revival a joke?"

"Some things don't revive, Rosie." He tried to mimic one of her sharp smiles.

"Since you're drunk, I won't kill you for calling me Rosie. Consider that your one and only pass."

Jack grinned, this time for real. He didn't know another woman like her—all sharp edges and threats, and yet she'd tried to get him laid and she was going to drive him home. Rose was one of those… Oh, what were they called? Two opposing forces existing as one.

He leaned forward on the bar, watching her while she efficiently cleaned and organized all her bottles and glasses and rags. "You know, I was telling myself that I should have some… What d'you call it? Restraint? Then I got to thinking I'm not good at anything anymore, so why not get really good at drinking?"

"Because you don't want to be a useless alcoholic. You've got friends and a job and a pretty decent place to live. So suck it up, Jacky Jack."

Anger, vile and heavy, bubbled up inside him. "I have a permanent limp, a quarter of my body is a giant scar that, oh yeah, I got watching my friend die. I have to look my nephew in his little baby face in a few weeks, and when I do, I have to pretend I'm not thinking about the fact that my brother fucked my fiancée. It's all been taken away. All of it. My pain-free existence. My friend. My future marriage. My future kids. My farm. It's either dead or all theirs now. So tell me, Rose, what right do you have to tell me to suck it up?"

"My dad used to beat the hell out of me when I'd lose a poker game for him, whether it was my fault or not."

Even with the liquor and anger flowing like hot lava through his veins, *those* words landed like an icy blow, but she kept going.

"And when I helped him win the poker game?" She shrugged, as if recounting a story that wasn't a damn tragedy. "He'd beat the hell out of my sisters and my mom in front of me. I've survived hell, Mr. Navy SEAL. Just like you. So maybe consider that not everyone has some amazing, wonderful life just because yours sucks."

Jack swallowed at the wave of guilty nausea flowing upward. He definitely did not take a sip of his last drink. "I'm sorry," he managed to say. Even though "sorry" didn't begin to cut it.

"Yeah, well, so am I. But I'm alive, and I'm making something out of it, so it's time for you to do the same. Now, what's your problem with women? You seem to have more sense about them than any of that group talking about firm hands."

"Did you tell me that horrible childhood story so I'd tell you what my deal with women is?"

"No, and if I could go back, I'd tape my mouth shut before I yapped all that crap. But I can't, so I'll use it. What's the deal?"

Either he was drunk enough to be stupid, or he was guilty enough to be stupid, or he was just Jack enough to be stupid. When he opened his mouth, the truth tumbled out. "Madison was the only woman I've ever done anything with."

"And when you say *anything*, you mean sex?"

"I mean everything. My mom and her mom were best friends growing up, and they had us a month apart. It was known from the very beginning Madison and I *belonged* together. Jack and Madison would grow up, get married, run the farm. I never questioned it. She was always going to be my wife. She's the only woman I've ever kissed, the only woman I ever took out on a date."

He scraped his palm against the beard he needed to shave off before his mother showed up. "I don't know how to talk to women. I don't know how to flirt or hook up. I never had to know. She was always there, and we just accepted that we were each other's future."

He laughed bitterly, twisting the still-full glass on the bar back and forth. "So I'm sitting there at your damn bar table with this woman you've thrown me at, who is very much not the woman I spent most of my life thinking I'd marry, and I don't know what to say. Or what to do. I just don't know."

He didn't dare look at her. He didn't want to see pity or disgust or whatever Rose would feel in the face of those pathetic admissions. He didn't want to know what the woman who'd been beaten by her father thought of his pathetic, small-town problems.

He firmed his grip on his glass, ready to raise it to his lips and drain it, but Rose put her hand over his from across the bar.

"How long has it been now? Since you found out about it?"

"Almost two years."

"Okay. Two years. You had your two years to wallow, and now, guess what? It's over. She did something shitty. They both did something really shitty to you. But it's been two years, and they have moved on with their lives, and now it's your turn. That's your revenge. That's how you get back at them. You rebuild your life. And no, it's not the life it was supposed to be—I get that. And I get that it's hard, but it's time to change. Which means you don't drink at my bar anymore. I'm not serving you."

He met her fierce, dark gaze, and he didn't know what to say. There was nothing but pain and confusion swallowing him, and all he really wanted to do was lay his head on the bar and cry like a baby.

He didn't.

"I'll text Gabe to come pick me up."

"No. I'm going to take you home."

"Why?" Alex and Gabe came at him like this sometimes. There'd been arguments. Becca joined in sometimes. Everyone seemed to think he needed to move forward.

But no one, not one of them, was telling him how to do it. Except Rose Rogers. Why her, of all people?

"Because, whether I like it or not, my lot in life seems to be wanting to help people. You might not want help, but you need it, and you made the mistake of letting me see it. So I'm going to help you."

"Whether I want it or not?"

"Damn straight, baby." She slapped the bar. "Sit tight."

And what else was there to do when someone who seemed to know how to live this life was telling him to do something?

So he sat tight.

⁓⁓⁓

Rose glanced at the man in her passenger seat. He was staring morosely out the window, and her heart did that annoying thing she wished she could eradicate.

She'd told him about her crappy childhood, and he hadn't recoiled. Oh, he'd looked damn sorry, but not disgusted. Not afraid to touch all that mess.

And she *was* a mess of all those mistakes she'd made, all the ways her parents' vices were stamped into her bones. She was the worst of both of them, and she had no business wanting to help a former Navy SEAL who'd been betrayed by the woman he loved.

When she got to the turnoff that would take her up to Revival Ranch, where she could drop Jack safely off with his *friends*, she didn't stop. She didn't slow down. She kept driving.

"Where are you going?" Jack asked as she missed the turn. "You're supposed to turn there."

Yes, she *was*, but she'd *felt* Jack's bone-deep despair. She'd seen that hopelessness in her own reflection, and no one else she'd encountered had ever made her feel like this.

Then he'd had to go and give those guys a lecture on firm hands and fifty-fifty and told that story of messing with the boyfriend who was mean to his sister. She hadn't grown up knowing men like him existed, but she was slowly learning there were good people out there. There was no doubt in her mind Jack was a good, upstanding, honest, trustworthy person.

Didn't mean what she was about to do was *smart*, but she was doing it anyway. "I want to show you something first."

"This better not be pity sex, because that's just stomping on my pride, and I'd have to say no."

Rose forced herself to laugh even as the thought of pity sex made her…well, a little hot and bothered, yeah. Jack was gorgeous, and she was on a sex sabbatical and…

Well, that wasn't the point. "Baby, if I was offering you any kind of sex, you *couldn't* say no. But that's not what this is."

He snorted out something like a laugh, and she drove on, farther out of town and toward her destination.

Her heart beat unsteadily and it was hard to breathe normally or act like she wasn't doing something so inherently stupid. Showing him this was like showing him a piece of herself she'd never showed anyone. She even tried not to show it to her sisters, and they meant everything in the world to her.

She owed them. She owed her sisters her strength and

her certainty and her power, and they didn't need the softer sides of her.

Jack meant nothing to her, which meant he couldn't hurt those softer sides, right?

So she drove to the place no one knew about. Not Delia or Caleb. Not her sisters or her parents or her bartenders. No one knew this little house in the middle of nowhere existed, let alone was hers.

She'd offer it up as some little slice of peace, and then he could go back to his life feeling lighter. And she'd feel better for having helped him.

She stopped in front of the dilapidated ranch house that had been built something like a hundred years ago. The majority of the land around it had long been sold off to neighboring ranchers, and the house had gone abandoned and falling apart for decades.

Last year, Rose had come across it on one of her long drives to clear her head, and something had kept her rooted in front of this falling-apart house. An improbable lilac bush had been blooming by the boarded-up front door, and the sunlight had reflected off the picturesque pond just down the slope of the hill.

Rose didn't believe in mystical bullshit, but she hadn't been able to deny that little frisson of excitement when she'd set eyes on this place. It had taken her two months to track down the owners, another month to strike a deal. It was still unlivable—especially in the winter months—but sometimes in the summer, she could come out here and spend the night if she didn't mind the mice.

Eventually she'd fix it up completely, not just the random little repairs she knew how to make. For now, regardless of how ugly it was, it was her escape. Her secret. The bar was her power, and this place was her sanctuary.

"Did you bring me here to kill me? Because that looks like the only possible thing you'd want to 'show me' at this place."

"Hey, that's my baby you're talking about there. Be careful. And get out." She slid out of the car herself and took a deep breath of the beautiful Montana summer night. These short stretches of summer weeks, when a person could go outside without a coat, always felt like magic. It was that brief period of time every year when she could pretend she lived somewhere warm and inviting.

"Seriously. What *is* this place?" Jack asked, stepping out of the car and looking around the starlight-dappled yard.

"This is my house," she said, spreading her arms wide.

"I thought you lived at the bar?"

"I do. For now. Once I get this place fixed up and maybe promote Tonya to manager, it'll be my full-time house."

"Why'd you bring me to your house?"

She ignored that question and walked toward the pond. Jack needed a little recalibration. When you were stuck in a shitty way of thinking, after a bunch of shitty-ass things happened to you, you needed to break free.

She had no business being the one to offer him a little solace, but she *had* solace, and growing up in a world empty of it meant she gave it when she could. No matter how often she tried to convince herself she was so much harder than all that.

She pulled her shirt up and over her head and let it fall to the ground. She didn't miss the little squeaking sound that came out of Jack's mouth when she did it, but she kept moving for the pond. Once she reached the bank, she shimmied out of her jeans.

"What are you doing?" he demanded.

She turned to face him, putting her back to the water. Moonlight shone on the sharp lines of his face—that perfect nose, high cheekbones, everything about him so angular and masculine, his expression so serious and stern. Even across the yard, lit only by the full moon, she could see the emotion in his eyes.

She'd been a little hard on him back at the bar, talking a little too frankly about Dad's heavy fists, because this guy had his share of troubles. Even if they weren't the same, even if they didn't quite compare. But trouble… oh, she was intimately acquainted with trouble, and what Jack needed was to find himself a little of the right kind.

That was one thing she had in spades.

So she flashed a grin and hoped he could see it in what little light they had. And then she jumped backward into the icy-cold water of her pond. No amount of Montana summer sun could warm this up, but it wasn't the sort of cold that would kill you. It was the kind of cold that reminded you that you were alive.

That was what Jack needed. She dove deep into the water, reminding herself of that, before coming back up to the surface.

She stood, letting her toes sink into the dirt, the water lapping at her chin. "Your turn," she called to him.

"I am not jumping into a pond. I thought *I* was the drunk one."

"Come on. I promise it will change your life. I bet you've never been skinny-dipping."

"I am not skinny-dipping. And, just for clarity, you aren't either. You still have your underwear on."

Rose laughed, stepping farther into the center of the pond, where she had to tread water to keep her head above the surface. "Okay, strip down to your skivvies and jump in."

"I'm not stripping down to anything."

"I thought you had some sense of humor in there. I guess I should've brought Gabe."

Jack stepped forward with an irritated grunt and pulled his shirt over his head.

Rose regretted very, very deeply that it was the middle of the night and there was no daylight to see the whole of him. Because what little she could make out was...

Well.

"Is that a tattoo?" she called, squinting at the mark on his bicep.

He stepped to the edge of the pond, and she could see the downward turn of his mouth. "Yes, I have a tattoo."

"And here I thought you were Mr. Clean-Cut."

"I was drunk when I got it."

She laughed at that. "You're drunk now. Lose the pants and jump in."

"I'm not taking off my damn pants."

"You can't swim in jeans."

"The hell I can't."

"What are you so afraid of?" she returned, scooping her hand through the water and trying to splash him.

"My scars are not for public consumption."

That shut her up for a second. Which was good, because she was letting this giddy feeling overtake her,

and then she'd say stupid things and probably do stu-
pider ones.

"This public can handle it. Take off your pants and
jump in the damn pond." Because she didn't know how
to be sweet or sympathetic, which was likely what Jack
needed. Someone like Felicity, who would know how to
give him a little peace and comfort that didn't involve
threats and icy water.

Who did she think she was, really? Like she was ever
going to know how to help some former Navy SEAL
who had voluntarily signed up to fight far away from
home. He'd actually been brave enough to *want* to do
that. She'd only ever fought because she didn't have a
choice, and sometimes she hadn't fought at all.

She opened her mouth to tell him to forget it—maybe
she'd even choke out an apology. Of course, that was
when he decided to take off his pants anyway and jump
in beside her.

Chapter 6

IT WAS COLD. WHICH SHOULDN'T HAVE BEEN A surprise. If there was anything Jack had learned about Montana in the handful of months he'd lived here, it was that everything always seemed to be too cold, even on a perfectly hot, middle-of-summer day.

He didn't know why that made him want to laugh, but suddenly he felt like laughing. Hysterically. He was in his boxers in the middle of Montana, swimming in some godforsaken pond with the most... He didn't have a word for what Rose was.

"I can't believe I'm doing this," he muttered, the water feeling less cold as he moved and adjusted to the temperature.

"Oh, believe it, baby."

She was treading water only inches from where he was standing on the cool mud. It reminded him of playing in the creek as a kid. Which might have been a fond memory if he hadn't spent all that time with his brother or Madison.

He didn't want to think about them or dwell on that. Not now, when the moonlight glinted against Rose's dark hair and made it silver. When her skin glowed like some magical, light-giving stone. When everything about her was so *present*.

"How does it feel?" Rose asked, something like laughter in her voice. Laughter—that bright pop of a reminder that life wasn't over just because it wasn't what he'd wanted it to be.

"Well, I feel cold. And baffled."

She laughed outright, that smoky, hazy sound that was like nothing he'd ever heard. So much of her was like nothing he'd ever experienced.

He knew he shouldn't drift closer. All of the things she'd done for him had been completely out of pity. She wasn't interested in him. And never mind that, back at the bar, talking to Felicity, he'd wished he could make a move and couldn't, but somehow, in this ridiculous moment, he felt like he could.

But that wasn't the point. Hitting on Rose wasn't why he was here, and it wasn't the right thing to do.

What has doing the right thing ever got you?

"Like a whole new man, right?" Rose asked, her voice suddenly hushed.

Even though he didn't remember moving closer to her, somehow he was. He could feel the water lap against him as she moved her arms and legs.

All of those stuttering, mood-darkening nerves he'd felt sitting across the table from Felicity were completely gone now that he was treading water across from Rose. His pulse beat hard in his neck, and something south of the border that hadn't voluntarily twitched in what felt like years was suddenly hard.

The water was cool, and the air was hot, and Rose glowed silver in the moon, and there were all these things he'd forgotten existed swelling inside him.

Excitement. Anticipation. Want.

"Why did you bring me here, Rose?"

He could see the way her eyebrows furrowed, but that didn't answer his question for him.

"Not sure I have a good answer for that, Jack." She smiled ruefully. "This is where I go when I don't know where to go. When I don't know who I am or where I'm going. I've never brought anyone here with me. So I have no idea what possessed me to bring you here, but here we are. And if you don't get something out of it, I'm going to take it very personally and think you're a total jackass. So you better find something to get out of it."

"Something to get out of it," he repeated, smiling. Because he didn't know anyone who talked like Rose.

He shouldn't have been thinking about all the things he wanted to get out of basically skinny-dipping with her. Because that's not what she meant—she meant his psyche or a therapy breakthrough.

But she was close, and she looked like a goddess, and he couldn't remember the last time he'd looked at a woman and not compared her to Madison. There was no comparison. Rose was an entirely different creature.

"What possessed you to come to my bar tonight when I told you I'd get you laid, even though that's not what you wanted?"

"I'm not sure I've got an answer for that, Rose," he said, repeating her response from earlier.

She grinned at him. "What's your tattoo? I can't make it out."

"It's an anchor and a banner with the phrase 'hold fast.'"

"Were you really drunk when you got it?"

"It was my twenty-first birthday. Alex and Gabe took

me out. I actually don't remember anything about it—I just woke up with this anchor on my arm. Not even a naked girl hugging the anchor. You'd think the guys could have thrown me a bone there."

Rose laughed her totally unique laugh, and they were close, and he wasn't the one doing it. She was the one drifting closer to him.

Her finger brushed against the spot on his bicep where his anchor was tattooed, and Jack forced himself to breathe slowly in, exhale evenly out.

"Hold fast," she mused. "What does that mean?"

"I told you I was drunk when I got it."

"Sure." Her eyes lifted to his. "It still means something to you. You could've gotten another tattoo to cover it. You could have gotten it removed. Hold fast—it means something though, doesn't it?"

"Because every tattoo on your body means something to you?"

"Every single one. Except maybe the one on my ass."

Jack choked out a laugh. "Do you really have a tattoo on your ass?"

"That's a question for the ages, Jacky boy." Her finger dropped from his arm, and she dived away from him, swimming to the opposite side of the pond. "Come on, Navy SEAL. Show me what you got."

"What I got is a bum leg."

"Okay, but aren't you guys supposed to be able to breathe underwater or some such?"

"Some such."

"Then I dare you to a contest—who can hold their breath under water the longest?"

"How would we possibly know who wins?"

"Whoever pops up first."

"The person who comes up first could just as easily go back down without the other person knowing."

She laughed at something about that, but then she shrugged. "We'll hold hands." She held her arms out, clearly kicking to keep herself above the surface of the water.

He didn't know why that, of all the things in the past ten minutes, would make him feel jittery. An offer to hold hands was nothing, but it somehow seemed more intimate than anything they'd done so far. More so than stripping and swimming in their underwear. More so than the moment in the hall when she'd pulled a knife on him and he'd neutralized the threat—by holding her arm, being able to feel her wild pulse jump under his fingertips. Those should have all been more intimate than a little hand holding.

"Chicken?"

He knew she was baiting him, and yet something about Rose made him want to give in to the baiting. When he never, ever wanted to give in to anyone else.

He took her outstretched hands. Rose seemed so large and in charge, but her hands were soft and small in his.

"Ground rules," he muttered, because they were just playing a stupid game, not…whatever. "When you need to come up for air, you squeeze my hand. The squeeze is admitting you lost to me, and we both come up for air together."

"Or you could lose to me."

"Keep telling yourself that, *baby*," he said, using that word she was always using on him. "And if we start to freeze to death, there better not be a *Titanic* situation where you get an entire door and I get zip."

Her laughter echoed out across the inky dark around them, and it slithered through his chest like something bright and viral.

Jack had the oddest sensation that this, right here, was the happiest he'd been in a very long time.

Not just the past two years, but before that even. Before… He wasn't sure. He wasn't sure he could ever remember feeling this kind of simple, unaffected joy.

Not with Madison, not on the farm, not anywhere but a picturesque Montana summer night in the shadow of a tumbling-down house with the most confusing woman he'd ever met.

When she counted to three, he sank into the water holding Rose's hands, wondering for the first time in a long time, with a sense of hope, what might possibly come next.

As much as Rose hated to lose, she knew winning against a Navy SEAL in *this* situation wasn't going to happen. Still, she held her breath for as long as she could, enjoying the cool water around her, the silence and the dark, with her eyes closed tight.

She did feel Jack's big hands gripping hers. They were the center of her universe for a few fleeting seconds— fleeting enough that she didn't fight that thought with everything she had, like she normally would have.

She let it linger.

Until she couldn't take the lack of oxygen anymore and she squeezed his hands and kicked to the top, Jack staying with her as they both broke the surface at the same time.

She blinked the water out of her eyes and gulped a deep breath of air. She settled her gaze on Jack, who seemed not at all out of breath despite however long they'd been underwater. He was *grinning* though, and that made her feel a little extra out of breath.

She'd seen a few smiles out of Jack, but she'd never seen a carefree grin on this gruff, stoic man's face.

She wanted to touch it. With her fingers, with her mouth. She wanted to find the source of that grin and breathe it deep inside of her.

Good men with good hearts are not for you, Rose Rogers.

"This might be the most nonsensical thing I've ever done," he said, his voice low, almost a whisper.

"I don't mind being the voice of the nonsensical." Her breathing was too shallow, and her skin was cold and shivery except where their hands were still clasped. Every atom of heat in her body centered there, where her fingers were threaded through his.

She tugged a little, but Jack's grip was firm, and his arms remained steady. She bobbed toward him instead, their legs brushing as they kicked to keep themselves afloat in the deepest part of the pond.

They didn't speak after that, and they didn't let go of each other's hands, and they didn't look away. Rose's mind was screaming a million things at her, but it seemed to be in a language she didn't understand, because she simply kept kicking and bobbing, her body occasionally brushing his, her hands always so secure and tight in his.

Would a kiss really be the worst thing in the world? The poor guy had only ever been with one woman after all. Wasn't Rose the perfect candidate for a rebound mistake? At least until the next upstanding girl came along.

She tugged again, drawing closer, and all she would need was to free her hands to be able to pull his mouth to hers. To give him what surely, *surely*, they both wanted—no matter how stupid it might be in the end.

"Jack, let go of my hand," she said, keeping that steady, blue gaze of his. Sounding as in control as ever, feeling as out of control as she never let show.

For a second, it felt as though his grip was loosening, but then he squeezed and pulled her firmly against him in one fluid movement. Rose inhaled sharply, watching the way his grin hardened into something she didn't ever think she'd seen on his face.

Determination.

"No, I don't think I will."

She was pressed against his hard, warm chest, their legs moving in tandem to keep them afloat, their hearts beating against each other. She could feel his warm breath against her wet cheek, and his lips were only a whisper away from hers. In any other situation, she would have taken control. She would have barreled forward and left regret for another time, but here and now with Jack, she waited. She soaked in the wild anticipation of what his mouth would feel like on her.

A phone went off from where they'd left their clothes, loud against the quiet country night. Loud against the heavy moment of stillness and anticipation that had settled over them.

"Is that your phone?" she asked in a hushed whisper.

"Ye—Oh, crap," he muttered, letting go of her hands and swimming for the bank.

She blinked at her new circumstances—alone in the middle of the pond, treading water in the cold, all by herself. "What?" she called after him.

"Well, considering the bar closed about an hour ago, I'm guessing I have a few people wondering where I am." He climbed out of the pond, and damn the moon for not shining where she'd like, including his leg that was supposedly all scar. She couldn't see any of it in the dark.

"And worried I'm off doing harm to myself," he added.

Rose swam after him, climbing out of the muddy pond as Jack fished his phone out of his pocket.

"Is there a chance of that?" she asked, her heart doing an awful cartwheel of worry at the thought.

"Not today," he muttered.

"That's not comforting, Jack."

He flicked a glance at her, any emotions on his face hidden by the dark around them. "I wasn't trying to be." He typed something into his phone and let out a hefty sigh. "I have to get back."

"Right." Right. She laughed, because of course. It figured she'd talked herself into doing something stupid, and *poof*, her stupidity was interrupted.

Jack was already pulling on his pants and his shirt, and Rose had to mentally shake herself into movement. Pick up her pants, ignore that her legs were wet and her feet were muddy. Pull her shirt on over her sopping wet bra.

Which was the best reminder, all in all. Stupidity only ever ended with wet, dirty discomfort, and an extra helping of frustration.

She pulled on her socks and her boots, glancing over at Jack doing the same.

"Thanks for this," he said, not meeting her gaze as he laced up his boots, sitting on the grass, moonlight dappling his hair silver and gold. "I don't know how to explain…"

"You don't have to," she said, pushing herself to her feet on a sigh. "I get it." There was something a little magical about this place, no matter how much she didn't want to believe in magic.

Because the truth of the matter was the magic was in the moon, in the pond, in anything and everything that wasn't her.

Chapter 7

JACK SAT IN THE PASSENGER SEAT OF ROSE'S CAR AS she drove up to Revival Ranch and tried to ignore the fact that he was sitting in dry clothes with wet hair and boxers. Tried to ignore the fact that he'd had Rose Rogers pressed against him and hadn't done a damn thing about it.

She hadn't said a word since they'd gotten in her car, and maybe that was all he needed to know. This whole bizarre night had been a trick of some liquor and the moon. Considering he was uncomfortable and his leg ached like a bitch, maybe all that back at the pond had been a dream and this was the waking up.

Rose brought her car to the end of the drive, pushing it into park next to Becca's truck. Becca'd have to drop him off at the bar in the morning to get the truck he'd left in Pioneer Spirit's parking lot.

The lights were on in the lower level windows of the ranch house, making the place where Becca and Alex lived look like, well, like a home. Nothing about that put Jack at ease in the least, because it wasn't *his* home.

They'd be able to see he was back though, and he could go to bed, and they could go to bed, and if Gabe tried to talk to him, Jack would...

Well, he didn't know, but he did know he had to get out of Rose's car. She'd done something for him tonight. He didn't know exactly what, and he certainly didn't know why, but he knew he'd used up all her pity or whatever it was that had possessed her to include him in this whole thing.

He pushed open his door. "Thanks for the ri—"

"I'm walking you to the door," she said, turning off the ignition.

"You don't have to do that. I can walk to the bunk-house. I can deal with my friends."

"Of course you can," she replied with a shrug. "But they're worried about where you were, and they're going to worry about what you've been doing. If I walk up there with you, lay on the fake-girlfriend thing a little thick, well, they won't ask questions. They won't worry, except maybe about your taste."

"I'm not going to lie to my friends. The fake-girlfriend thing is for my family and my family only."

She shrugged. "Your choice. Doesn't mean I can't go to the door with you and prove you weren't out... How did you phrase it? Doing yourself harm."

"Why are you doing all this? You don't even know me."

Rose stared straight ahead as she squared her shoulders. She shook her head as if she couldn't believe what was transpiring.

Which would make two of them.

"You ever just want to help someone? And maybe you don't have a good reason for it, it's just there?" She glanced at him then, and he couldn't make out much of anything in her expression, but he knew that feeling.

All too well. "Yeah, I guess I know what that feels like."

She laughed, shaking her head. "So I don't have an

answer to any of your whys, Jack. Let me walk you to the door. Consider it a practice run."

He agreed if only because he did understand that inclination, and it would make his life easier, and a few more seconds in Rose's presence wasn't a hardship. Like everything else in his life right now, she made no sense. But like nothing else in his life right now, it didn't twist him up into guilt, fear, and bitterness.

So he walked toward the ranch next to Rose, and where he might have veered off toward the bunkhouse, Rose was clearly dead set on delivering him to the front door of the ranch house, based on the fact that she'd grabbed his hand and was tugging him that way.

"I'm not going to hurt myself, if that's what you're afraid of."

She didn't stop walking toward the house, but she did drop his hand. "No."

"Because I'm not that bad off. I wouldn't give Madison the satisfaction of thinking it was over her."

Finally Rose stopped her persistent march forward, but before she could say anything to that, the door to the ranch house opened, and Alex, Becca, and Gabe all stepped out onto the porch.

When no one said anything, Jack rocked back on his heels. "Beautiful night, huh?"

"Is everything okay?" Becca asked, though in the porch light, it was clear her gaze was on Rose, a questioning kind of concern in that expression.

"Sorry I kept him out late and didn't call. Got carried away," Rose returned, everything about her voice light and cheerful. She sauntered over to him and moved onto her toes.

Jack held himself perfectly still as she brushed her lips featherlight across his jaw. He watched her, and her gaze held his, an amused little quirk tilting the corners of her mouth as she dropped back down to her heels.

"See you later, sweetie." And then in a completely unnecessary display, she smacked his ass as she sauntered back to her car.

Maybe it should have irritated him, but all he could do was laugh. Rose was... He blew out a breath, the laughter dying. Because Rose was something a lot more complicated than he probably needed right now. But he preferred *half-naked swim in a pond* complicated over *facing his ex and his brother* or a *doctor's office waiting room* kind of complicated.

"Come inside, Jack," Alex said, the first to interrupt the silence.

"I don't believe you're my commanding officer anymore, Alex," Jack replied, but something about tonight had unwound that tight spiral of panic he'd been fighting off with anger and bitterness. So despite the snappish words, he stepped up onto the porch and walked inside.

Alex, Becca, and Gabe followed, and they all stood in the entry way, three pairs of concerned eyes on him.

The scrutiny didn't press down on him like it usually did. It wasn't the stilted silences he'd sat through while talking to his family over the course of the past year and a half, or the bitter arguments he and Gabe and Alex sometimes got into when one of them was having a bad day.

There was something okay about this. They were worried about him, and it wasn't in the way his family worried—the *please be okay so we don't have to discuss the elephant in the room*. And it wasn't the way Alex and Gabe had worried before coming here—*if we just keep moving forward, eventually it'll be okay*.

This was something simpler. Something about *him*, instead of them, and that was very nearly new.

"My family is coming to visit," he blurted when it was clear no one knew quite what to say.

Everyone's eyes went wide because, yes, everyone knew exactly what that could mean.

"Your whole family?" Alex asked carefully.

Jack nodded. "Mom. Dad. One sister can't make it, but big bro, cheating ex-fiancée, and their kid are sure going to be here."

"Like hell they are," Becca retorted, fisting her hands on her hips. "You tell them neither of them are welcome. And if you don't want to tell them, I sure will."

Jack had to force himself to breathe through the heavy thing on his chest, because the thing about your fiancée cheating with your *brother* was that you never quite got that unequivocal support Becca was showing him now. No doubt Alex or Gabe would have shown it, but all three of their lives had been blown apart before they'd had a chance.

So no one had ever simply blamed Madison and taken his side without anything else muddying the waters, and he didn't know how to respond to that. He didn't know how to *thank* Becca for that.

"I'm serious, Jack," Becca continued when no one said anything. "I will call your mother up myself, and I will tell her that's unconscionable and awful, and no one should expect you to—"

"It's okay," he managed.

"No, it isn't."

"Rose had a good point tonight. It's been something like two years, and I can't go back and change anything. So maybe it's time to move forward. And if that means them coming here, well, I can take it." He hadn't been so sure of that until right now, thanks to some combination of a woman jumping into a pond and Becca standing up for him.

"What exactly does Rose Rogers have to do with all this?" Alex asked.

"Ah. Well, in a weird twist of fate or something, I was talking to Mom in Pioneer Spirit's parking lot, and Rose called me over. Mom overheard it, and suddenly she was asking about women and yapping about how Madison was worried I hadn't moved on."

Becca made a squeak of outrage. "That two-timing, lying, horrible sack of sh—"

"Easy, tiger," Alex murmured, giving Becca's shoulders a squeeze.

"Anyway, Rose and I agreed to trade favors. Like I mentioned the other night, she needs a little extra security at the bar on weekends, and I need a fake girlfriend."

"Fake?" Gabe asked, raising an eyebrow and looking pointedly at his clothes. Which, yes, were rumpled and a little dirty and… Well.

"We were just talking." Jack didn't think explaining they'd gone swimming would be met with unquestioned understanding.

"You're awfully muddy for just talking," Gabe returned blandly, neither censure nor much of anything readable in his tone.

"We went for a walk. Look. She's… I don't know.

There's nothing going on, and she's going to pretend to be my girlfriend while my family is here, and all you guys have to do is play along. That's all I ask."

Alex, Gabe, and Becca exchanged glances, and Jack knew exactly what those looks meant.

"I really am okay," he said firmly, taking time to look each of them in the eye. "It might be temporary, but you know how that goes. Now, it's late, and we all have a lot of work to do in the morning, so why don't we go to bed?"

There were murmurs of agreement, and Alex and Becca moved toward the staircase that would lead them up to their bedroom, and Gabe moved toward the front door.

Call it the booze, stupidity, or some other thing, but Jack couldn't let it go. "Hey, Bec?"

She turned. "Yeah?"

He thought about how best to express it. All he could think about was the day at the diner a few months back when he'd told her about Madison, and she'd told him she'd always wanted siblings. "The, uh, whole offer to call my mom and give her a piece of your mind? Thanks, Sis."

Becca's face crumpled a little, and suddenly she'd recrossed the room and was squeezing him tight, something that sounded like a sob escaping her lips.

Jack stood stock-still, arms in the air. A million years ago, he might have known what to do with this outburst—he did have two little sisters after all. And he'd been Madison's go-to for when she was upset.

An entire lifetime existed like a brick wall between that Jack and this one, and he didn't know how to... He didn't know.

Jack looked over Becca's head at Alex. "A little help here?"

"Hey, you were the one who made her cry, so you have to deal with the consequences."

Becca sniffed into his chest, and he patted her back awkwardly. She finally pulled away, wiping at her cheeks.

"You don't need any help, Jack. You're doing just fine."

He could almost believe it.

Rose groaned and swore and eventually gave in to the relentless pounding on her door. She glanced at her clock. It was nearly one in the afternoon, which wasn't *that* terrible considering she ran a bar that was open until two in the morning.

But usually she was up and moving by noon, dealing with distributors, schedules, receipts, or what have you.

She swung out of bed. She didn't have any appointments, and her one-man cleaning crew, Cletus, never let anyone back here.

Except family.

A cold dread grabbed her by the throat and she hurried her steps, jerking the door open to find Delia on the other side. She was calm as could be, Sunny wiggling in her arms.

"Hey," Rose greeted breathlessly, moving aside so Delia could step in. "Everything okay?"

"That was going to be my question for you. You're usually up by now."

"Had a late night." Rose scratched a hand through her

hair. She'd showered the pond off her when she'd gotten home last night, but she hadn't bothered to do anything beyond wash up and fall into bed. And now she was a sleepy, tangled mess.

And a little too curious about what Jack was thinking this morning.

Rose shook her head and held her arms out for Sunny. The one-year-old gladly nose-dived into Rose's chest.

"Rose, what aren't you telling me?"

Oh, a whole slew of things. She looked up at Delia and smiled. "About what?"

Delia stood there in silence, staring that imperious older-sister stare. Her jaw worked. "I know," she said gravely.

Rose frowned and walked over to the little playpen she kept set up for Sunny's visits. She placed the girl down onto the mat and handed her one of the toys before turning back to Delia and lowering her voice. "You know what?"

"I know Dad's out," Delia said, her voice not breaking exactly, but weakening. "The lawyer called me."

"What?" Rose said on a gasp. An actual, soap-opera gasp, because. No. No. *No!* Delia was *not* supposed to know. "I told that little weasel not to tell you." She shook her head vigorously. "You shouldn't be worrying about this. Forget that asshole ever called you and focus on growing that baby. You can't worry about this."

"Maybe I shouldn't," Delia said, absently patting her stomach. "But you didn't want Mr. Rombach to tell me *before* you knew I was pregnant, so I'm going to have to toss out that excuse. Why the hell did you think you should keep this from me?"

Rose blew out a breath. She hadn't even had her coffee yet. Why had that bastard *told* Delia? "Oh God." Rose grabbed Delia's hand. "Who else? Did he call everyone?"

Delia sighed. "Yeah. Elsie and Billie and I talked yesterday. We all decided I'd break the news to Steph this morning, then come ask you what the hell you think you're doing."

So all her sisters knew. She'd been trying to *spare* them, and they knew. Why could she never get it right when it came to them?

"Rose."

She couldn't face that note of hurt in Delia's voice. This wasn't supposed to hurt. Not anymore. She was going to make up for all her old mistakes. She thought she had, saving Steph, getting Dad thrown in jail once and for all.

But he was out now, and that was on her too.

Delia stepped close, her fingers curling around Rose's arms. "Sissy, this isn't like it was. We're in this together."

Rose forced herself to face Delia's sad, all-too-empathetic gaze. "I know we are, but I can handle this. I handled Steph. I can handle this. You guys have lives—"

"And so do you."

"You have a kid and one on the way. Steph has to get ready to move into her dorm in a few weeks. Billie and Elsie are out there making Seattle their bitch. And *I* can fight this. *I* can fight him." *I owe you. God, how I owe you.*

Delia couldn't seem to listen to reason. "We're not

separated anymore. I won't let him separate us again.
We fight this together. We fight *him* together. Just like
when we were kids."

Except it hadn't been like that at all. Oh, Rose had
always pretended to be one of them, as though she were
part of the fight, but she'd been Dad's favorite. She'd
been his secret weapon. And for so very long, a part of
her had *relished* that.

She wanted to cry, but hell if she was going to cry
twice in one week. "In all likelihood, he's back in that
hellhole with Mom and he won't bother any of us."

"I hope so," Delia said, watching Sunny happily babbling away at a mirror. "Everyone at Shaw is on high
alert. I don't think Caleb's even sleeping, the idiot. Dan
suggested hiring a private investigator, someone who
could keep tabs on him."

"We can't afford that," Rose whispered. Maybe she
could take out a loan. The bar could be collateral—

"Dan can. And as much as I hate taking charity from
my brother-in-law, this is about everyone's safety. It
isn't as though the ex-hockey player doesn't have the
money. Even Caleb's considering it, and you know he'd
rather eat his own arm off than take money from Dan."

"I, um, have a guy doing a little extra security for
me at the bar, but I guess someone keeping tabs on
him wouldn't be bad." Like it did for Caleb, the idea of
accepting help burned and frustrated, but she couldn't
possibly argue with Delia when she had a kid to protect
and another one growing in her freaking stomach.

"Who?"

"Who what?"

"Who's this guy *you* trust to do security for you? You

don't even trust Tonya with the keys to your bar, and you're thinking about making her manager."

"He's just a guy."

"And now you're being cagey." Delia studied her face, and Rose looked away. Delia had an uncanny way of getting to the bottom of things, and Rose didn't want to talk about Jack. Not when she felt all weird.

"What's his name? Why'd you pick him? Where'd he come from?"

Rose groaned. "You know I have work to do, right?"

"And you know I'll get out of here a lot faster if you spill the details already."

"Fine." Rose unsuccessfully tried to rake her fingers through her tangled hair again. "His name is Jack. He's a former Navy SEAL." And that was all she was going to say.

"Jack what?"

"Why? So you can google him?"

"Is he one of those guys over at the Maguire ranch? They're doing some sort of injured military rehab thing? What are they calling it now? Re…Re something?"

"Revival Ranch," Rose muttered.

"Yes, that. And you hired this injured former Navy SEAL to watch after you?"

"No, I traded him a favor to stick around here on Friday and Saturday nights and be on the lookout. He doesn't even know who he's looking out for, just what Dad looks like. He is most certainly not protecting *me*."

"It's not the worst thing," Delia said, her voice hushed.

"What?"

Delia sighed, walking over to the playpen. She looked down at Sunny, who was still happily busying herself with toys. "It's not the worst thing to let someone look after you. To trust someone. To let go a little."

Rose didn't know how to control her face. She didn't know how to fight all this. It was too early and she was too tired and Delia didn't *get* it.

It wasn't other people she didn't trust. It was herself.

"Rose, if you want to be a good sister, you want to take care of me while I'm pregnant, then you listen to me. I want you to let me in. I want you to tell me everything. I don't ever, *ever* want secrets between us."

"It wasn't a secret. It was just—"

Delia crossed and grabbed her again, this time giving her a little shake instead of a squeeze. "This is our chance, Rose. To have whatever we want, *be* whatever we want. We get to live and love, without fear and without holding back. Do not shut me out. Do not shut the girls out. We are in this together. Always. Forever." Delia's lips quivered, but she pressed them together. "Puking my guts out or no, I can handle this as long as we're all in it together."

"We are."

"Good, because we aren't helpless little girls at his mercy anymore. We are five grown, kick-ass women, and we have the Shaws behind us one hundred percent. He can't do anything to us anymore."

Rose wished she could believe it, but for her sister, she nodded. For her sister, she did the one thing Delia had asked her not to do.

She lied. "You're damn right he can't."

Chapter 8

JACK ARRIVED AT PIONEER SPIRIT AROUND SUNDOWN, per Rose's previous instructions. Tonya quickly ushered him to a table close to the door, gave him an iced tea, and that was that.

He didn't get a greeting from Rose. Not even a glance.

So he did what she'd asked him to do. He sat there and sipped his tea and watched the door. He'd stared at the picture long enough, trying to read the hidden danger in a sixty-something-year-old man's face, but much like in a war zone, you couldn't read sins in the supposed enemy's eyes or wrinkles.

Regardless, this was his mission. Never mind that he hated sitting still, whiling away hours in a bar. He was working, so he couldn't drink away all the crap that whirled around in a constant loop in his brain. A mission was a mission, and it didn't matter if you hated it when it was for the greater good.

He scanned the bar, not even able to catch a glimpse of Rose working behind the line of customers sitting and standing, waiting for their drinks.

Good thing his family wasn't here yet. If they knew he was sitting around a bar for hours on end, they'd have quite a few things to say. In their own special code, of course. Armstrongs never came out and said a bad word about anyone. It wasn't considered moral or neighborly. That didn't mean judgment wasn't passed though.

If this was happening at home, his family would very quietly express concern over the amount of time he was spending "in town." Mom would suggest other ways he could spend his evenings. Dad would make noises about farm duty without ever coming out and actually telling or asking Jack to do something.

Jack smiled ruefully. Why did he miss that? Who wanted veiled disapproval and constant suggestions about better ways he could spend his time? He didn't, but it was all part of being a part of something bigger than him. Being an Armstrong. Being a family. Working together.

Maybe eventually Revival would feel like that, once they opened. It wouldn't be much longer—by the new year, if Becca the Hun had her way. But it wasn't here yet, and his chest still ached with a vague kind of homesickness he couldn't ever give into. Because the home he wanted, the home he remembered…it was long gone.

Thanks to two people who were supposed to love him.

Damn, he wished he had a real drink. Or a pond to jump in to remind him of all those things he'd felt last night. For once, he'd been hopeful about the future and grateful for the people he had. But he had hours to go and no pond on hand, so he pissed away the hours making up stories about every patron who walked in the door. Ms. Leather Vest ran an outlaw biker gang somewhere out in the vast Montana landscape. Sunglasses Inside Guy was a famous country singer incognito.

And Rose Rogers was the beacon his gaze kept drifting to when he could catch a glimpse of her. Even as the crowd thinned and it became a little too obvious, he kept watching her. The longer he sat there, not seeing any sign of the guy in the picture anywhere, the less he cared about how obvious his staring was.

He watched as she emptied the tip jar and handed the contents to Tonya, sending her on her way home. He watched as the crowd dwindled down to fifteen, then ten, then three. He saw Rose making a beeline for him, surely to tell him to go home, and he didn't know why he wanted to avoid that as much as he did.

But when someone grabbed her attention before she could reach him, he headed for the bathroom, leaving the room while she was busy telling Mr. Sunglasses that he didn't have to go home, but he couldn't stay here.

Jack stepped into the dimly lit bathroom and washed his hands, looking at himself in the grimy mirror. He'd avoided mirrors a lot more lately, not really wanting to see what stared back at him. He still wasn't sure he wanted to, but for the first time in a long time, he felt compelled.

Compelled to look at his own blue eyes and the way his face was too thin and sharp these days. There was the beard he'd have to shave before his mother showed up, and all the scars no one could see but him.

This was Jack Armstrong, this man staring back at him, his plans all gone and his future a big question mark. The familiar panic settled somewhere beneath his breastbone, and he had to look away.

He'd never had to deal with question marks. His life had been a string of periods, of knowing exactly everything that was coming next from the second he was living till the day he died.

And now it's all gone. When are you going to accept that?

The panic beat harder. He was used to pushing the anxiety away, down beneath that will of steel that had gotten him through SEAL training and a tour in Afghanistan. That heavy thing that had allowed him to survive watching Geiger die, to survive his own injuries and make it through all the physical therapy he'd needed to be able to move his body right again.

He didn't have that thing to work toward anymore. He was alive. He had friends, a job, and a place to live, and that iron anchor that had kept him grounded against panic didn't seem to be working anymore.

Now what? Now what? Now what?

"I don't know," he whispered, staring at a rusty sink in a hole-in-the-wall bar bathroom in the middle of rural Montana.

Who the hell was this guy he was somehow living in and for?

Maybe, just maybe, a hole-in-the wall bar bathroom was not the place to figure it out.

He forced himself to move away from the sink and the mirror. Maybe he couldn't anchor his panic like he used to, but that didn't mean he couldn't beat it. He might not be a SEAL anymore, but he was a SEAL at heart. He wouldn't be beaten.

Not by anything.

He stepped out of the bathroom to find the bar empty save for Sunglasses Guy sitting on a stool and grinning at Rose.

She was not grinning back.

"I don't think you know how things work around here," she said, her voice edged with the kind of fury that would have sent a smart man running.

Sunglasses did not run. "Come on, baby. Bet if you let me buy you a drink, I could change your mind."

"The bar is closed, and you were told to leave."

"Don't be an uptight bitch."

"Did you know acting like a dick won't actually make yours any bigger?" She flashed her sharpest grin and then jerked her chin toward the door. "You have five seconds to get out the door."

"Or what?"

"Or I escort you out," Jack said flatly, stepping forward and making sure he didn't limp, no matter how it hurt to move his leg like that. "And we might have a little accident with my fist and your nose along the way."

The man turned to face Jack and scowled. "I don't believe you were invited to this party. Bye, now."

"Jack—"

He ignored whatever Rose was going to say. He stepped forward and grabbed Sunglasses by the back of his shirt, jerking him to his feet.

"Hey!" The guy tried to fight Jack off, but Jack was holding his shirt tight enough that the collar would start to choke him if he did more thrashing. "Hey!" the guy yelled again as Jack started propelling him toward the door.

Jack was sorely tempted to slam the guy into it, considering he apparently thought it was okay to harass women when he thought they were alone. For the sake of not having to clean blood off Rose's floor, he opened the door with his free hand and shoved the guy out.

"Please let the door hit your ass on the way out," he muttered, slamming it hard and smirking a little when it clearly did hit its target.

Jack flicked the lock, something like a smile spreading across his face. That had felt good. To do something. *Something*.

He didn't know what he'd expected Rose's response to be, but it certainly wasn't the cold fury she was aiming right at him.

"You should not have stepped in."

"Excuse me?"

"I don't need any macho display interrupting *my* business in *my* bar." She whirled away, slamming dirty glasses down and flinging towels about behind the bar.

"Looked like it came in pretty handy right then," Jack returned, and maybe he shouldn't be pissed that *she* was pissed over him doing something that finally felt *real*.

But he was.

"Yeah, well, so does this." She reached under the bar and pulled out a gun and slammed it against the hard surface of the bar. "I'm armed, remember? Don't get it in your head you need to swoop in and save me. I asked for your help for one thing and one thing only. Keeping an eye out for one guy. I don't need muscle. Especially yours."

"'Thanks for the help, Jack' is the actual appropriate response."

Her nostrils flared, and she leaned over the bar as if it were the only thing keeping her from going after him. "You're not a Navy SEAL anymore, Jack, and I'm not the country you swore to protect. So, no, I won't be thanking you."

It landed harder than it should have. He *knew* he wasn't a SEAL anymore. He'd come to grips with that. What else was there to do? He couldn't even walk right.

Of course he wasn't a SEAL anymore. He'd looked into that bathroom mirror and *accepted* that.

And yet the thing about swearing to protect, about feeling good over *having* protected her and her throwing it back in his face. Yeah, it landed like the hard, solar plexus blow it was.

"Okay," he forced himself to say, and if he wasn't so rattled, maybe he'd have been irritated or embarrassed that his voice was hoarse. "Point made," he added and turned for the door.

He was not a Navy SEAL. No one wanted him to protect them. He didn't know who he was or what he wanted, and it was all fine. Great. *Amazing*.

He didn't need a mission. He didn't need anything.

He walked out the door and tried not to worry about her locking it behind him. Of course she would. Rose wasn't an idiot, and she didn't need his help.

No one did.

He had a family who loved him, complicated and from afar. Friends who cared if he was okay and wanted to defend him to those who'd wronged him. He had work to do. All of that was important and better than a lot of people had.

But not one person in the universe *needed* him. He didn't know how a guy was supposed to breathe with that knowledge sucking all the oxygen out of his body.

Rose swore and internally lectured herself a million times over. Her hesitation lasted maybe two minutes before she went after him.

She shouldn't do it, because Jack had seen her true

colors right there, in the nasty temper and the words designed to hurt. Her parents' legacy passed on to her—with just enough conscience for it to bother her, but not enough to change.

She unlocked the front door, practically jogging to catch up with his long-legged strides, never mind the limp.

"Jack!"

He didn't stop, and why should he? She'd been purposefully mean and twisted the knife right where it would do the most damage.

She shouldn't run after him and prolong that damage. Fixing things now would only give her the opportunity to do it over and over again. She didn't want to feel that rush of shame and hurt every time, and she didn't want to see the way his face registered a blow, the way those ice-blue eyes widened, and his mouth lost that hard-edged military firmness. In that moment, he looked like any other vulnerable man instead of the superhero he so often resembled.

Let him leave. Go inside. Save him from yourself.

"Jack!"

He finally stopped next to his truck. It was dark, and she could only see him as a shadow.

"What? I'll be back tomorrow night if that's what you're worried about. A deal is a deal." He opened his truck door.

She had to close her eyes against that perfectly executed slap. Oh, he wouldn't see it that way. This trading of favors was his duty, the right thing to do. No matter how she treated him. No matter all the ways she would eviscerate him before she could stop herself. Why on

God's green earth had she allowed this to happen? She'd stuck her nose in his business, and suddenly they were all tangled up in something.

Cut the ties.

"You don't have to come back."

Even though she wasn't sure she'd said that in any more than a whisper, the whole night around them seemed to hold its breath, heavy and quiet and so, so still.

Then he slammed his truck door closed, and she jumped. When was the last time she'd been scared enough to *jump* at something? She'd beaten the fear of overt threats out of herself long ago.

But Jack, or at least the shadow of him, stormed across the parking lot to where she stood at the end of the sidewalk. She didn't have to see his face to know he was furious.

"You will not dismiss me. You are not my commanding officer, you are not my boss, and you are damn well not my ex. I am not disposable, and I'm not letting another person treat me that way."

"Jack." It came out like the pained gasp it was, and she reached out for him, but he sidestepped it, the two of them a pair of angry, hurting shadows dancing away from each other in the night.

"I will be back tomorrow night, and I will look for the mysterious guy you want me to look for, and you are going to pretend to be my very happy girlfriend so Madison can shove it up her ass. And you know what? If I see a guy harassing you, I'm going to step in. I don't care how many guns and knives you have under there. It's *my* life. *I* get to decide."

Which gave her at least a little inkling that this wasn't

all about what she'd said. "It's my life too," she said quietly, and that seemed to still some of that angry agitation coursing through him.

This whole outburst softened her, because Jack wasn't an outburst guy. He kept it all bottled up tight— and maybe he needed to let some of it go. Not alone though. "Come inside. We'll have a drink."

"Yes, because it's a hell of an idea to keep drowning it all in alcohol."

Maybe it wasn't the best idea she'd ever had, but he couldn't head home emotionally bleeding all over the place. He needed to take a breath and get a handle on himself before she let him go off in his truck all half-cocked.

"Come inside."

"Remember when you said you weren't any country I swore to protect? Well, I'm not some sob story you need to soothe your conscience with."

"That's not what I'm doing," she returned through gritted teeth, because maybe he wasn't too far off the mark. She didn't exactly see him as a sob story, but there might have been a flash of truth she recognized in the whole *soothe your conscience* bit.

"Then what are you doing?"

"I don't know," she threw back at him, frustration and guilt and some other thing that felt a whole lot like panic fluttering in her chest. What was there to panic over? What did she care if Jack took off? They were maybe friends at best, and he'd just made it clear he was coming back. Panic was nonsensical. Frustration was pointless. Guilt was...

Well, inevitable.

"Seems to be a theme," he murmured, his voice suddenly soft. "Not used to that, are you?"

She wanted to tell him he didn't know her, but she couldn't form the words, couldn't push them out of her mouth.

"Me neither," he said, as if she'd agreed instead of remained silent and still. She felt his fingertips on her cheek, hot and rough against the cool of her skin. A gentle caress.

He was touching her like something delicate and precious, and her breath got all tangled in her lungs. She swallowed, trying to find some sense of power, some sense of her usual cool detachment.

"W-what are you doing?" Had she just *stuttered* that question? Unacceptable. Rose Rogers didn't stutter.

"I thought we established I don't have a clue what I'm doing, so it might as well be this," Jack returned, his voice a dark rumble.

And in the dark night, like so many of her dreams lately, Jack's mouth was on hers. Hot and somehow demanding. None of the timid, only-been-with-one-girl stuff she might have imagined.

His beard was a rough scrape against her chin and his tongue a velvet whisper across her lips, and no matter the little voice in her head telling her to stop this before it hurt them both, she opened her mouth for him.

His tongue swept in, and everything inside her shut up and hummed with a pulsing life. It might have been dark around her, but she felt like a beacon of light, like the center of something. And when Jack's warm hand slid behind her neck, cupping it firmly, as if she was somehow *his* to cherish and protect, her body simply loosened and relaxed in a way it never, ever had.

That was quickly followed by a bolt of panic so hard and so potent, she pushed him away. It was only then she realized she was shaking, maybe shaking *apart*, against the brick wall of her bar.

Her bar. Her power. She was in charge. She was...

Broken, just like me.

She pushed away her father's voice, pushed away everything except the feel of the cool, rough brick behind her back. This was her center, this rough-and-tumble, hole-in-the-wall bar she'd worked her ass off for the past few years.

She took a deep breath in and a deep breath out, almost able to laugh at the fact that she could hear Jack doing exactly the same thing.

Calming himself. Finding center.

"I'm not going to pretend I didn't... Well, that was a hell of a kiss, Jack."

"Okay," he replied, his voice frustratingly devoid of any readable emotion.

"I imagine sex would be great too."

"I would imagine," he replied blandly.

"I need you to understand something, okay? You're not disposable, but I'm not...good guy material. I'm attracted to you, God knows, and I'd even break a few personal rules and sleep with you, but that's all it would be."

"Did you think that kiss was me asking for a pity fuck?" And *there* was a hint at some emotion—rage or wounded pride or both.

"No. No, that's not what... Look, guys like you

do not have *relationships* with foul-mouthed, tattooed bar owners."

"Guys like me."

"Yes. Good, upstanding—for heaven's sake, you were a Navy SEAL, engaged to the girl next door that your family expected you to marry. You're like an American fairy tale. Let me tell you, a princess gets that guy. Not me."

"Did you mistake me kissing you for a marriage proposal?"

She blew out a breath and something almost like a laugh. "No. But… One woman. You've had one life-long relationship, and I just need to be clear that this ain't going to be that. This can be something temporary and fun, but nothing like a *relationship*. That's not what I'm after."

"I see."

"So you can take it or leave it."

He was quiet for the longest time, and it was stupid to hold her breath or worry. Of course he would take it. It was sex without strings. It was the modern American Dream.

But Jack never seemed to do the *expected* thing.

"Leave it," he replied, a firm, commanding response that brooked no argument.

Chapter 9

"WHAT?" ROSE SPLUTTERED, AND THERE WAS SOME satisfaction in that. Not as much satisfaction as her melting against him like candle wax when he'd kissed her, but still some.

"I said leave it," Jack repeated, unable to keep from smiling, though he doubted she could see it clearly in the dark.

"I'm sorry. You're turning me down because *why*?"

"Temporary and fun doesn't sound... Well, it's not what I'm looking for anyway." Because he was looking for *something*, and he hadn't figured that all out yet. But for as much as had changed in the past two years, he was still Jack Armstrong, and he was not a man who jumped into things without understanding what he wanted out of them.

He'd followed Alex and Gabe here, moaning and bitching, but there'd been a hope that Montana and Revival Ranch would offer him some insight. He'd come here with *hope*.

If he slept with Rose, he wanted the hope there too.

Because the moment his mouth had touched hers and that sharp, whiskey taste of her had infiltrated his system, he'd realized the answer to all the panic he'd felt in the bathroom not so long ago.

For the first time in twenty-eight years, he finally and fully realized that this was his life. Not his parents', not

Madison's, not his country's. This was *his* life, one he was in charge of. There was no one to give him orders. No one on some faceless other side wanting to lob grenades at him. There was nothing but this whole empty stretch of years in front of him.

Kissing Rose had loosed something in him. There was no one waiting for him to come home. There were no old plans to make a reality. There was nothing except whatever he wanted.

And damn if he didn't want Rose Rogers.

Not like this though. Oh, his erection argued with that a little bit, but something quick in an empty bar wasn't going to solve anything, and there'd been a few too many years recently where he hadn't solved a thing. He wanted that feeling that had rushed through him when he'd taken out the guy at the bar. Rose had made a very good point that it was her life too, and she got to do what *she* wanted, and she didn't want him stepping in to protect her.

Fair enough, all in all, but he needed to find something that gave him that same sense of control. Of choice. For the first time in his life, he needed to decide what it was he was going to accomplish, regardless of what anyone else said.

As much as he wanted one of those accomplishments to be getting Rose into bed, Rose was used to being in charge. Quite honestly, he wasn't. He'd met the expectations of everyone in his life, followed his superior officers' orders, and ever since the explosion that had rocked his whole life, he'd followed Alex around with only a few adolescent tantrums to counter.

Maybe it was time for a switch.

"Let's go back inside."

"For what? You kissed me and then rejected..." She cleared her throat, and it was dark, so he couldn't see her, but he could picture her squaring her shoulders—he could envision her clearly drawing that armor over her expression again. "You rejected my offer. I think we're done here, sweetheart."

"Has your *offer* never been rejected before?"

"Um, no. *I* do the rejecting around here."

"Well, maybe this will be good for you."

She made a squeak of outrage, and he knew he shouldn't laugh, but Rose held herself so together. Sure, he'd seen cracks in that tough-as-nails demeanor, but they had always been to let her kindness seep through.

He hadn't seen her surprised yet, or affected. He hadn't seen her spluttering or unsure. He couldn't get over the crazy thought that he needed to find some surety in life and maybe Rose needed to find the opposite.

Wouldn't it be fun to find it together?

"You know, Jack, I've been waiting around my whole life to have a man tell me what would be *good* for me."

He was not the smartest man who'd ever walked the earth, but he knew that syrupy-sweet tone meant nothing—*nothing*—but trouble.

"I didn't mean..." Only he kind of had meant that. He edged away from where he was standing, still way too close to her.

"Go to hell," she whispered vehemently, and only about a second later, she crushed her mouth to his. If he'd thought *his* kiss was a little pushy, it had nothing on *hers*. She was all teeth and tongue, and her fingers scraped through his beard and into his hair—a rough, delicious friction.

It was an invitation, or maybe a deliberate show of all she could offer, and his body had tightened so painfully, he wasn't sure when it would ever unwind. He questioned all those things he'd just assured himself of.

They could have sex *now*, and he could convince her of other things *later*. Much, much later. That seemed like a much better thing when her mouth was like the sun he wanted to revolve around. When for the first time in years, someone was touching him as something other than a patient or a friend. It was about him. And her. And so many parts of himself he thought had died felt as though they were pulsing to life.

Rose released him with a shuddery exhale that did all sorts of things for his ego.

"I hope that keeps you up all night, Jack," she said. He didn't think it sounded nearly as sharp as she wanted it to, but she turned, and he heard her footsteps retreat toward the bar.

She jerked the door open and, bathed in the small swath of light from inside the bar, flipped him off before disappearing inside. The bang of the lock clicking into place echoed through the night.

All Jack could do was laugh.

―――

Rose stomped around the bar, flinging glasses into the dishwasher with too little care, wiping down the bar with as much force as she could muster. Sweeping and cursing in equal measure.

Usually Cletus handled half of this, but Rose knew she wouldn't be sleeping tonight. If she wasn't so irritated with smug, irrational, condescending *men*, she might have chased after Jack and insisted he put her to sleep *real* good.

What right did he have to kiss like that? What right did he have to sweep into her life—very uninvited—and suddenly make all her old choices and plans feel...

Wrong wasn't the right word. *Less*. Not having someone around to kiss her like that suddenly felt like *less*.

That rat bastard. She didn't even know his last name! Or what he liked to eat. And even though they'd all but skinny-dipped together, she didn't know what the man looked like naked.

Except in his expression. She'd seen raw and naked emotion in those cool-blue eyes a few too many times to count, and it always pulled at something inside her that she'd thought she'd eradicated long ago. There was too much *wrong* flowing through her blood to ever do something right.

Which was self-pitying bullshit she didn't have time for, much like she had no time for that macho stunt he'd pulled kicking that douche out of her bar. Though it had been nice for once—just once—not to have to fight her own battles. Wanting was one thing, but she didn't *need* help and she didn't *need* nice, and she sure didn't deserve it.

She slammed into her apartment with tears burning in her eyes and emotion clogging her throat. She wanted to go to her house out in the middle of nowhere and sleep under the stars and dream of...

She had a terrible feeling she'd only dream about Jack.

She needed a shower. Shower. That was a thing she'd do. She pulled her phone out of her pocket and slammed it onto her nightstand and then glared at it.

It was the middle of the night, but Sunny wasn't the best of sleepers, and Delia usually had trouble sleeping when she was pregnant and...

"You are not bothering your sister at two o'clock in the morning." She said it firmly and determinedly into the empty room.

She stalked to the bathroom and got into the shower, trying to wash the bar grime and smell off herself. It didn't help, because she didn't feel like the sticky, sweaty mess she usually did after a Friday night at work. She still felt *Jack*.

The hard edge of his body. The scrape of his beard. The taste of his mouth somehow different than any other man who'd dared put his lips to hers.

She'd never touched anyone like Jack. Never allowed herself even the glimmer of an idea she might be good enough for the likes of him. She didn't date a whole heck of a lot, but when she allowed herself the luxury of a man in her bed, she went for the slick and the mean. Men she could fight, whether with her words or her actual fists—people like her, ugly inside and out.

And there was that urge to cry again, no matter that she was clean and dry and wrapped in her favorite pair of sweats. So she grabbed her phone and typed a quick awake? text to Delia.

When her phone rang in the next minute, Rose curled up into bed and breathed a sigh of relief. "Sunny or baby?"

"Baby," Delia replied, groaning. "I've been puking my guts out for the last hour."

"You okay? I could bring you something."

"Caleb's already served me four glasses of ginger ale

with varying levels of ice, a bottle of water, a bag of crackers, and a Snickers bar."

"A Snickers bar?"

"He's getting desperate. I told him to leave me alone to die in peace, so I can probably talk for fifteen minutes before he brings me some other thing. What's up?"

"Well, since you're married to one, I figured you could tell me why men are so stupid." Although she never could quite think of Caleb as stupid. Especially not when he fussed over Delia like a mother hen. Caleb was good and sweet, and Delia deserved that more than anyone Rose knew. Definitely more than Rose would ever deserve.

"Hm. Well, that depends on the man, I suppose," Delia returned. "Who are we talking about?"

Rose paused and considered doing something she'd never done—not as a teenager or even in the past two years when life had gotten somewhat normal for the Rogers girls. She considered actually telling her sister everything that was going on.

"Just a guy."

"Hm. The guy you hired to look out for Dad, I'm assuming?"

Rose blew out a breath. "Poor Sunny isn't ever going to get anything by you, is she?"

"From your lips to God's ears. What was his name again? Jack?"

"Yes. Jack."

"And what did this stupid Jack do?"

Rose sighed, thinking about that moment outside her bar. She couldn't picture it since it had been dark, but that somehow made it worse. She had to relive the feel of it every single time. "He kissed me."

"Did you decapitate him?"

Rose smiled, burrowing deeper into her pillow. "No."

"Castrate then."

Rose burst out laughing, but the answer was that *feel* of Jack all over again, and the laugh died. "I kissed him back," she muttered, picking at a small tear in her comforter.

"Hm. Interesting. I'm guessing you aren't calling me to talk about a shitty kiss at two in the morning, so it must've been good."

Good did not begin to describe what had transpired between them. No word did. From the idiot hitting on her to Jack escorting him out, from their fight to their kiss, from Jack's *leave it* to her flipping him off. There were no words for any of it.

"No one's ever kissed me like that," Rose murmured before she could think better of it.

"Like what?"

Everything inside her rebelled against saying it out loud, like a curse that would take if she did. And yet the truth of it bubbled up inside her, a poison she *had* to let out before it killed her. "Like I might have the answers he's looking for," she all but whispered.

Delia was quiet, a long, drawn-out moment that sat in Rose's stomach like a weight.

"Well, Sissy," she said at last. "Maybe you do."

"I don't have anyone's answers," Rose replied, fighting that stupid tide of emotion all over again. Answers? She was never an answer. "Even if I wanted to, which I don't, I'm not…"

"Let me tell you a little story that might help you sort through some things."

"Don't you dare *once upon a time* me."

"Once upon a time..."

"Delia," Rose tried to growl, but it ended somewhere on a laugh.

"There was a man who was the last man I ever thought I'd end up with. Granted, I didn't think I'd ever end up with anyone, but really, most especially not him."

"I'm going to hang up on you."

"And then a magical thing happened, Rose. I gave him a blow job."

Rose howled with laughter, gratified Delia managed to do the same without retching. And maybe she cried a little bit too, laughing with her sister over something as simple as sex jokes.

"Rose, in all seriousness, if he's a good guy and things feel different with him, trust me, honey, it's... it's a... I don't have the words. It's big and it's wonderful and it'll hurt like hell half the time, but it can change your life in the most wonderful, beautiful ways. And I'd hate to think you, my brave, take-no-shit little sister, would be too scared to take a chance on something good."

"I'm not scared," Rose shot back, holding the phone too tight.

"Then what are you?"

Not good enough. She opened her mouth to say it, to finally let it out. Put everything at her older sister's feet. That's what they were for when your parents were assholes, right? A big sister was there to guide you through all the crap you thought about yourself.

Except Delia had never had anyone to do that for her. She was the oldest, and she'd protected all of them, and all Rose had ever done was protect herself at the expense of anyone else.

Apple of my eye, Rosie girl. The one apple that didn't fall too far from the tree.

Rose swallowed against the rising tide of nausea that went with the memories of her father's voice saying those words. The way her mother would say the same thing whenever Rose lashed out at her.

Only Dad had been gleeful, and Mom had been disgusted, and it was all too, too much to lay at her sister's feet. Or anyone's.

Delia groaned long and loud. "Sorry, I gotta go." The line clicked dead, thankfully before Rose had to listen to the inevitable follow-up.

She set down her phone and stared at her ceiling.

Saved by the puke.

Chapter 10

Jack hated sessions with Monica. Of course, he also hated the label "PTSD" and doing obnoxious breathing exercises and yap, yap, yapping about all the stuff he'd rather leave behind three times a week.

On the other hand, the nightmares had started to go away. The headaches that he'd blamed on his physical therapy, on the pain pills the doctor had prescribed, and a million other things, had dissipated to almost never. Even the random bouts of shaking panic that used to grab him out of nowhere had diminished.

So he kept going back. He might not *like* therapy sessions, but damn if they hadn't worked. Jack only wished Gabe would get over himself and do the same.

That was a worry for another day, because now he was standing in a stall with Monica, brushing down one of the horses. He supposed that was half of why this worked. They got to concentrate on the horses, on their hands, and the conversations that followed felt all the more natural because of it.

"Are you excited about your family visiting?" Monica asked, brushing out Pal's mane carefully.

Jack focused on the side of the horse he was sponging down. "It'll be good to see Mom and Dad," he said, hedging. Which was pointless, because he had no doubt Monica would maneuver him into talking about the subject he was avoiding.

"You said you were having trouble sleeping again lately. Do you suppose it's to do with the visit?"

He glared at her over the horse. "I hate 'do you supposes.'"

"Hmm," was all she said, her blue eyes on the horse's mane.

Jack blew out a breath. "Yes, I *suppose* it does."

"You're excited about seeing your parents?"

"Yes. Them. And my sister. Not so excited about the rest." Which he didn't have to elaborate on, since he'd already told Monica the whole Mike and Madison story.

"Naturally. However, it might help to look at it as an opportunity for closure. I imagine whenever they told you about it, there wasn't an opportunity to really discuss it."

"Oh, we've never talked about it."

"What?" Monica demanded, looking at him with wide-eyed surprise.

"My father was the one who called and told me Madison was pregnant and would be marrying Mike."

Monica's jaw actually dropped, which might have been funny if they'd been talking about anything else.

"You mean, your brother and Madison never..." Monica paused and smoothed out her features, pressing her fingers to her mouth before she continued. "They've never spoken to you directly about what happened?"

"No."

Monica frowned at that, pressing her lips together so tightly, they all but disappeared on her fair face.

"What?"

"Nothing," she replied and again smoothed out her features, though there was still a downward turn to her lips. "I'm an impartial listener."

Jack was surprised to find...he didn't think that was true. Clearly, she had an opinion, and she was trying very hard to mask her disapproval.

Which was oddly warming.

"Well, this will be an opportunity to get some closure with them. For all of you. Not talking about it...not speaking at all?" She focused back on the horse as if that might keep the emotion out of her voice. "I can't speak for them, but typically when something bad happens, the best way to deal with it is head-on."

"Oh, Monica, you do not know my family at all."

She chuckled at that, but she sobered quickly. "Jack, you had an incredibly traumatic experience in Afghanistan, compounded by a complex relationship betrayal. While you've made incredible strides the past few sessions, if you don't address this piece of it, you'll never fully be able to accept the events of that day."

"She's married to my brother and they have a kid. What more is there to address?"

"Just because some events are irreversible doesn't mean we don't have to deal with the emotional fallout."

"Yeah, well, they're not getting the satisfaction of seeing my emotional fallout."

"Okay. I can understand that desire. We all want to keep our personal pride intact, and I don't think that's a necessarily wrong tack to take. Ignoring it isn't going to help *you* though."

"I'm not going to ignore it. I'm going to flaunt my new happy life, girlfriend and all."

"Wait. You have a girlfriend?"

"Well, someone who's agreed to pretend anyway." Rose hadn't said a word to him since Saturday night, but he figured if she had decided not to honor their deal, she would have come out and told him that. So he'd spent all week giving her space. He'd thrown himself into ranch work during the day, had his therapy in the afternoon, and pored over vet candidates with Becca, Alex, and Gabe at night.

And yes, he'd spent a *lot* of that time thinking about Rose, but there was something comforting about that. Thinking about something that wasn't his limp and pain, his mental state, or the impending arrival of his family made him feel more normal than he had in a long time.

"As your therapist, I can't condone that plan of action," Monica said very carefully, frowning as she hung up the mane comb on its peg.

Jack shrugged, dropping the sponge in the bucket. "I didn't ask for your approval."

"No, you didn't." She stepped out of the stall, and he followed. He could tell she wanted to say something—she kept opening her mouth, then closing it and shaking her head. Finally, she threw her hands up in the air. "You know what, it's unprofessional, and I should keep my mouth shut, but for what it's worth, as a friend? I don't just condone it—I want to see your brother's face when you show up with a girlfriend."

Jack barked out a surprised laugh. That was the absolute last thing he'd expected. It wasn't so much that he didn't consider Monica a friend—aside from the whole therapy thing, she was part of his business, and her kid was a riot. Friendship had oddly made it easier to trust her with the therapy stuff. She was actually a part of all this. This weird question mark of his life.

"Can I ask you a question not about me or my stuff?"

"Sure."

"What kind of things would make a person think…" Rose's words about not being "good guy material" and not the princess who ends up with a decent guy had rattled around in his head, not making any sense. "Well, that they're not good enough for someone."

"You're sure this isn't about you?"

He blinked at that. He knew he was a little broken. Okay, a lot broken. He knew he wasn't good or perfect, but he'd never considered that a reason to stay away from people. Or to think all he could ever have with Rose was something *fun and temporary*.

"No, it's not about me."

"Self-worth is a complicated thing. The loss of it can stem from a tragedy, a trauma, or something as simple as consistent undermining from an important relationship or maybe from childhood."

"Abuse?"

"Definitely." Monica frowned. "What's this all about?"

Jack shook his head. "Just thinking about a friend, I guess. How do you help someone find that, then? Self-worth."

Monica ran a hand over her braid. "Well, that's complicated too. It has to come from them first— encouraging them to find confidence in things they're good at, learn new skills, really engage with life. It's a lot about giving them the space to feel good about themselves, but it's far more than that. And usually they have to accept some things about the cause of the problem as well, which you can't do for them."

Jack considered all of that. Complicated seemed to

be the theme for this whole post–Navy SEAL, post-planned-out life he was living.

"Which goes a little bit back to what we're talking about with the whole family visit thing. It's an opportunity, Jack, for you to accept some things—or at least address them."

"Oh, look, time's up."

Monica rolled her eyes, but there was a smile on her face. "Okay, but if there's anything I can do to help, just let me know."

"Thanks, Monica." He offered a wave and headed for the barn. Hick had the day off, and Jack had haying to do. Haying that would be spent wondering if Rose had anyone to talk to. About her problems. About him. About anything at all.

Because he'd been there, with no one to talk to. He'd never talked to Madison about his fears about being deployed and definitely never shared that with his family. He hadn't wanted to worry them. He'd never discussed anything too difficult with anyone, because that wasn't what you did. You worked, you dealt, and you lived. Everything else was between you and your nightly prayers.

Here at Revival, he had nothing but people to confide in. Whether he was feeling like crap or had no idea where his life was going or whatever. He had this entire group of people who not only *would* listen to him, but actually wanted to hear what he had to say.

He didn't know much about Rose's life, but she seemed like such an isolated figure. Tough and strong, yeah. She had that old, run-down house in the middle of nowhere to escape to, but she didn't seem to have any*one*. She seemed to make sure not to.

Maybe that meant she didn't *want* anyone, at least for the long haul. Maybe that was something he should respect and accept.

Maybe.

~~~

Rose was so not in the mood for a Friday night at the bar, which was unusual. Usually the crowd—and the money coming in—revived her spirits no matter how low they were.

But Jack being in her bar made her edgy. Of course, somehow Jack *not* being in her bar had made her edgy too, and she'd been waiting around all week for him to show up. He and Gabe usually came in at least one night a week, but he'd been completely absent since Saturday.

She'd *known* he would come in tonight, since that had been their deal. She'd told herself all week she would not pay him any mind tonight, but her gaze kept finding him…always staring at her from his seat at a table.

The absolute worst part of this was that she didn't know what to *do*. Talking to Delia had only confused her more, and a week with no Jack sightings hadn't clarified anything either.

Because, much as she didn't really know the guy, she knew *parts* of the guy, and the way that all worked together to make her feel…soft. Damn it. She couldn't allow herself to be soft.

She focused on her customers instead, amping up the charm as much as she could. It wasn't to keep her mind off Jack. It was to get better tips to help Tonya out.

There were people with real problems in this world,

and that didn't include Rose. She could take care of herself and deserved anything that came her way.

The crowd dwindled, and Rose did everything in her power to ignore the moment that Jack got up from his table and started ambling toward the bar. How could a man make her heart beat faster and her stomach flutter like she was nervous?

When he got close enough, she decided to nip this in the bud. "Crowd's small enough now. You can go."

He slid onto a bar stool instead. She scowled. He smiled.

"Are you busy tomorrow morning?"

She raised an eyebrow, a perfectly practiced look of disdain. Most men withered. Stupid men winked. Jack simply sat there and waited.

Oh, damn him.

"I thought we should prepare," he continued. "It looks like my family will be here Thursday. I've got quite a bit of work to do all this week, but you can tag along some morning and we can talk about things boyfriends and girlfriends usually know about each other."

"The only thing my *boyfriends* have ever known about me is that I have a mean right hook."

He didn't even blink. "And whether or not you have a tattoo on your ass, I'm presuming."

She wouldn't laugh. She wouldn't smile. But he was grinning, and if she thought he was hot when he was broody or drunk, it had nothing on *happy* Jack. "I don't think your parents will ask about that. Though your ex might want to know."

His smile dimmed at that, and maybe that was why she had been feeling soft around him. Pity. She felt bad for the guy. It wasn't about *answers* or all that crap Delia had been yapping about before she'd hung up puking the other night. It wasn't about *her*. It was about the sob story in front of her.

If she could only convince herself of that, then she didn't have to feel nervous. She could help Jack out without getting all weird about it.

"You ever ridden a horse?"

She blinked at the non sequitur, but when she noticed where his gaze had dropped—her shoulder—she swallowed and adjusted the sleeve of her shirt to cover it.

She tried to step away, and she wasn't sure why panic beat in her chest. She didn't have to explain her tattoo. She didn't have to answer his question. She didn't have to do anything she didn't want.

Luckily, Jack reached out and wrapped his fingers around her wrist, which centered everything right there. Panic and nerves not gone but settled a little under the bloom of outrage. "Let go of me, sailor, or I'm going to have to cut you."

He didn't let go—her own fault, since she wasn't about to cut him, and they both knew it.

"You have a horse tattoo."

"Do not," she retorted stupidly.

He leaned forward, his upper body leaning against the sticky surface of her bar. He pulled her wrist closer, so she had to lean forward. She should fight him off. She should throw a fit and kick his ass. The problem was—and this seemed to always be the problem with Jack—she didn't want to do any of that.

He used his index finger, just that one finger, to nudge the collar of her shirt back down over her shoulder, where it naturally fell. Even though she didn't want him to see her tattoo, the gentle way he touched her was hypnotizing. There was no manhandling, no jerking or heavy-handed pawing. It was all very soft. Intoxicating.

Pity. You pity this guy. She tried repeating it over and over to herself until she believed it.

Jack's blunt fingertip traced the small, black horse inked on her shoulder as a reminder that nothing good ever came from promises. Rose had to swallow against all the unwanted emotion swamping her.

Jack smiled up at her again, and this time, it was a soft, amused thing, not that flash of charm. Somehow it was worse to see him soft, feel his gentleness. Yes, that was most definitely worse.

"So, why do you have the tattoo of a horse?"

"I like horses."

"You said every one of your tattoos meant something."

"It means I like horses," she said through gritted teeth. Gritted because he kept tracing it, and the touch waved across her skin with goose bumps and heat, and she didn't like that her heart felt all mushy, and she wanted another try at that angry kiss from last week—all at the same time.

"Tell me," he urged.

If he'd been anyone else, she'd have told him to fuck off. She didn't like people poking at her or trying to poke into her, but...

Well, her heart was mush, and her brain was apparently dead. Besides, maybe telling Jack the straight-out truth was the best way to handle this whole thing. Maybe he'd finally get the picture she was nothing but trouble.

"My dad used to take me with him to his poker

games. He taught me to play, coached me how to cheat so he could win. One time, when I was ten and obsessed with horses, like most ten-year-old girls, Dad promised if I was really good, and he won, he would buy me a horse. Just for me. I even had a name picked out."

"Why do I get the feeling this doesn't have a happy ending?"

"How astute," she returned, embarrassed at the way her tone had turned bitter instead of matter-of-fact. "He lost the game. I never got a pony, which I suppose was good, since he said if I *did* have a horse, he'd have shot it after the way I'd blown it for him."

Rose met Jack's gaze, because she wanted to see his pity. She wanted to make sure they both understood what this was—two screwed-up people who were interested in each other because of that and that alone.

He didn't look like he pitied her. He had that thing that so few people had. Not detached sympathy or the kind of pity where you handed off a five-dollar bill and hoped the skinny girl with bruises got a meal that night. Jack had empathy. He didn't tut-tut *poor Rose*, but simply listened like he could have some understanding of what that situation might have been for a little girl.

She looked away, but Jack's hand was still curled around her arm, though his finger had stopped tracing her tattoo.

"What did you want to name the horse?" he asked, his voice a hushed whisper. She looked around the bar, but it was nearly empty except for Tonya, who was laughing with two of the regulars.

Rose blew out a breath, knowing she would regret

telling him. She already regretted all of this, but Jack's thumb was brushing back and forth across her inner wrist and she wanted to live in that sensation. "Libby."

"Why Libby?"

"Short for Liberty. Don't have to explain that one to you, do I?"

Which shut him up for a second. He didn't let go of her wrist though, and she didn't try to pull away.

"Come riding with me."

Which gave her enough impetus to tug her hand away. "I don't know how to ride a horse. It was a pipe dream when I was a kid, and the tattoo is a reminder that promises don't mean anything."

"I'll teach you how to ride," he said, as if she hadn't just laid a private piece of her heart she didn't want him to see right there on the bar.

"I'm not going riding with you. I'm not..." She was tired, mostly of the way his presence seemed to keep her in a state of panic and indecision. She needed to harden up again. "Look, I agreed to be your fake girlfriend. I agreed to come to a dinner or two and lay on the screw-you-Madison, but I don't need to know anything about you to pretend we're dating."

"My parents will expect you to know some things. They'll expect—"

"Madison Number Two?" She expected that to dim some of his determination, but it didn't.

He shrugged. "Maybe. That's not what I mean though. I don't confuse you with Madison. I consider that a very good thing. But I'm not a superficial guy, in case you haven't noticed. They're going to expect us to have a certain level of understanding. They're going to expect me to have talked about my family to you. They're going to expect you to know some things. What's the harm in you knowing them?"

Which was a trick question, and she knew it. Because the more she knew about Jack, the more she wanted to know—and the more this confused, don't-know-what-to-do feeling consumed her. But explaining that meant exposing her weakness, and she'd learned to never, ever do that.

"I guess I could spare a few hours," she said, slapping a rag to the surface of the bar and pretending to be very engrossed in cleaning. "I'm not getting up early for it though."

One way or another, she'd prove to him, and herself, that she could handle this. She was Rose Rogers. She could handle a charming former Navy SEAL. No matter how he looked. No matter how he kissed. No matter how he talked.

She could absolutely handle him.

"Great," he said, sounding easy and light, which she wasn't sure she'd ever heard him sound like in all the months he'd been coming here.

He slid off the barstool, and she thought that was that, but in a too-easy move, he leaned over the bar and brushed his mouth across her cheek.

"See you then, Rose."

Then he ambled out of her bar as if he didn't have a care in the world. She'd thought she'd had the upper hand for most of that conversation, but watching him leave, she quickly realized she had lost.

Damn it.

Chapter 11

JACK GOT UP EARLY THE NEXT MORNING. IF HE COULD get the majority of his chores accomplished before Rose arrived, he'd have time to give her a real riding lesson, check the fences, and still have a conversation.

He probably wasn't the best candidate for teaching, considering he had trouble getting on the horse due to his leg, but he didn't want to bring Becca or anyone else in to help. Wrong as it might be, he very much wanted Rose to himself.

For all those very important *learn some things about each other* reasons. Imperative to learn, so they could show a very functional-looking front to his family, of course.

Maybe he could admit to wanting her to know some things about him too, but this was mostly what two people in a fake relationship did to prepare. He was pretty sure.

It was only eight, and Rose hadn't texted that she was ready to come over yet, but he still headed to the stables anyway. He could get everything lined up, and if Rose still hadn't texted him by then, he'd maybe ride out and check half the fence or so.

"Why are you getting two saddles ready?"

Jack turned to find Gabe at the entrance of the stables. He hadn't exactly expected company this morning. So he hesitated. He didn't want to tell Gabe what was going on, because Gabe would definitely read into things beyond the fake relationship.

Probably read into them correctly too and then razz him mercilessly. Jack was used to taking Gabe's harassment, but mostly over things that didn't matter.

Rose mattered somehow.

Unfortunately, there were no possible lies here, so he could only go with the truth and hope Gabe didn't blow it out of proportion. "Rose is coming out."

Gabe didn't reply. He stood there looking vaguely disapproving, but Jack wasn't about to get sucked into a debate. He just kept focusing on getting the two saddles together.

"So," Gabe said.

"So," Jack repeated.

"Acting like it's not weird doesn't make it not weird."

"I'm not acting like it's not weird. I know it's a little out there, but welcome to my life," Jack returned.

"Look, the pretending for your ex or whatever, I guess it's no big deal in the grand scheme of things. What I don't understand is why that has to include you and Rose spending a lot of time together *now*."

"We don't have a lot of time to sit down and talk. This will be a nice, quiet place to figure out how this whole thing is going to go down."

"I get you want to stick it to Madison. And part of me wants to full-fledged support this, but…"

Jack stopped what he was doing, surprised at Gabe's disapproval. "But what?"

"Honestly? The more I think about it, the more I've watched you the past week, the more I think it's a mistake."

"I expect this from Alex, not from you," Jack returned. "I can make my own choices."

"I know you can, but I thought you might consider the opinion of someone who cares about you. My mistake."

Jack took a deep breath. He didn't want to lash out at Gabe for no reason. And there was no reason to be irritated or even angry that Gabe was expressing an opinion. It took a bit of work to not have that reaction though. Lashing out had been his MO for about two years, and he wanted the next couple of weeks to be weeks of change. He wanted to evolve into something else—a guy with a future, instead of one hung up on the past. So he worked very hard to make sure his tone was genuine instead of antagonistic.

"What's such a mistake about it? It's a lie, yeah, and maybe it's childish to want to prove something, but I have to accept that she and Mike are married and have a kid. I *don't* have to accept her pity. And quite frankly, I won't give my brother the satisfaction of knowing he broke me."

"It's not that I object to that. It's that I object to and maybe have concerns about the woman you're bringing into this whole thing."

"You have concerns about Rose?"

"I like Rose and all, but I don't know a thing about her, and neither do you. Are you sure you can trust her with this?"

"Trust her with what? All she has to do is pretend to be my girlfriend."

"Do you trust her to watch your back? Actually help with what you want help with? She could just as easily fly off at the mouth and say something stupid. She could take whatever information you tell her and twist it. Maybe she's great and nice and everything, but the bottom line is, you don't know her. Much like Madison, you only think you do."

Jack tried to keep his angry first response buried deep. This was Gabe trying to protect him. Gabe had trust and loyalty issues, and he cared about Jack. This was a friend thing, but the comparison to Madison hurt, and the need to defend Rose bubbled up inside him.

He took a deep breath and swallowed down all those twisting, emotional reactions and tried to come up with a tempered response. "I appreciate your concern," Jack said stiffly.

Gabe scoffed and interrupted. "But you're not gonna do anything about it. Great."

"Maybe I thought I knew Madison, and that turned out to be very much not the case, but Rose isn't... It's a favor. She's not going to fly off at the mouth or anything else. She's a friend."

"That you've known how long?"

"Rose is a good person," Jack replied firmly, keeping a lid on his temper by sheer force of will. "And she's been good to me for no reason."

"Everyone always has a reason, Jack."

"So is this about my baggage or yours?" he snapped at Gabe.

"Or mine?" a female voice asked from the door.

Gabe closed his eyes and swore. Jack could only stare at Rose, standing in the sparkling, early sunlight shining through the open stable doors.

"I thought you, uh, said you weren't waking up early."

"I didn't plan to, but my body had other ideas. I didn't know arriving early would mean hearing questions of my character."

Gabe stared back at her, blank and fierce. Which was not usually Gabe's way of doing things. He kept the blank and the fierce well hidden under a layer of pretend good nature.

"I don't know shit about your character, Rose. I believe that was my point. And if you hurt my friend—"

"Oh goody, threats. Were you hoping I'd run away crying or try to fight you?"

Gabe rolled his eyes. "I'm out of here." He disappeared out the doors before Jack could come up with anything to say to fix this situation.

"He's just protective," Jack offered lamely to Rose.

"He's just right. I'm nobody to you, Jack. I'm not a good person, and you probably shouldn't trust me."

"But you're here."

She blinked at that. There was some deep, dark emotion swirling in the depths of her eyes he didn't know how to label, and he really didn't know how to fix.

It also wasn't any of his business. He and Rose were friends of sorts, and okay, they'd kissed. And yes, he would like to do a whole lot more than that, but that didn't make it his job to fix her. She'd made it really clear that she didn't want him to try.

He'd watched for nearly a year as Alex had thrown his whole life into trying to fix everything—himself, Gabe and Jack, the ranch and the foundation—and make it perfect. Even before everything that had happened overseas, Jack had known that would never work. You couldn't fix the past, and you couldn't fix people. There was too much midwestern practicality in him to feel otherwise.

There was also such an incredible desire to fix something for someone and feel useful. To feel as though he had a purpose aside from moving cattle from one pasture to another or checking fences to make sure they didn't escape.

In a few months, this ranch would be more than that, but for now, it was just cows. And he was just a man scrambling and failing at feeling whole. A broken man had no business trying to help a broken woman.

But it felt like that was exactly what they could do for each other.

"So are you going to teach me to ride or what?"

He smiled at her, because what else was there to do? "If you're ready, I'm ready."

Rose hadn't known what to expect with this whole *learning how to ride a horse* thing. She'd spent the walk over to the stables berating herself for agreeing to it, not to mention showing up early—and just about every other moment she'd spent in Jack's presence. The inward berating had only increased when she'd overheard Gabe voicing his very intelligent concerns. If she had half a brain, she'd have been walking away from Jack too, not letting him teach her how to get on a horse. She wouldn't be following him around on said horse, listening to him talk as he checked fences and did other very manly looking things.

The cowboy hat so did not help. He looked like every fantasy cowboy that had graced the covers of Billie's romance novels—so much so that Rose fell into a few too many fantasies as Jack led her all around Revival Ranch on Pansy, the very calm and gentle horse he'd saddled for her.

Rose *knew* she had no business walking this very thin and dangerous line, but it didn't stop her. After all, she'd done a lot of things she had no business doing in her life.

Jack chatted on about his family, and Rose found herself rapt. She was supposed to be learning to pretend to be the girlfriend, but instead, she actually wanted to know. He had the kind of family she'd only dreamed about while she was growing up. He had two loving parents, his grandparents and aunts and uncles and cousins nearby. He made it sound idyllic even though she knew the idyllic was tempered. Because he didn't mention Madison, and surely if the woman had been his intended since he was born, then she would've featured in the memories he was sharing with Rose.

Still, he talked about his sister who was in med school with a certain awe and big-brother pride. He talked about his other sister who would be visiting and how she had some hipster store or stand or something, selling jams and jellies and pies and whatnot. And there was that same odd thing in his voice. Pride and awe, even if he was a little disdainful of the end result.

He spoke about his parents as if they were angels. If the stories he told about his grandfather, who had some bizarre little airport in the middle of nowhere, were all true, the man was a god among men.

Rose had nothing to share back. All the family she'd ever known was her parents. If her grandparents were alive, she didn't know it or them. Her mom had a sister who had stopped trying to help them long before Rose was born. Apart from that, Rose had no sense of family except her sisters.

So she understood the pride Jack had for his—if she had that, she'd be proud too. But that tone in his voice wound inside her like hope, and what did she have to hope for? There was nothing to hope for when it came to Jack Armstrong.

Armstrong. Even his name was perfect.

Rose refused to feel disappointment when they arrived back at the stables. She had work to do at the bar. She had a life to lead that didn't allow for this flight of childhood fantasy. Pretty horses and strong men.

No matter that this reality had lived up to the fantasy of a little girl who'd always wanted a horse. She knew what it was like now to have the feeling of the wind in her hair and a beautiful Montana ranch spread out before her as if she had all the freedom in the world— the dream she had dreamed with singular ferocity for her entire childhood.

Then she'd grown up and found it on her own without a promise from any man. It was important to remember that every time Jack made her feel completely like a ball of emotion and softness and, well, feelings for him in particular.

She had built a life of her own creation, and no one could take that away from her if she didn't let them. No one could make her *feel* against her will. Well, no one could make her act on it anyway.

Jack dismounted, and she winced as he landed on what was clearly his bad leg. He sucked it up and played it off, but it must've hurt. Did riding the horse bother his injuries? His limp was significantly more pronounced than it had been before they'd gotten on the horses.

She wasn't about to mention it though, because that would not be what he wanted to hear, and it was not the conversation she wanted to have.

At least she'd thought that would be the last conversation she'd want to have—until Becca walked into the stables. Rose didn't know Becca very well, but she knew the look of a determined woman.

Which meant Rose needed to get out of here and fast.

"Well, I should get going," Rose blurted, and then realized how stupid she sounded, considering she was still sitting on top of the horse.

Jack smiled up at her. "I think you're going to have to get off the horse first."

Heat flamed into her cheeks, and Rose was absolutely horrified. She hadn't blushed when one of the teachers from school had asked her point-blank if she needed help. She hadn't blushed when someone had caught her pulling a half-eaten sandwich out of the cafeteria trash can.

Now she was blushing because she'd done something stupid in front of Jack? This crap had to stop. Rose cleared her throat, ignoring the easy humor in Jack's blue eyes, the way little wrinkles fanned out from the corners. Never *mind* that he was younger than her.

She tried to remember what lessons he'd taught her about getting off the horse, but it was all gone because he'd had his big hand on her leg half the time. How was she supposed to pay attention with all *that* going on? She'd been too busy dreaming about things she had no business dreaming about.

Mainly something other than a horse between her legs.

"Let me help," Jack said when she sat there like a mute lump. He put his hand on her hip and talked her through leveraging herself up and over the saddle and back down to the ground.

When she stumbled, Jack held her up, and she could smell him. The Montana summer. The horse. The leather. And it all worked together to scream *Jack Jack Jack* and *want want want*.

"Well, thanks for all that stuff," Rose muttered. "I better get going."

"No!" Becca all but shouted, stepping forward. "That's why I came out here. We put together a picnic lunch, and you two are coming."

A picnic lunch? What was this place? *Little House on the Prairie*? "No. Thank you. I can't. I have work to do."

"But you have to eat lunch. It makes sense to eat here. Then when you go home, you can get straight to work."

And as if it was the most normal thing in the world, Becca linked arms with Rose.

"It'll be great, and it's all packed up. If you don't come, food will go to waste."

Rose looked helplessly at Jack, but he was only grinning.

"You're supposed to help me," she hissed at him.

"This is more fun," he replied, adjusting that ridiculous cowboy hat on his head.

She glared at him, but she knew she wasn't getting out of this. Clearly Becca had some plan. Maybe Rose wouldn't be so nervous about going along with it if she hadn't caught Gabe airing his concerns this morning, or if she hadn't felt like her guts were tying themselves into knots. She knew she was letting herself down a path of incredible destruction, and not for herself. Not destruction *of* herself either. Destruction of poor Jack.

She didn't know why she couldn't stop it. She didn't know why she was powerless here when she was powerful everywhere else.

Rose was not a good person, but she was a *strong* person. That was the foundation on which she'd rebuilt her life. Jack Armstrong made her completely weak. It was alarming and frightening and panicking, and yet here she was being led toward one of the trucks in front of the house.

"Why are we getting in a truck?"

"Oh, we've got this place all set up down by the creek. I packed all sorts of goodies, so I promise you won't go hungry. And it's an absolutely stunning view."

"Well, who can say no to a stunning view," Rose muttered.

Becca let go of her arm and pulled her keys out of her pocket, but before Rose could catch a breath, Jack slid his arm around her waist. Casual and easy as you please.

She sent him one of her most felling looks, but he was not felled. Even a little. He grinned instead. "Relax. We'll have fun."

"As fun as Gabe talking about how you can't trust me?"

"Think of it this way—you'll now have ample opportunity to make Gabe squirm. You like to make men uncomfortable."

"I do not," she blustered.

He leaned close, his mouth almost brushing her ear, sending a spark of unfair lust straight to her core. "Liar," he murmured right up against her ear.

And yes, she was a liar. She was practically vibrating from the inside out from the simplest of things. He wasn't even whispering in her ear. He was talking. He wasn't kissing her. He just had his arm around her waist. His mouth wasn't touching her ear, and yet everything in her wanted to center on that point of no contact.

She couldn't even think about that or process it, because they'd stopped at the bed of the truck.

Alex was sitting in the passenger seat, and Becca slid into the driver's seat. Gabe and a kid were squished into the back seat. Apparently she and Jack were supposed to hop in the cab with a blond woman.

"Rose, this is Monica, our on-site therapist."

"Hey," Rose managed, forcing a smile.

"Hi," Monica said with one of those knowing smiles that meant Jack had talked about her. He'd mentioned her to the *on-site therapist*.

So great, she wasn't just faking a relationship. She was now a circus sideshow for his friends.

If it hadn't been Jack, if it had been anyone else pulling this, she would've reverted to classic Rose behavior: off-putting, harsh, and sharp. She'd refined that kind of persona over the years of scraping by on her own and then being a female bar owner in a tough town. But this was *Jack*, and she didn't want to piss off his friends. She didn't want to piss off *him*. Her brain wanted her to be angry and treat him like dirt, but when he helped her into the truck cab, her heart knew it was the last thing she could possibly do.

She wanted to do the right thing with Jack. The good thing. She wanted his friends to like her, and she wanted him to *like* her.

She wanted to be the person she knew, deep down, she wasn't.

But if this was pretend, her acting like his girlfriend for his family, giving it a little practice in front of his friends, even though they knew it was pretend, then maybe for the next few days that could be *her* pretend.

She could pretend to be the woman she wanted to be. Dangerous, yes, but when Jack scooted next to her, slinging his arm across her shoulders, how could she resist?

Chapter 12

JACK WASN'T SURE WHAT BECCA WAS UP TO. SHE'D insisted the rest of them head down to the picnic spot while she and Alex lugged all the stuff. Normally, Jack would have argued, but letting it go meant he got to sit next to Rose on a blanket in the warmth of a beautiful summer afternoon and feel alive, really *alive*, for the first time since that grenade had gone off.

A memory that came back a little too easily due to how badly his leg was killing him. He didn't know what it was about riding that screwed him up so much, but it sucked. Becca kept talking about getting some kind of all-terrain vehicle that might work better for him, but he hated the idea of spending foundation money on something just for him. Just for his weakness.

Thoughts for another day.

Gabe had gone down to the creek with Colin to throw rocks, while Monica kept a watchful eye from a safe distance and Becca and Alex bustled back and forth, chatting and laughing with each other.

"So," Rose said, her voice low enough that no one around them could hear. "What did you tell your shrink about me?"

Jack had sprawled out on his good side to hide the fact that he was trying to stretch out his leg. Rose was sitting cross-legged next to him, and he squinted against the sun to look up at her face. Her hair was dark and straight, and he'd enjoyed watching the way the wind played with it when they'd been on the horses. Now he enjoyed the way the sun profiled her sharp nose and sharp chin, because as much as he didn't think she was half as sharp as she pretended to be, he liked that she *looked* it—that she could be it and still have that softness underneath.

"I told her about you pretending to be my girlfriend."

"And that's it?"

She still didn't look directly at him. Her gaze was focused down at the creek, either on the sway of the trees, or Colin's gleeful cheering over rock splashes, or something else altogether.

"Did you expect there to be something else?"

She turned to him, her expression all narrowed-eyed suspicion.

He merely smiled, because every time he did, she got the oddest softening around her mouth, no matter how hard she tried to keep her scowl.

He couldn't have explained to Gabe why or how *this* woman had crawled under all his ugly defenses, but the more time he spent with her, the more he wanted. Friendship, sure, but more.

Yes, he wanted more out of something for the first time in a long time, and that felt too good to back away from.

"What's the deal with the kid?" she asked, jerking her chin toward the creek and effectively changing the subject.

"Monica's husband died when Colin was a baby. Helicopter pilot. Colin's still not quite jazzed about living here, but he's taken a shine to Gabe. And Ron Swanson."

"Ron who?"

"Becca's pet goat."

"Pet…goat. I guess I shouldn't be surprised. My sister's brother-in-law has a ranch full of llamas. It seems Blue Valley is the capital of odd pets and ranch animals."

She didn't say anything else, just sat there like a picture, and Jack didn't even bother to pretend he was looking at anything else. He was drinking her in, drinking this *feeling* in, and he was going to enjoy this easy contentment for as long as it lasted.

Which was why, when he noticed the little edge of ink peeking out from her sleeve, Jack leaned forward and nudged the sleeve of her T-shirt up so he could see the entire tattoo on her bicep. "What's this one mean?"

She looked down at the colorful and delicate design. Unlike the dark horse on her shoulder and the menacing wolf on her left forearm, this was a bright and feminine infinity sign made out of pastel flowers and random letters.

"My sisters and I got matching tattoos last year. Those are all our initials," she said, pointing to each flowing, flowery letter.

"And it's an infinity sign," he said, tracing the figure eight. He glanced up at her, knowing he'd find that dark gaze on him.

"Sisters forever. Blooming. No matter what."

He wanted to press a kiss to it, to her, but it wasn't the time or the place. When it was, when he *finally* got her naked—because it was feeling less and less like an *if*—he'd kiss every last tattoo, every last piece of her story that she'd had inked onto her skin.

"Mom!"

Both he and Rose looked over to where Colin raced

up the bank. The boy reminded Jack of a gangly, excitable puppy, with old-dog Gabe slowly following.

"Mom! There's a rope you can swing on to jump in. Gabe said I have to ask first. Can I? Can I?"

Monica frowned, glancing down at the creek and what appeared to be an old—if sturdy—rope hanging from a thick tree branch.

"Is the water deep enough?" Monica asked, voicing her question to Alex and Becca, the two people who knew the land the best.

"Well, it was when I was a kid," Alex offered, glancing down at the creek. "And it even looks a little higher than it used to."

Monica pressed her lips together. "I don't know, Col."

"Please, please, please, please, please—"

Monica held up a hand. "Not today. Maybe another day, we'll put on our swim gear and check it out, but for today—"

"It's *hot*," Colin whined. "I'm so bored."

That clearly hit Monica where it hurt. She frowned down at the creek again, studying it carefully. Then she shook her head. "We don't know if it's safe. The rope could break."

"Can't an adult test it first?" Colin pressed, looking hopefully up at his mother.

She laughed. "No."

He turned his gaze to Gabe, an endearingly cheesy grin spread across his face.

"Sorry, kid," Gabe replied. "I'm not walking around in wet jeans."

"You'll dry," Colin replied, pointing up at the sun.

"I'll do it." Rose hopped up to her feet, earning

surprised looks from just about everyone. Rose shrugged. "If it's okay with your mom, I'll test it out."

"Oh. Well."

Colin went through another round of a hundred pleases crammed into under a second.

"Okay. If Rose tests it out and gives it the okay…" Monica took a deep breath, clearly wrestling with mom instincts and wanting Colin to have some fun. "Then I guess you can."

Colin let out a whoop and raced over to Rose.

"Come on, kid. Let's see what we're dealing with," Rose said, sauntering down the bank toward the rope. "I didn't know a bunch of ex–Navy SEALs would be afraid of a little water," she added loudly.

Monica stifled a laugh as Gabe glared after Rose.

Jack got to his feet. "Well, I know a challenge when I hear one. You guys coming?"

"Ah, hell," Alex muttered, following after Jack. But Gabe didn't leave.

"She impugned your manhood, Gabe. Aren't you going to go give it a try?" Becca offered with a sweet smile.

"Fuck no," Gabe returned, still looking surly and pissed off, standing by the blanket with his hands in his pockets.

Jack made a few chicken noises. Becca giggled, and Gabe glared at her.

"You're all children."

"Oh, come on. Have some fun, Gabe," Alex called. "We'll see who can jump the farthest."

Gabe muttered a few more curses, but he fell into line behind Alex. Jack couldn't stop himself from grinning. It had been a long, long, *long* time since the three of them had done something purely fun together.

"Take off your shirts!" Becca yelled after them.

"Your girlfriend is objectifying us, Alex," Gabe muttered.

"My fiancée," Alex corrected. "Can't say as I mind." In a rare act of humor and fun, Alex pulled off his shirt and dropped it next to the bank.

Jack shrugged and followed suit, laughing when Monica and Becca cheered and whistled from the blanket.

"What a bunch of fools," Gabe muttered before pulling off his own shirt.

They reached Rose and Colin, Rose holding the rope between her hands. "Ready to be impressed?" she offered, flashing a carefree grin, no sharp edges in sight.

"Don't break your neck," Jack returned.

She rolled her eyes, taking a few steps back before running and jumping off the bank. She swung out into the middle of the creek before she dropped, spreading her arms and legs wide. Rose landed in the middle of the creek with an impressive splash.

Jack realized he'd been holding his breath waiting for her to resurface, and even once she did, it wasn't easy to catch that breath. She looked like some mythical creature, her hair wet and gleaming in the sun. Rose flashed him a victorious smile, which seemed to fill his lungs beyond capacity.

"You got it bad," Gabe muttered, and Jack didn't bother to try and read the tone there.

"What's he got bad?" Colin asked, frowning.

"Nothing, runt. Let's get you out there."

Jack glanced back to find Alex staring at him with that old Navy SEAL–leader stare—trying to determine what was right and if he should step in.

Jack looked away from Alex. "Got something to say?" he asked, preparing himself for another lecture like Gabe's from that morning.

"Nope. It's just good to see you smiling, Jack."

Jack didn't have a thing to say to that. It felt good to smile. It felt good to do something fun and stupid. He felt *good*, and he wanted to hold on to that.

⁓⁓⁓

The water was cool, the sun was warm, and the view was *helllooo*. Alex, Gabe, and Jack might have been *former* SEALs, but they were still in excellent shape. Really excellent, drool-worthy shape as they jumped into the water one by one, Colin yelling in delight every time.

A splashing fight ensued and Rose drifted away from the group of men, trying to decide if she wanted to wade in or escape back to the picnic. Before she could make a choice either way, Jack drifted along with her.

She kept her gaze on Colin, Alex, and Gabe, the two older guys taking turns putting Colin on their shoulders and letting him fall off in a great splash.

"We seem to end up swimming together in our clothes a lot," Jack said casually, his gleaming shoulders drifting closer and closer.

"There were a few less clothes last time." And sadly, it had been too dark to properly appreciate the breadth and strength of those shoulders.

"Oh, I remember," he replied, that lethal, brain-killing, heart-fluttering smile gracing his too-perfect face. The water made his hair and beard look darker, and the sun made his eyes seem an impossible sky blue.

"You couldn't see anything," she reminded him.

"I have a rich fantasy life."

She laughed—couldn't help it. He took away all her self-control, kept her in this ridiculous push and pull between what she *knew* was the right thing to do and what she *felt* was the right thing to do.

The sun was shining on the water and there were shouts of laughter and fun all around them. Jack had a perfect smile, and self-control was some distant memory on some faraway planet.

"You know I don't have time to play all this hooky," she said, more trying to remind herself than him that she had a bar to run and a life to live.

"And yet here you are."

"Becca didn't give me much of a choice on the whole picnic thing."

"I'm pretty sure Rose Rogers had a choice," he murmured, drifting still closer. He couldn't do things like that in front of *everyone* who might start taking this all the wrong way, which she had a bad feeling would encourage Jack to keep taking everything the wrong way.

And you. You aren't stopping any of it, are you?

He reached out and tugged down the front of her shirt, just a centimeter or two, and didn't even have the decency to try to look down her top. "What's this one?"

She looked down at the edge of the tattoo. A straight line between her breasts, something that wouldn't have been showing at all if not for the water dragging down the collar of her T-shirt.

There were a million things she could say in response that wouldn't be flirtatious promise, but…

Well.

She was wet, and he was shirtless, and she'd lost

control of her brain. *It's all pretend, right? What's the harm?* "I think that's a question for another day," she returned, her voice too husky, her smile too sly.

"Why?"

"Because I don't feel like stripping off my shirt in front of your friends."

"You could tell me."

"I could. I think I'd rather show you when the time's right." And with that little bit of idiocy, she swam away from him and climbed out of the creek.

Jack didn't follow, which was good. She needed a breather, a reminder to herself that no matter what she *pretended*, she couldn't get so wrapped up in the game that Jack started thinking it was real.

Rose tried to wring out her sopping hair as she climbed up the bank and back to the picnic, but she froze when she realized Monica and Becca were sitting on the blanket. Crying.

"What's wrong?" she asked before she could think better of it.

Monica waved a hand in front of her face. "Nothing. Really. It's a happy-tears situation."

Rose glanced back at the creek, where the guys were still splashing around. She didn't get it.

Monica cleared her throat and handed Rose a pop. "It's just that Colin's been slowly accepting the move here, but I haven't seen him truly enjoy himself like that for a long time. A really, really long time."

Which Rose supposed made sense. Delia cried over just about anything Sunny did, and Delia was so not a crier. But Becca crying right along with Monica didn't compute.

Becca waved a hand toward the creek as if in answer

to Rose's unspoken question. "I haven't seen the three of them goof around like that, all grinning and stupid… ever. It's just…" Her voice squeaked. "Really good to see," she choked out, more tears falling.

Rose didn't have anything to say to that, so she sank onto the grass next to the blanket, not wanting to get anything wet. She popped the pop can top and took a long, slow drink, watching as the guys started climbing out of the creek. They got out one by one, helping Colin up and out, and then somehow making an easy joke out of helping Jack.

It was the first time Rose was really looking at all of them and could see the toll of war on their bodies. She couldn't see any obvious marks on Alex, but he was walking with a limp that hadn't been there before. Gabe had some uninterrupted lines and what Rose assumed were burn scars on his shoulder. Jack had clearly gotten the worst end of whatever happened though. He had marks up his side and down his arm, and his limp was as pronounced as she'd ever seen it.

All three of them were grinning and laughing, tousling Colin's wet hair or giving each other friendly shoves. Rose got it then, Monica's and Becca's tears. While she'd seen all three of them brood in her bar, clearly war hadn't beaten them.

And that was a beautiful thing. Enough that she felt her eyes sting a bit too.

"So, it's really just all pretend?" Becca asked quietly.

Rose blinked, startled out of her reverie. Still, she stared straight ahead and didn't pretend to misread Becca's question. Best to nip any possible speculation in the bud. "Yup."

"Jack's a good guy," Becca replied so very not subtly. Which was funny—that anyone would think *she* needed to be sold on Jack.

"I know," she said, looking at Becca. "He deserves a good woman."

Rose didn't miss Becca and Monica exchange a glance, but she ignored it. She watched as the three scarred men and one excited boy made their way back to the picnic site. And she really hoped Jack found that good woman before Rose did any damage.

Chapter 13

JACK COULDN'T HAVE SAID A PICNIC WITH HIS entire friend group plus Rose was high on his "things he'd like to do with Rose" list, but it turned out he liked it all the same. He wasn't surprised at the ease she had with Becca, Alex, and Gabe. They came into her bar enough. He was a little surprised how friendly and easy she was with Colin, if only because she rarely showed that laid-back, soft side of herself.

Which often evaporated anytime Monica spoke to her. There was a stiffness there. It wasn't that sarcastic, edgy thing she applied with people she didn't like at the bar. This was more genuine discomfort. A nervousness almost.

He imagined it was the therapist thing, but that didn't make it any less weird to see discomfort on self-possessed Rose.

He wanted to understand more of her, and he knew she didn't want that to happen. Actually, it wasn't that simple. Clearly some part of her liked him, or she wouldn't have been here. She wouldn't have gone riding with him, and she definitely would have begged off when Becca suggested the picnic. It couldn't all be pity that had her here.

She had a lot of baggage, that he knew, and she'd certainly built herself an armor against the world. Anyone who'd done that wouldn't easily lay that armor down.

So he might have to get a little sneaky. Something he wasn't sure he'd ever been, but the prospect of trying something new was appealing. Far more compelling than dwelling on the fact that his family would be here in a few short days.

"We should get back to Hick," Becca said, standing up and brushing the grass off her pants. "You two can stay out longer if you want," she said, smiling hopefully at Rose.

"I need to get back," Rose said, hopping to her feet with a speed that was a little over the top. She jumped into helping Becca and Monica clean up the picnic, so Jack did the same. Colin chattered about the creek, and there were conversations about the perfect summer weather or having the picnics become a regular thing. Everyone talked and laughed on their way back to the truck.

Except Rose. Rose was silent. And not smiling.

Jack wanted to understand that. There were so many things about Rose he wanted to understand—the tattoos, the armor, why she was here if she didn't want to be.

He needed more time, so when they piled out of the truck back at the ranch house and Rose was still silent, he knew what he had to do.

She tried to bolt for her car the second her feet hit the ground, but he reached out and rested his hand on her elbow.

She stopped on a dime, and he tried not to grin at that.

"Bye, Rose," his friends chorused, already focused on unloading the truck and getting back to ranch work.

"Bye," Rose muttered, then shook her head as if disgusted at something. "Thanks for the picnic, Becca."

"No problem. You're invited anytime."

He could tell Rose was trying to smile, but it was more of a grimace. Then her gaze moved to his hand on her elbow, and he wasn't sure he understood what it was in her expression. He knew she wanted it to be irritation, but there was something else. Something closer to panic or fear than *I will kill you with one of my many weapons*.

Rose flicked a glance to the dispersing group, but Alex, Becca, and Gabe were heading toward the house with the picnic supplies, and Monica and Colin had headed for the stables. There was no one around for her to make excuses for.

"I do have my own life, Jack."

"Of course you do."

She sighed gustily, but he noted she didn't even try to pull her elbow out of his grasp.

"We should go out."

Her eyes widened, and then she stepped back and away, pulling her arm out of his grasp harder than necessary considering he hadn't really been holding on to it. Just resting his fingers there.

"Jack, don't—"

"A trial run. Not a real date," he amended, trying for innocent.

"What was this?" she asked, waving her arm to encompass the ranch, which he supposed meant the picnic and the ride beforehand. Maybe there was something wrong with him that he enjoyed the way he made her panic a little, but if she panicked, that meant he got to her. If she'd had no investment, she would have eradicated him already.

"This was getting to know each other and giving you a riding lesson. It was something, but we need a little more. My sister is super nosy, and she's going to ask about our first date. It can't be a picnic with my friends. So we'll have one. Then we won't have to make one up and remember details because it'll be real. Fake real." He smiled.

She scowled. "I don't have time."

"What about breakfast?"

"Breakfast is not a date."

"Sure it is. My sister would eat that up with a spoon. She'd call it unique or some hipster word that wouldn't make any sense to me."

"She'd think we had sex is what she'd think," Rose said firmly.

Jack winced at the thought of his sister thinking about anything related to sex, but then he rubbed his jaw, considering sex and Rose. He let his gaze move over her, then he flashed a grin. "I mean, we could work that out too, if you were willing to compromise on your whole no-strings-attached deal."

She scowled deeper, crossing her arms across her chest. "I am not."

He shrugged. "Okay, name the day and time before Thursday we could have a date."

"A fake date."

"Sure."

She let out a hefty sigh. "Fine. But it is fake, and just so we have something to tell your jerk of an ex."

"Of course."

She rolled her eyes at his overly officious tone. "Tomorrow. Seven. Pick me up at the bar."

"Yes, ma'am."

She shook her head and muttered something that sounded an awful lot like, "why am I such an idiot," before stalking toward her car.

Jack watched her go, more than pleased with himself.

———

Rose looked at herself in the mirror and told herself for approximately the millionth time she was an idiot.

"The biggest idiot ever," she muttered to her empty apartment.

She had promised herself she wouldn't dress up. So she hadn't. Well, mostly. She had worn her nicest, most form-fitting jeans and had replaced her usual T-shirt with something more blousy, that had a bit of a V neck she wouldn't be caught dead in behind her bar.

She was pretty sure she'd never worn it. She wasn't even sure how it was in her closet.

She was about to rip it off and exchange it for some kind of big, lumpy sweater no matter the temperature, but her phone buzzed.

She glared at the message on her screen. From Jack. *Outside*.

What was she doing?

She took a deep breath. She was having a fake date so they had a common story to tell Jack's parents. It wasn't that big of a deal if she didn't make it one.

Jack couldn't force it to be anything more than that, and the fact that she was afraid, down to her bones, showed her just how important it was to do this dumb thing and prove to both him and herself that she could handle heart-tripping smiles and polite gestures and endearing compassion under a gruff exterior and…

She wrenched her door open and huffed out a breath. She wasn't afraid of anything. Not anymore. And Jack couldn't make her afraid.

She stepped outside into the warm night, and pretty much every admonition she'd given to herself over the past few hours turned to ash and floated away.

Jack was standing next to his truck looking at his phone. The sun was beginning to set in a delicate pink on the horizon, and he was in nice jeans and a button-down short-sleeved shirt and that cowboy hat that shouldn't look so perfect on him. But of course it did.

He glanced up and smiled. That smile that said *I think I'm sneaky*.

Which was absolutely one hundred percent not at all cute.

"Hey," he offered casually.

"Hey."

"You look nice."

She sauntered toward him, trying to find Rose under all this weird uncertainty inside her. "Baby, I look spectacular."

He grinned full-on at that, and she couldn't help but grin back. He moved around to the passenger side of the truck and opened the door. "You ready?" he asked.

She stood and stared for a good thirty seconds. "You don't really open car doors for every woman?"

"Not every woman—my grandmother, my mother, and my date, and jeez, that sounds warped."

She laughed, couldn't help it. "I don't want to know what you got up to on that farm of yours," she said, purposefully brushing against him as she got up into the passenger seat.

"I believe it was called manners," he returned, leaning close and handing her the seat belt she very well could have reached for herself. "Watch your feet," he murmured as if he was whispering sweet nothings into her ear, and then he shut the door.

She fastened her seat belt and reminded herself she had the upper hand. She always had the upper hand. Just because his ridiculous little gestures and whispers made her edgy and needy didn't mean she wasn't the one in control.

He'd been with one woman. She knew way more about maneuvering men than he'd ever know about maneuvering a woman. The end.

He climbed into the driver's side and tipped his hat back a little on his head. He started the ignition and pulled out of the bar's gravel lot. They headed west down Main, the sunset morphing slowly from those pale pastels to streaks of fire.

"Does the sun set like that in Iowa?"

"I assume you mean Indiana?"

"Sure. Whatever I-state you're from."

"It does indeed, Rose. The sun sets that way everywhere. Montana, Indiana, Afghanistan. It never fails to amaze me."

Why did he have to be sweet? Touch something deep and vulnerable inside her that she thought she'd eradicated a long time ago.

When they got close to Georgia's, he didn't slow down and he didn't stop. "Where are we going?"

"Bozeman."

"Bozeman?"

He glanced at her for a brief second before returning his gaze to the road leading out of Blue Valley. "We could eat at Georgia's, but I don't think my family would be impressed by it as a first-date place. Besides, people know us there. You'd get all sorts of questions."

"Right." And she didn't want questions. At all. Certainly not when this was as fake as it got.

Silence, aside from the low strains of the radio, settled into the cab of the truck. Jack grimaced as a new song came on.

"This isn't country. He's talking."

"I like it," Rose returned. "Regardless of what it is."

"It's hard to listen to," he said, reaching for the dial.

She slapped his hand away. "I like it," she repeated.

"Women," he muttered, which turned into a heated debate about country music, only finding common ground in Willie Nelson and Waylon Jennings. When they reached the restaurant some thirty minutes later, Jack once again opened her door for her.

She wrinkled her nose at him as he held out his hand to help her down. "I do not know what to do with this, Jack."

"Go with the flow," he returned as if it were simple as that.

Maybe it was. She let him hold her hand as she stepped down from the truck and followed him into a nice restaurant that she wasn't sure any man she'd ever dated would have even known existed, let alone taken her to.

They were escorted to a table, and Rose slid into the booth across from Jack. It was one of those places that kept the lights so low, you could barely see anything, but that faint, warm light only accentuated the sharp features of Jack's face and the way even more of that hollowness he'd shown up to Blue Valley with had filled out, even in just the past few weeks.

Her chest felt all jittery, and it wasn't the same as before the date. It wasn't fear or worry that she didn't have control of the situation. It was so much worse than that. She was nervous.

She never got nervous during a date. She always knew where something was going. And she had no idea at all where this was going.

It's going nowhere. It's fake.

"Have you been here before?" he asked casually, studying the menu.

Rose stifled a snort. "Ah, no. This is not my style."

He glanced up at her over his menu. "Did you want to go somewhere else?"

He didn't ask it in that manipulative way that would have made sense to her. He asked it like he cared. Like he'd get up and walk out if she said yes.

"No, I…I just…" Good God, she was stuttering. She looked down at her menu. "It's nice," she grumbled.

They ordered, and Jack chatted on about something to do with cattle and beef and steak, and Rose didn't know why it seemed so interesting when Jack talked about all that, but it was.

"Are you going to tell your sister we talked about cows on our date?" she asked, desperate to feel like she had some kind of handle on this whole thing instead of sitting across from him and hanging on every word.

"Maybe. She's very into the whole slow-food thing."

"This is the non-med-school sister."

His mouth quirked. "You do pay attention."

"I'm supposed to, right? They've got to think we've been dating for, like, months." They were supposed to show up and believe she and Jack loved each other. Her stomach turned on one nauseated roll.

"That would be ideal."

A mouthwatering steak was placed in front of her, and still her stomach roiled. She needed non-love type topics. Topics that would remind her she did not belong anywhere near Jack's orbit and this performance for his family wouldn't just be about pretending to be someone involved with Jack, but pretending to be someone Jack's family would approve of and think was better than Madison. "Tell me about your mom," she blurted. Whatever woman had raised Jack would be the kind of woman who would find Rose abhorrent, she was sure.

"She's a mom. A force." He smiled fondly. "She had four kids and helped run the farm with my dad and just always made us feel like we could do whatever we wanted—as long as we went to church every Sunday and had a real job, that is."

Rose couldn't help but laugh at that, even though it was completely foreign to her. Church and mothers who were forces as much as the rest. "So she'll be super thrilled about a girl who's never stepped foot in church, runs a bar, and is covered in tattoos."

"You aren't covered." His mouth quirked at something.

"What?"

"I still haven't told her *I* have a tattoo." He rubbed a hand over his chin. "And I'm going to have to shave my beard or she'll express severe disappointment."

"Such a good son."

"I try to be."

She should have something sharp or nasty to say to that, but how could she? He was good. Dutiful. "I was not such a good daughter."

"From what little you've told me about your parents, I'd say they didn't deserve a good daughter."

"No, I suppose they didn't."

"Do you have siblings?"

Everything inside her turned to ice. "I don't want to talk about my family. This is about your family."

She could tell he didn't like that. "They'll want to know about you too, not just what you know about me."

"I don't want to talk about my family with anyone."

She let him think that was because of what she'd told him about her father, and maybe, in part, it was. She was embarrassed of who and what her parents were, and Jack knew she had sisters, but aside from that, if he knew their names, if he ran into Delia in town and knew who she was... It would all get too complicated and twisted. She had to keep them separate.

"Tell me about your sister in med school," she said instead, and he did, telling stories about both his sisters with the kind of awe and protectiveness Rose understood.

They ordered dessert and lingered there, him asking her about running a bar until she finally told him how she'd won Pioneer Spirit in a poker game. She didn't know how he'd maneuvered that story out of her, considering it reminded her of where she'd learned her poker skills. Something Jack also knew, because she couldn't keep her big mouth shut around him.

When it was finally time to go, Jack once again opened all doors for her, and she didn't fight it, because what was there to fight? This decent, good guy wanted to open doors and say please and thank you, and somehow, he thought her worthy of that kind of attention.

This wasn't fear or nerves anymore, it was outright confusion. Didn't he get it? Who and what she was? Didn't she wear that pretty clearly?

He pulled his truck into the bar parking lot, and he turned off the ignition and got out of the truck and not because he thought he was going to talk his way into her bed. He was probably going to walk her to her door like this was some movie about wholesome teenagers.

He rounded the truck, and she sat in her seat until he opened the door, and then she furrowed her eyebrows at him. "Are you for real?"

He cocked his head as if he couldn't quite figure out what her confusion was. "Far as I can tell."

She shook her head and let him hold her hand as she got down from the truck again. Then he did, indeed, walk her to her door.

He stood there in the faint parking lot light, so close that she wanted to fling herself at him, but she was stronger than that. This was fake, and she couldn't let him make it real.

"I guess I shouldn't kiss you," he murmured, leaning closer and closer until she could practically feel the faint whisper of his whiskers. "You might get the wrong idea."

She laughed, though God help her, she didn't know why. None of this was funny.

"Of course," he continued, his voice low and sensual, a very lustful promise all wrapped up in those syllables, "you could admit this was a real date and we could go inside."

That scared her more than anything. She couldn't feel soft about him and have sex with him. She'd ruin him and everything before his family even showed up. "No. No, we can't do that." But she wanted him. His hands, his mouth, that good heart.

You can't want that, Rose.

Which irritated the hell out of her. That he could work her up like this and not take the simple, good thing she'd offered him.

"Why won't you take an offer of no-strings sex?" she demanded.

"Because I want more than sex from you, Rose." He leaned forward, brushed his mouth chastely across her cheek, and then turned and walked toward his truck. "Good night."

It wouldn't be though, because once again, she'd spend it tossing and turning, yearning for Jack. Damn him.

Chapter 14

JACK STOOD IN FRONT OF THE MIRROR IN THE bunkhouse bathroom and tried to keep his mind blank as he ran the razor over his beard. He'd gone into Bozeman yesterday and gotten a quick buzz at the cheap barbershop there, and now every time he caught sight of himself, it was like seeing a ghost. The reflection showed him the man he'd been a few years ago, a needling reminder that his family would be descending soon.

Today.

Any minute, really.

Which was fine. Great. He hadn't seen his parents or Vivian since they'd visited him in the rehab center last Christmas. He missed them. Mike and Madison and kid were a bitter pill to swallow, but it was a small price to pay for the rest.

He set down the razor and gripped the sink. It was a giant price to pay, and he hated it. It felt like a poison, seeping in to ruin the past week. It had actually been really good—a combination of hard work and fun that hadn't existed in his life for a very long time. And Rose, whether on the periphery or smack dab in the middle of it all, had become a bright light of hope.

So much hope he'd almost been afraid to touch it, really touch it, for fear she would simply disappear in a puff of smoke. Their fake date had been, well, the opposite of fake, and he wanted to revel in all that instead of the pain and confusion.

He wished he'd taken her no-strings offer now, because the impending week—or two, as Mom had been delightfully vague—felt like nothing but a black, torturous cloud.

There was a knock at the bathroom door. "Uh, I think they're here," Gabe called.

Jack swallowed and leaned forward in the sink, washing the excess shaving cream off his face. Maybe the cold of the water would kick him into some kind of functioning gear. He dried off his face, pulled on the shirt he'd picked out, and felt like a zombie walking through life short on brains.

Stepping out of the bathroom, he forced himself to smile blandly at Gabe. "Thanks."

"I think Becca's got Rasputin ready to attack if anything goes bad."

Jack managed a weak chuckle at the mention of Becca's mean-ass rooster that wouldn't die. "Great. Attack chicken at the ready." He ran his hand over his alarmingly short hair and forced himself to breathe naturally. Like any other mission, he just had to focus on getting the breath to come in and out, not on the task ahead.

Gabe clapped him on the shoulder. "You know we got your back."

Jack nodded. He did know that, but unfortunately, none of his friends could do this for him. No one could.

He put one foot in front of the other and left the bunkhouse. It seemed wrong for the ranch to look the way it usually did. It seemed wrong for the sky to be a bright, cloudless blue and the mountains in the distance to sparkle like magic.

He'd prefer a gray, drizzly sky with plenty of mud to maneuver around. The bracing chill of a Montana spring or whatever a Montana winter would bring. He wanted anything other than to have this pretty summer day tainted by...

The RV Dad must have rented chugged up the drive and came to a stop. Jack hadn't realized he'd started to backpedal until he felt Gabe's hand on his shoulder.

"Only way out is through," Gabe muttered.

Which was true. Unfortunate, but true.

The door to the RV swung open. When Mom came into view, it wasn't so hard to move forward anymore. She stepped down from the RV looking exactly as she looked in all his memories. Seeing her short, curly, dark hair, perfectly made-up face, and pleasant smile—which was almost always on it—was like stepping back in time.

She turned to grin at him and came hurrying across the yard as he strode toward her. He didn't even bother with a greeting. He just leaned down and pulled her into a hard hug. She smelled like his childhood—she'd worn the same perfume since he was born—and it took about every last thing he had not to cry like a kid right then.

"My, you're barely even limping," she said, muffled into his shoulder as she squeezed him back tightly. "They got you fixed up all right, and just look at all this." Mom pulled back and gestured toward the mountains. "My goodness."

"It is that."

She reached up and touched his face. "Oh, I've missed you, sweetheart."

"I've missed you too, Mom."

She sniffled and looked away, straightening herself as she waved Dad over. Jack held out his hand for his father to shake. It was how they'd greeted each other since he'd turned thirteen. Even in the hospital, Dad had gone for the handshake greeting, no matter that Jack had seen tears in Dad's eyes for the first time since his great-grandmother's funeral—making that twice altogether.

Dad took Jack's hand and squeezed, shaking once before pulling him into a hard, quick hug.

And that about brought Jack to his knees, but they both released each other, cleared their throats, and exchanged rough-sounding greetings.

"Looking well, boy."

"You too, Dad."

His sister was the next one out of the RV. Vivian bolted toward him, launching herself at him with a wild abandon he'd *always* envied about her. "Jacky." He caught her even though his leg threatened to buckle. His impetuous, somehow grown woman of a baby sister.

"I'm not hurting you, am I?" she asked, holding on for dear life.

"As if," he scoffed, giving her a little twirl before he placed her on the ground.

She flashed him a grin. "My *God*, this place is fantastic."

"It is. You're going to love every last thing about it, I have no doubt."

As the next person climbed down the stairs, a horrible, awkward silence descended, everyone's smiles going strained. Except Vivian. She scowled.

God bless her.

Mike stepped out of the RV, not looking at the assembled crowd. Instead, he looked back to help Madison down, since she had both arms full of kid.

Jack made half-assed introductions to Gabe, who cheerfully greeted all of them with his usual easy facade, but Jack's chest felt like it was in a vise. He didn't know how to do this.

You do it the Armstrong way. Pretend everything is fine and normal.

He tried to smile, but he knew it didn't actually move his mouth. If anything showed at all, it was a grimace.

"Mike. Madison." He managed to greet them as they approached. He didn't make a move to shake hands or hug, and thank Christ, neither did they. Jack looked at the tow-headed one-and-a-half-year-old in Madison's arms. "And this must be...Croy." Yeah. They'd named the poor kid Croy of all things.

Madison smiled up at him, and he tried to tell himself this woman was a stranger. Just like the Jack he'd been a million years ago was a stranger, this woman was not the girl he'd once loved and been so certain he'd spend the rest of his life with.

Except she looked exactly the same. Dark-blond hair, bright-blue eyes, and fair skin that freckled in the summer no matter how much sunscreen she put on. He'd seen her naked, told her he loved her, and promised her forever.

And she was holding his brother's child.

"Croy," Madison said to the little boy, her voice the same sweet thing he remembered from his youth. "This is your uncle Jack."

The little boy, who looked like every childhood

picture he'd ever seen of Mike and himself, merely blinked in Jack's direction.

Jack turned away. Away from some weird, warped version of his lost future, away from the two people who'd hurt him the most in the world, and toward his parents.

"Are you up for a tour?" he asked, his forced cheer failing so hard, he thought he saw Vivian and Gabe cringe.

"Yes, that sounds lovely," Mom said overly brightly, hooking her arm with his.

Jack didn't look back to see if Mike or Madison followed. He couldn't. He could barely breathe through *this*, because he'd known seeing them would suck. And it did, but he hadn't considered the worst of it. That now there would be memories of *them* together in this place that had been his sanctuary.

The only reason he was able to breathe through that horrible realization was his mother next to him, chattering on about their drive.

Rose had no idea how Gabe had gotten her phone number, but it was hard to be pissed about it when she read the message.

> This is Gabe. Jack's family is here. If you've got a few mins to play girlfriend, now might be a good time.

Why he thought *she* would help matters was beyond Rose, but the fact that it was *Gabe* asking, when he'd been so untrustingly opposed not so many days ago, made Rose feel like it was important. Important enough to do something she hadn't done once since she'd taken control of Pioneer Spirit.

"If anything goes wrong—"

"Rose, I know you mean well, and trust me, I get this is a big deal for you. But, sweetheart, I know how to open the bar on a Thursday afternoon," Tonya said, crossing her arms over her chest.

Rose nodded, not sure if her nerves were more over what she looked like, what she was about to go do, or that she was trusting someone else to open her bar.

All three. Definitely all three.

"I didn't realize you were going to be in a play though," Tonya said slyly.

Rose scowled at one of the few employees she trusted and one of the few employees she wouldn't snap at for a comment like that. Even if it was true, because she was definitely dressed to play a part. "If Ginny doesn't show up for her shift, you call me. If the delivery doesn't come through, you call me. If anything, and I mean *anything* goes wrong—"

"I call you. I got it. You can trust me."

God, but it wasn't easy. Still, she forced herself to smile at Tonya. "I know I can." Then she did it. She handed her spare key to someone else.

"I'll give it back when you get back," Tonya assured.

Rose shook her head, and no matter how it made her stomach churn, she did what she knew she should have done a while ago. "Keep it. You're my right-hand man. You should have a key."

Tonya raised her eyebrows, but she didn't say anything else as she slipped the key into her pocket.

"I'll be back," Rose muttered before heading out the back exit.

Everything about today was screwy, and she wanted it to be over now. *Now.* But the only way to make it over was to do it, so she got in her car and drove to Revival Ranch.

The pretty scenery of the drive did nothing to calm her, and it was so irritating to be nervous, to be worried. She shouldn't have been self-conscious. This wasn't their fake date he could take the wrong way, and apparently *hadn't*, since he hadn't even tried to really kiss her. This was for his family. For him.

When had she ever been self-conscious?

It wiggled through her nevertheless, all nerves and worry. She wanted to be what Jack needed. A *fuck you* to his ex and his brother, and someone his upstanding, church-going parents wouldn't look down their noses at. She wanted to pretend to be someone his parents would think was just as great as Madison, if not better.

It was why she was wearing a dress with long sleeves, despite the warm weather. She'd hidden her tattoos as best she could, put on the demurest amount of makeup she could muster, and braided her hair to hang over one shoulder.

She looked sweet and good, and now she just had to keep up the act long enough to make them believe it. God help her.

She parked her car next to a giant RV and tried to remember why she was doing this. A favor, nothing more, nothing less, for a guy who'd been treated pretty shitty by his family. She was a metaphorical middle finger, and her feelings about the man involved weren't at stake. Beginning and end of story.

Rose stepped out of the car, smoothing her hands down her borrowed clothes. God bless Summer Lane for lending her the sweet-looking dress and not asking any questions. Delia's sister-in-law always looked like some kind of hippie fairy princess, and Rose figured that was just the kind of look she needed for pretending to be someone's girlfriend.

Rose studied the ranch but, aside from the RV, didn't see signs of anyone. At least not until the RV door swung open and a blond woman holding a kid stepped out.

They both froze and stared at each other.

Rose supposed it could be Jack's sister, but between the baby and the lack of any kind of resemblance, Rose absolutely knew this was Madison. Of course it was. She was blond and blue eyed and beautiful, even in jeans and a T-shirt.

Despite the baby wriggling in her arms, she didn't look the least bit frazzled, like Delia so often did when wrestling with Sunny. Surprise was clearly written all over her face, but mostly she was serene and perfect grace.

Rose wanted to scowl and shrink away, because she could never pretend to compete with that—no matter that Madison was a cheating asshole. That was the thing to remember though. Madison might *look* perfect, but she was definitely *not*.

So Rose fixed the brightest smile she could muster on her face. This was the woman who had cheated on Jack—sweet, ridiculously good Jack. And with his *brother*. "Hi there!" she greeted, forcing out a kind of cheer she'd never used before in her life.

"Hello," Madison returned cautiously.

"I'm Rose," Rose continued, stepping toward her.

She didn't know if Jack had told anyone her name, but she figured the best course of action was to assume everyone would know who she was. That she had the right to be there. "You must be Madison."

Madison blinked. "Y-yeah. Yes, I'm Madison. And you're...Jack's..."

Rose smiled sweetly. "I am Jack's," she said cheerfully. "And who's this little sweetie?" Rose asked, touching a finger to the kid's waving fist.

Rose didn't miss the way Madison shifted so the baby was farther away from her.

"This is my son, Croy," Madison muttered, her gaze going up to the ranch house.

"Cory?"

Madison frowned, her gaze going back to Rose, clearly assessing everything. "Croy."

"Oh, sorry." Rose laughed airily. "How unique." It was probably mean, but she was feeling mean. Meeting Madison in person filled Rose with a renewed sense of fury. Seeing the sweet little boy in Madison's arms, as if the woman deserved that kind of gift.

All Rose's anger at the way Jack had been treated returned with a vengeance.

"Well, I can't wait to meet everyone," Rose said, turning her attention to the ranch house. "Are they in the house?"

"They were taking a tour of the stables when I had to come change Croy's diaper."

"Let's go then."

Madison didn't say anything to that, but she did fall into step next to Rose, Croy babbling happily.

A group of people started filing out of the stable

doors—first Alex, Becca, Gabe, and Jack, then what must have been the Armstrong family.

"Just what has Jack told you about me?" Madison asked, her eyes ahead on the group of people, her tone hushed.

Rose tried to decide what answer would irritate this woman the most. She didn't know Madison enough to really know, so she could only guess. "Oh, he mentioned that you two dated years ago," Rose said offhandedly.

"Is…is that it?"

Rose studied Madison and then decided that the *best* course of action was to say as little as possible. If Madison was curious enough to ask a stranger what had been said behind her back, then the worst thing for her would be to never find out.

So Rose shrugged and picked up the pace of her walking. "Not *it*, exactly." Then she made a beeline for Jack, effectively cutting off any more conversation.

Her step hitched for about a second when she got her first good look at him for the day. He'd cut his hair and shaved off his beard and was standing there, all military ramrod straight, looking like the perfect, way-too-handsome soldier that he was.

When he looked over at her approaching form, he stared at her as if she had two heads. The outfit she was wearing was probably the equivalent of two heads, she had to admit. Or maybe he was staring like that since she was walking next to Madison. Either way, she smiled and sidled up next to him. "Hi, sweetie," she said, staring up at him and fluttering her lashes until he clearly had to suppress an amused smile. "Sorry I'm late."

"Late," he echoed. "Right." He turned his gaze

to his family, his arm coming around her shoulders. "Everyone, this is Rose," he said, and it was the weirdest thing how *proud* he sounded. Completely disconcerting how *real* it felt to have Jack's arm around her, her arm around his waist, and his family waiting, what seemed like eagerly, to meet her.

An act, Rose told herself as she was introduced to the Armstrong clan. *All a fucking act.*

Chapter 15

JACK DIDN'T KNOW WHAT TO MAKE OF ROSE'S outfit. He didn't know what to make of Madison walking up alongside her, his mother pulling Rose in for a hug, or his sister gushing over her *adorable* dress.

Because Rose was wearing a *dress*. And it was all flowery and flowy and sweet. She'd braided her hair, and it fell over one shoulder, and she looked like some completely different person than the Rose he knew.

He didn't like it. Because as much as this was fake, he still wanted her to be…her. When she talked with his parents, he wanted…

Things he probably had no business wanting.

They went through the rest of the tour of the ranch, and Rose held his hand and acted like everything was a marvel. She chattered with his parents and his sister all afternoon, mostly ignoring Mike and Madison and the baby. By the end of it, Mom was charmed, Dad was blushing, and Vivian kept mouthing *I like her* anytime Jack met her gaze.

Which had been the plan and the point, and he didn't miss how silent Mike and Madison were. But something about the fact that it was Rose *acting* bothered him on a deep level that he couldn't seem to rationalize away. He wanted the Rose from their date night—the snark, the laugh. The way she slowly opened up to him and there was something softer underneath, but it wasn't this. His family would no doubt be as charmed by that real her as much as this fake version of her.

In the evening, his family filed into the living room of Becca and Alex's house while Gabe and Alex took care of some chores. Becca had insisted on making dinner for the whole crew, no matter how he'd argued or Mom had insisted she didn't have to.

Eventually Mom drifted off to the kitchen, intent on helping the preparations, and without Mom's influence, Dad and Mike drifted into farm talk.

Jack thought he could have accepted that. He could have dealt, because he had this whole new farm-like endeavor that he did actually enjoy, no matter that it wasn't the family farm *he* had been supposed to take over. Then Madison joined in. Talking about crop yields and rotation, rain levels and soil testing, and Jack could only stare at his hands and try to convince himself it was all a very real alternate reality.

Didn't matter that those were supposed to be his conversations with his wife.

They were not his.

At some point, Rose excused herself, and Jack didn't totally listen to what excuse she used. Whether she was going to help Becca or go to the bathroom, or she was just going to disappear. It didn't feel like it mattered. He was untethered either way.

Croy toddled over to him, grabbing on to Jack's knees when his balance wavered. Blinking blue eyes stared curiously at him before he shouted something with a little jump. "Ba! Ba!" He held out his pudgy hand, a red fabric ball clutched there.

Jack swallowed and took the outstretched ball. He pretended to examine it. "A very nice red ball."

Croy repeated him, though the syllables were a little baby garbled. Still, it made Jack smile, and he held the ball back to Croy. He took it, then hurled it at Jack's chest.

"Easy, slugger," Jack murmured as Croy squealed in delight. They repeated the process a few times before Rose's voice interrupted.

"Jack, Becca wants us to dust off some chairs in the office and bring them to the table."

Jack looked up. Rose stood in the entrance to the kitchen, and she nodded down the hall toward the rarely used office.

"Oh. Sure." He looked down at the kid holding on to his knees. His nephew. It was easier to separate him from what Madison and Mike had done when it was just him and the kid and the ball, but Rose standing behind him and Madison staring at them with pink-cheeked embarrassment, he suddenly didn't know what to do with Croy.

Madison got off the couch and scooped him up without making any eye contact with Jack. "Look at your puzzle, baby."

Baby. *I don't know, baby. Let's wait.* Madison's voice was a constant loop in his head. Should he have known all along? Should he have read into her not wanting to actually *get* married before he was deployed?

"Jack." Rose's hand squeezed his shoulder, and he looked up at Rose in costume.

Except she didn't have that fake, wide smile on her face. She looked a little grave, a lot more like the Rose he preferred.

"Right." He stood and followed Rose down the hall, everything inside him feeling hollow. They stepped into the old office that had once been Alex's father's and wasn't used much these days.

"Was this a real errand or a fictional one?" he managed to ask.

"Both," Rose replied with a shrug. "I asked Becca if there was anything we could do to get away from dick-bag talk."

"Dick-bag talk?" he echoed, standing in the middle of the office, wishing he could will himself back to present-day life.

"Yeah. Your brother, sitting there talking about all the things that were supposed to be yours? Dick. Bag."

"I'm sure he didn't mean—"

"Well, I'm not sure," Rose replied, searching the room before she found a stack of folding chairs. "And for the record, *Croy* isn't a name. It's a drunk person trying to spell Cory."

"Rose," he admonished, trying not to be amused.

"It's like a noise a British person makes when they're frustrated. I can't get the pickle jar open! Croy!"

He tried to swallow down the laugh, but no matter how childish it might be, it felt good to be around someone who didn't ignore the past or wasn't faintly embarrassed by it. Someone who thought it was the affront it was.

Because no matter what he had or hadn't done, whether or not he should have realized Madison didn't really love him, what she and Mike had done was a betrayal.

"And you're sitting there playing with the kid, and I don't know how, Jack. I really don't."

"He… Well, it isn't his fault."

"No, but…" She shook her head. "And your brother!" Rose continued, sharp and hard as she wiped down one folding chair and moved to the next. "I've run a bar long enough to know that sometimes you get a gut feeling about someone, and mine is always right."

"And what's your gut feeling?"

"That he's a turd." She glanced back over her shoulder at him. "What's the deal there anyway?"

"Deal?"

"I mean, I never had a brother, but I'd chop my own arm off before I hurt my sisters the way he hurt you. So I doubt it was a great relationship."

"I didn't think it was a bad one," Jack muttered. "Competitive, I guess. We're only about eleven months apart."

"And?"

Jack sighed. "And I was—and this isn't conceit, it's just the truth—better at everything."

Rose grinned, forgetting the chair. "Everything?"

"I got good grades. I was the star of the basketball team and led us to state twice. Mike was a fair student, always pissed I had more playing time, and couldn't join the military because of his asthma."

"That doesn't excuse what he did."

"I've spent two years trying to find a way to excuse what either of them did," Jack replied. "Nothing does."

"Damn straight."

He found himself walking toward Rose. Not to help, but to soak up the orbit of *actual* Rose.

"She asked me what I knew, you know," Rose said, so patently pleased with herself.

"What did you say?"

"Oh, I was vague. I said I knew you'd dated, and when she asked if that was it"—Rose flashed one of those grins he wanted to sink into—"I said it wasn't *it* and walked away. I hope it eats her alive."

Then he didn't resist. He sank into her smile, pressing his mouth to hers, gathering her close. It wasn't like the parking lot—no. Not frustrated confusion and attraction pumping through him. He knew exactly what he wanted, right here.

Her mouth. Her words. Her support.

She was stiff for all of two seconds before she melted into him and the kiss. Her hands slid up his arms and up his neck. "I miss your hair," she murmured against his mouth before scraping her teeth across his bottom lip.

"It'll grow back."

She laughed into his kiss, and he breathed it in, the beautiful, sharp reminder, *this* was his life. Mountains and ranches and *Rose*.

Which made him forget everything else. He slid his hands down her back, over her ass, pulling her closer, wanting *all* of her.

She pulled her mouth away from his with a breathless laugh that wasn't the same as the one she'd made before. "Jack, your family." Something about her tone sounded all wrong. Like that syrupy-sweet thing she'd used when everyone else was around.

Then he realized she was glancing over his shoulder. "Oops," she said, all fake embarrassment.

He looked behind him to see Madison standing there, her expression pinched.

"Sorry," Rose said, leaning her head against Jack's

chest and patting him on the abdomen. "Hard not to get carried away with this one."

It hit him hard and unwelcome that this wasn't what he wanted, no matter that Madison was clearly rattled. Maybe in some part of his brain or betrayed heart, he wanted her to hurt. But he wanted that kiss with Rose to have been real a lot more than he wanted to perform for Madison.

"Mom wanted me to let you know dinner is ready," Madison said.

"Mom," Jack echoed.

"Yup. I'll let her know you're on your way," Madison muttered, turning on her heel and hurrying out of the room.

Jack glanced at Rose, who had a self-satisfied smile on her face.

"You don't have to lay it on quite so thick."

She blinked at him, something in her expression shuttering, that Rose armor clicking into place. "That's the point though, isn't it?"

"The point was never a fake Rose. It was a fake relationship."

"Lucky you, Jacky boy," she said, hefting two folding chairs under her arms before walking past him. "You get both."

Which was not what he wanted. At all.

⁓

After dinner, Rose stood on the porch of the Revival Ranch house and told herself not to bolt. Becca was trying to convince Mr. and Mrs. Armstrong they would be more than welcome to sleep in the main house, while

Vivian enthusiastically took Becca up on the offer. Jack stood as he'd stood all night, stiff and straight and unsmiling. The worst part was she thought he was *trying* to smile. All the while, a perfect, starry sky stretched above, and everything looked like a beautiful, heavenly dream.

All Rose could do, all night since that kiss, was think about it. Relive it. She could fight attraction, and she could even fight confused, frustrated kisses in bar parking lots. She'd fought that fake, wonderful date tooth and nail, but she didn't know how to fight whatever *that* had been.

Sweet and maybe a little sad, but like a kiss from her could soothe the sad.

Then she'd opened her eyes to look at him, to read him and that heart-shuddering kiss, and she'd seen Madison in the doorway and remembered why she was really there.

Jack might not want fake Rose, but he did want *fake*. Maybe he'd convinced himself he liked her outside of that, but she didn't believe it for a second.

Couldn't.

"Mom. Dad. Spend the night in a real bed. Maddy and I will be fine in the RV. More than fine," Mike said, sliding his arm around Madison's shoulders.

Madison clutched the baby to her chest, misery all over her face, and Rose didn't have it in her to feel bad for the woman. She might have a little more conscience than Mike, but that didn't erase what she'd done to Jack.

Jack. Who was somehow immeasurably sweet and good and clearly saw the best in people if he was kissing Rose, for heaven's sake.

"Oh, well, if you're sure—" Mrs. Armstrong turned to Becca, who was already steamrolling over the excuses.

"We have plenty of room for you three, and I made up both extra rooms, so if you don't sleep there, I'll have done all that work for nothing."

Mrs. Armstrong let out a hefty sigh. "All right, you've twisted my arm. We'll sleep in the extra room. Vivian, maybe you should—"

"Two extra rooms, Mom. I'm sleeping on a real bed without a kid screaming in the middle of the night." Vivian grinned in Jack's direction. "Unless you and Gabe have room in the bunkhouse."

Rose didn't know Vivian all that well, but she had the sneaking suspicion Vivian kept flirting with and making innuendos about Gabe to get a rise out of Jack, not because she had any particular interest in Gabe.

"Here's fine," Jack all but growled, earning him a tinkling laugh from Vivian. There was a brief flash of humor on his face before it was gone. Rose wanted to slide next to him again, say something silly and over the top so he'd show that smile again, laugh, or roll his eyes or something other than that horrible blankness.

Mrs. Armstrong got there first, stepping forward and pulling Jack down into a hug. "Good night, sweetheart. We'll see you in the morning."

Jack hugged his mother back and nodded, and again there was maybe the glimmer of *something* before it was gone.

Then Mrs. Armstrong turned to Rose, all soft, sweet, *motherly* smiles. Rose could only imagine what this woman would think of *her* mother, a cold, bitter woman who'd hurled insults at her children like her husband had hurled fists.

Rose swallowed. It was as though that stupid kiss before dinner had dismantled everything, and she didn't even know *how* to be pretend Rose anymore. She was just this bleeding, armor-less idiot.

"It was so good to meet you, Rose. I hope we'll see more of you."

Rose forced the fake smile and opened her mouth to say something overly sweet, but Mrs. Armstrong pulled her into a firm hug before she could get words out. It was motherly and soft, all those things she'd never had growing up. She knew Mrs. Armstrong wasn't perfect. Hell, this whole family was dysfunction personified. There *was* love here, even if it was a little warped around the edges.

"Thank you," Mrs. Armstrong whispered, and Rose didn't have the first clue what she was being thanked for, but Mrs. Armstrong released her abruptly and then bustled into the house. Mr. Armstrong and Vivian followed at her heels, while Mike, Madison, and Croy headed across the lawn to the RV.

"I've got this all covered if you want to go down to the bar and get a drink or something," Becca said with a sympathetic smile.

"Thanks, Bec," Jack replied, his mouth still doing that horrible thing where Rose thought he was trying to smile and failing.

"Night, guys." Becca disappeared inside, leaving Rose and Jack alone on the porch.

"She's nice," Rose murmured about Becca, feeling somehow less. Becca had opened her home and fed Jack's family simply because it was the right thing to do.

"Yeah, she is."

That never would have occurred to Rose. She wasn't nice or selfless. Even getting herself into this mess had been tit for tat, a favor for a favor. She didn't know how Jack thought otherwise, but she needed to put an end to it before this got...

She wanted to laugh at herself, because as much as she wished she could stay in denial, this was already complicated. *Go home, Rose. Get the hell away from this mess.*

"You want to go to the bar?" she asked instead, because she needed him to stop looking so bleak and desolate or she was going to do something *really* stupid.

"No," he replied, his voice gruff, his eyes on the crescent moon glimmering in the distance.

"You want to go to my house?" she asked on a whisper. A whisper, because it was not an offer she could extend him. Yet here she was.

It's pretend. Just for a little while. What's the harm?

"Yes," he replied simply, his gaze never leaving the moon.

"Okay." It didn't matter that she was an idiot. She'd made the offer, and something inside her chest expanded at the thought of being there for him. Of soothing him.

Of kissing him over and over again.

Jack's hand slid over hers, twining his long fingers with hers. He didn't look at her or anything other than straight ahead, but her heart squeezed all the same.

No guy had ever done something as innocuous as *hold her hand*. Which was a stupid thing to think, being that they were walking past the RV and this was all for show.

The main door was open, so the only thing keeping Rose from looking inside was a screen. Madison was standing there, watching them.

So Jack wasn't really holding *her* hand, no matter that he hadn't so much as glanced at Madison watching them. He probably had some Navy SEAL sixth sense, and he was holding on to her hand for dear life to prove a point.

Not because he needed it—or her.

Which was right and for the best and damn necessary. Anyone who had ever needed her ended up hurt. Emotionally. Physically. All the kinds of hurts.

She released his hand once they reached her car, but he held on. For the first time since they'd stepped out onto the porch, he finally looked at her. Really looked at *her*.

Why her breath caught at that was beyond her, but what wasn't beyond her since he'd kissed her like she mattered?

You cannot let yourself matter. Do not let him think you matter.

"For the record, fake Rose is not invited," he said, his voice so serious.

Tell him to fuck off, this is your party, and you'll invite who-damn-ever.

"Okay," she whispered instead.

Chapter 16

THEY DROVE IN SILENCE TO ROSE'S HOUSE. HE DIDN'T know why she'd suggested coming here, but he knew it was exactly where he wanted to be. Clear, starry night. Abandoned, falling-down house. Beautiful, complicated Rose Rogers. It felt like everything he needed after this day.

It hadn't been the explosive, angry tragedy he'd expected. It hadn't been the easy, *oh this doesn't actually hurt so much* gathering he'd hoped for. It had been all those things and a million other things on top of them, to the point where he'd gone completely numb.

Numb to Vivian's happy recounting of her strange customers. Numb to Madison and Mike feeding Croy at the dinner table, a clear partnership. Numb to Mom's good-night hugs.

He felt nothing.

He supposed it was some natural, biological function—shutting down completely so he didn't have to actually deal with the pain.

Rose pulled her car all the way up to the steps of the house. Without a word, she got out and so did he. He shoved his hands into his pockets and stared at the pond glittering in the distance.

"Want to go for another swim?" Rose asked from somewhere that sounded a million miles away. *He* felt a million miles away. When he turned to face her, she was a lot closer than that, still in that overly feminine dress, her hair in that ridiculously demure braid, simply standing at the top of the steps and looking like the sweet, accommodating queen of the dilapidated manor.

Something swept through him then, a tide of emotions he couldn't have named if he'd tried. They weren't sweet or nice or easy. It was fire, and it was pain, and it was some edgy need with teeth.

He stalked over to her, taking each step with no thought to the ache in his right leg, and he noticed and yet didn't mind the wariness that crept into her expression.

Maybe someone should be wary. Maybe someone should have a goddamn care.

He reached out and tugged the band out of her hair. She didn't move. She stood there like a disapproving statue. So he unwound the braid until her hair hung loose over her shoulders, all bent in the places it had been twirled together.

"I hate that dress," he all but spat, that edgy, needy thing building in him more and more the longer she looked at him with nothing but detachment.

Her eyebrows raised a fraction. "Do you now?" she murmured, all cool, collected, in *charge* Rose.

Thank Christ she was back. He couldn't take another second of fake her.

"I hate the syrupy-sweet way you said my name all day," he continued.

She crossed her arms over her chest, icy, regal, and cool. "Well, I just live for the critique of my performance. Maybe you'd like to do a review in the *Valley County Gazette*."

He had no reason to be mad at Rose. Hell, maybe he

didn't have any reason to be mad period, but it roared through him like fire, and he wanted to get under her facade. The dress, the hair, that distant way she spoke.

So he got up in her face, gratified when she stepped back. And then again. He kept going until he had her backed against the door. Still she looked at him with nothing more than icy disapproval. He leaned his face into hers until their noses were practically touching. "I hated that fake fucking kiss."

She didn't back down, but that cool disapproval went hot and angry, and something inside him roared in triumph.

"Well, *I* hate the way your ex stares at me as though I'm some fungus growing on you. *I* hate the way you walked around all day like a zombie when they should be the ones marinating in their own awfulness. *I* hate the fact that your mother *thanked* me." Something changed in her posture then. A slump, a ragged breath. "She… Why, Jack? What the hell was she thanking me for?"

She looked very close to miserable with it, and he didn't understand that reaction, but what *did* he understand today? "I don't know," he answered, something like gentleness blanketing all those jagged edges.

"I didn't do anything," she said, shaking her head, and he thought maybe she was attempting fierce and failing.

He reached out and traced his finger over a strand of messy hair. "Now, that isn't true." Because he couldn't stand her misery, and it was the antidote to the anger swirling inside him. He wanted to soothe that lost note out of her voice over and over again.

"I'm not your salvation, Jack," she said, and this

time, she was all fierce, her dark eyes blazing in the moonlight.

"No," he returned, still tracing the path of that one strand of hair with his index finger. "Nothing is." Was that what he'd been waiting for? Salvation? Everything to click into perfect place? He felt like he'd been waiting for *something*, and anytime one little, jagged piece found its match, another million shards turned on him, making him just as miserable as he'd always been. And no, Rose was no salvation, but she seemed to know exactly how to dull the edges of those shattered pieces of himself.

He pressed his finger to where the strands of her hair ended just below her shoulder, on a cluster of cheerful, yellow flowers. Then he traced the modest collar of the dress, everything in him tightening hard with want.

He wanted Rose. He wanted underneath all those ways she protected herself. He wanted to hear her sigh his name. He wanted to know, more desperately than he had this entire time, what it would feel like to be deep inside her. Joined. Naked.

Just them.

Even as she let out a shuddery, shaky exhale he could feel down to his soul, she straightened her shoulders. She hardened the softness that existed deep inside her whether she wanted to admit it or not. "You want to fuck your way to feeling better, that's fine, but you better know that's all this is."

He pressed his forehead to hers and laughed, which he knew was not the answer she wanted. But it was *funny*. Funny that she could soothe those sharp things and poke at his temper all at the same time. Because he'd be damned if Rose ever, *ever* thought he was using her just to make himself feel better.

"You should know me better by now," he said.

"You *don't* know me better, because in case you've forgotten, everything about this is fake. Made up. You're all riled up because your brother's an asshole, and yeah, it'd feel pretty good to stick your dick in something besides that woman, and I bet it'll feel pretty good period. For both of us. But I'm not throwing myself into that if you're going to pretend there's anything *really* happening here."

He lifted his head from hers, but he used his body to crowd her more, until she was plastered against her door and he was only a whisper from being pressed to her. "It's not all fake. The kiss in the parking lot wasn't fake, and the kiss today wasn't all fake. Our fake date was the realest thing that's happened to me in two years." He pressed his palm to the door right next to her ear. "A quick *fuck* isn't ever going to be all this is."

She lifted her chin, and he didn't think she had a clue the way *fear* shimmered in her eyes like starlight. Not fear of him exactly. She wasn't fighting or bolting, and it'd be more than easy to do both.

No, she was afraid of *this*—the thing that beat between them. So afraid that she had to pretend it didn't exist. And maybe he'd be afraid too, but he'd watched his friend die and been blown apart by a grenade, and he'd be damned if he'd waste that kind of fear on something that felt good.

"Don't kid yourself, Jack," she said, more whisper than slap.

"Don't lie to yourself, Rose." He leaned in, but he

didn't kiss her. He swept his thumb over her cheekbones and watched her eyes flutter shut as her lips parted. He soaked in that moment of painful anticipation, remembering her taste, the feel of Rose melting against him—in surprise, in anger, in hope.

And still he didn't kiss her, because he was not conceding this point. No matter what it cost him. He needed her hope. He needed her…real. Rose.

"I'll kiss you when you tell me the truth," he whispered, so close to her he wasn't sure he could live up to that threat if she didn't give in.

Her eyes flew open, and she quickly turned her expression of surprise into a sneer. "Ha!" she returned defiantly.

"You're not quite the closed book you think you are. And the fact of the matter is, actions speak louder than words. You feel something for me, Rose. You've helped me, and you can fake a lot for my family, but my family hasn't been here very long."

She pressed forward, a seductive slide of friction, and he very nearly had to close his eyes to fight off the pounding desire to give in.

She had to give him what he wanted first. She had to.

She tried to kiss him, but he pressed his palm to her chest, gently pushing her back into the door, before he slid his hand up to her throat. Bare and soft, her pulse hammered against his fingers as he brushed his thumb on the underside of her jaw.

"Tell me the truth, Rose," he said, never looking away from that dark, desperate gaze.

He could feel her shuddering under his loose grip, against his body. Her breathing was a ragged thing, as if he was already touching her everywhere like he wanted to.

But this had to be... Well, it had to mean something. He'd analyze the whys of that when he wasn't so hard that it hurt.

"Okay, fine," she said, still that defiant tilt to her chin. "Not *everything* going on here is fake, but it damn well should be."

"Close enough," he muttered before crashing his mouth down onto hers.

~~~

Rose had never romanticized a thing, a man, or a kiss in her damn life—other than Jack's mouth devouring hers, his body pressing her against the rough, aging wood of her house, her refuge. This place no one but them knew about. She'd invited him here, twice now, and he was changing it. Changing her. Rearranging all the pieces inside her chest that she'd resolutely kept separate. He was stitching them together with light and hope, and she couldn't let it happen.

This wasn't like either of their previous kisses. Though he'd initiated both, though they'd both been ridiculously potent, there had been a weakness in them—a sense of being lost, of searching to be found.

This wasn't that. Jack wasn't the least bit lost as his tongue swept into her mouth, as he pressed the hard length of his erection against her, his hand still on her throat. He was in charge, a soldier on a mission, and the mission was to have her melted from the inside out.

The ache inside her was so deep, spread so wide, she didn't even care. She relished his mission, would give it to him freely over and over again, if only he found a way to unwind all the pressure building.

The cool evening air whispered against her legs, and it was only then she realized Jack was pulling up her skirt. While one hand corralled that fabric, the other hand slid down her neck and over one breast, his fingers finding the outline of her tightened nipple.

He splayed his hand across her abdomen, the skirt of the dress hanging over his arm as his finger slipped beneath her underwear.

He gritted out a curse as he traced her intimate folds. She was a raw, throbbing nerve, and his touch was the only thing that soothed it. The more he explored her with his rough, blunt fingers, the more she forgot all the things she'd tried to convince herself.

It was fake.

It was once.

Nothing more.

"More," he said in that commanding military voice, the one that shivered through her. As though she could trust him to take care of anything and everything. With his fingers moving inside her, finding all the slick parts of her desperate for him, she couldn't think to fight it all off. Her release was just out of reach, and somehow that was best. She didn't deserve anything from him.

She shut her eyes against that thought, swallowing down all this crazy emotion. Sex wasn't about feelings. It was about getting off. Period.

And she wanted to get off on more than just his fingers. She fumbled with the button of his jeans and then the zipper, reveling in the loud exhale of his breath against her neck as she found him. Hard. Thick. Hot even through the thin cotton of his boxers. She wanted all of that, for them to be chasing that edge together. She pushed at his pants, and he nudged down her panties until they fell onto the porch floor.

His hand slid down her leg, then hooked under her knee, bringing it up and around him, her underwear falling off in the process. Then his hand slid down her other leg, and she hesitated, hooking her arms around his neck. "Jack, I don't think this position is possible."

He hefted her up without any extra fanfare, and her legs hooked around his waist, her arms holding on to his neck.

"Anything is possible for a former Navy SEAL," he said, that beautiful smile lighting up his face and her heart and…

No. She couldn't feel that. So she adjusted her weight, rubbing herself against him until he groaned. She couldn't seem to stop chanting his name. She couldn't seem to remember that a world around them existed. It was only him.

"Jack. You. You." She wanted him so desperately, she couldn't even find a way to make it happen. They *needed* to stop. They needed… She didn't know. She could only say yes. She could only beg.

He slid deep inside her in a slick, perfect glide. They groaned in tandem, and he simply held her there, joined.

She let her head fall back and hit the hard wood of the door he had her half pressed against. He held her up and she wanted to stay there, right there forever, on the brink of the orgasm trying to wash over her.

"I'm doing this all wrong," he muttered.

She laughed, her arms holding on for dear life, her body eager to *move* against this perfect invasion.

"Laughing doesn't help my ego, Rose."

"Everything feels pretty right to me, Jack." Which

was too close to a truth she wasn't capable of accepting. This. Him. Right.

"Do you have something to lie on in there?" he asked, his voice a rough, delicious scrape.

"There's a bed."

He stepped away from the door, hefting all her weight in what shouldn't have been an incredible show of strength. She held on to him, and somehow she was weightless and easy in his arms, with him still lodged inside her.

"Open the door," he ordered.

She let one of her arms unwind from his neck and reached over to turn the knob. "Jack, you can't carry me. Your le—"

"Like hell I can't," he growled, shouldering the door open. "And I'll lecture you about the unlocked door later."

Every step moved her against him in a way that had her panting from unfulfilled pleasure.

"Where?" he demanded, that *soldier on a mission* tone back and wonderful. *Perfect.*

She grabbed the battery-powered lamp she kept on the little table by the door, though she nearly dropped it when he adjusted her weight and slid deeper. "I-In the back," she managed, clicking on the lamp and wrapping her arms back around his neck.

Jack did limp as he carried her the entire way into the one inhabitable room in the house, but he never lessened his grip. Nor did he stride with enough movement to give her everything.

Damn it, she wanted everything.

Just sex everything. Not him everything.

He made it to the bed and laid her down on the

mattress, and she groaned in distress when he slid out of her.

"Scoot back."

She wanted to tell him she didn't take orders anywhere, let alone the bedroom, but she *wanted* to take his orders if that would get him back inside her faster. So she put the lamp down on the floor next to the bed, then scooted back, spread out, and he crawled between her legs, hovering over her.

"Take off your shirt," she said.

"Take off your dress," he returned.

They both stripped off their clothes in a flurry, and *oh* naked Jack was something truly special. Something that deserved more than a weak, battery-operated camping light.

She opened her mouth to say something about doing this in the daylight, but her heart shied away from ideas like another time, another place. There was only now, there was only him, between her legs, gazing at her like she was made of some precious thing.

You are nothing precious, Rose Rogers, and if he knew anything about you, he'd know that.

"I need you inside me," she said, to fight off the urge to cry or tell him, confess all her sins, and make him run away. But then she'd be unfulfilled, and she was selfish. Wasn't that what everyone always told her? She was selfish, so she'd use Jack for her own ends, and he'd never know all the terrible things she'd done.

"First," he murmured, his finger brushing down between her breasts. "Tell me."

She swallowed, looking down at the column of the

tattoo between her breasts that he was tracing, as gently and fascinated as he'd touched her below.

"It's the poker hand that won me the bar," she replied in a shaky voice she didn't recognize.

He cocked his head, something like a frown gracing his perfect face. "Why here?"

"Because that bar is my everything—my heart, my soul." *My power. My freedom.* Words she barely managed to keep inside. Speaking them aloud would lead to too many questions and too many terrible answers.

He made a considering sound but that was it before he was over her again, kissing her so fervently, she could only give in to it, move with him, meet every slow, far-too-meaningful thrust.

He scraped his rough palm up her hip and over her abdomen to cup one breast. He thumbed her nipple until she was moving her hips, urging him faster, deeper.

This was taking too long, allowing too many cracks in her heart to fill up with lies. Lies like sex could ever be more than something he was getting out of his system because he was sad. Something she was getting out of hers because she was desperate.

"Hurry," she whispered, digging her nails into his shoulders, and then she used a word she'd never in her life used during sex. "*Please.*"

It spurred him on, harder, faster, deeper, until the wave of pleasure crested through her, wave after pulsing wave of light and joy and *release*.

He held her close, wrapping her up in his arms, against his chest, pushing deep one last time as he whispered her name and fell over his own edge.

Her name. As though it were something beautiful. Perfect. Precious.

And she knew, without a shadow of a doubt, she could never, ever let it happen again.

Chapter 17

JACK WOKE BEFORE DAWN. ROSE WAS NAKED NEXT to him, though curled away from him in a tight ball. She was sleeping soundly and somewhat loudly. She wasn't snoring exactly, but she sure did make a lot of sleeping noises for such a tiny thing.

He had to leave. Not only did he have chores to do, but his parents were also sleeping at his friends' house, and sneaking away last night had been irresponsible and unfair.

He watched Rose's chest rise and fall. Years ago, irresponsible and unfair would have been the worst things he thought he could be. In the wake of Rose, they seemed necessary and right.

She was like nothing in his life had ever been. She was vibrant. Dynamic. She seemed so absolutely certain of who she was and where she belonged in the world— and considering how little he had of that right now, she felt like a miracle.

He didn't want to move. He didn't want to leave. He wanted to stay here in this private world of theirs for as long as he possibly could.

Would it really be that wrong? Would it really be so awful to do something for himself? To enjoy Rose and life and live for *himself*?

Maybe not at some other time, but his family was visiting him, and they deserved his time and attention, so he had to get back. Which meant he had to wake Rose up and have her drive him back to the ranch.

He was not a stupid man. Waking her up would complicate that feeling inside him, that truth that he knew—but wasn't so sure she did—that this was real, that what he felt was real. That they were at the beginning of something. A seed planted.

Rose wasn't ready for that kind of acknowledgment.

He wanted to be strong and certain and steady enough to wait her out, to take the time to prove it was all true, but there was something dark and ugly whispering from a part of him he kept locked down.

All those black thoughts and questions he'd had lying in his hospital bed, reeling from the death of his friend, from his injuries, from the knowledge his brother had slept with and impregnated his fiancée.

He'd always thought of himself as good. Moral. Hardworking and right. Instead, he'd lain in that hospital bed thinking that he'd been wrong. That there had to be something fundamentally wrong with him for all that to rain down on his head.

In his world, if you did everything right, you were supposed to be rewarded. If you were punished, there had to be some *reason*.

Something in him had been deserving of that punishment.

He stared at the ceiling of Rose's dilapidated house, much like he'd stared at the ceilings of a hospital room, a rehabilitation center room, the Revival Ranch house, and then the bunkhouse. He'd spent years now staring at ceilings, wondering when he'd be able to figure out what he'd done to deserve this fate.

Answers hadn't come to him before, but here was

Rose. Beauty and hope, like a drink of cold water in the middle of a harsh, dry desert. He ran his palm down her spine. She was *here*, and she was something like his. At least for a while. Wasn't that worth something?

Naked, she somehow looked vulnerable. In need of protection or support. That had to be a figment of his imagination, because Rose needed none of those things. He still wanted to give them to her.

She shifted, the scratchy blanket she'd pulled over them last night sliding down her hip. He traced the tattoo there. It was small but dark. A black feather with blood dripping down it. It was the most disturbing of all her tattoos, even more than the wolf on her arm. It seemed the most vulnerable. The saddest. What on earth did a bloody feather mean?

She rolled over onto it, facing him fully now. Her eyes were still closed, but she curled into him. He wrapped his arm around her, holding her against him. He thought her snuggling in had been some sort of sign, some acquiescence, but then bit by bit, he felt the tension creep into her body.

When her eyes opened, they were wary.

"What does the feather mean?" he asked.

She simply stared at him, those dark-brown eyes fathomless. She was beautiful and special, and he knew there were a million secrets swirling around in there that he would have to fight tooth and nail to hear about. But he wanted to. Rose felt like an impossibly beautiful thing he didn't know how to hold on to, no matter how hard he fought.

There was something invigorating in *wanting* to fight though. He hadn't wanted that in far too long.

"You have to get back," she said, ignoring his question about the tattoo.

It was true. He did. So he didn't have time to press his question, no matter how much he wanted to. He had to believe there would be time. "Yes, I do."

"I think I dropped the car keys on the table by the door. Take my car and drive back. I'll call my sister to pick me up after I've slept longer."

"You want me to leave you here?"

She lifted a shoulder carelessly. "I'm going back to sleep. Besides, if you take my car without me, it'll give Madison something to think about."

He frowned at that. He didn't want to think about Madison right now. But she was there, with his family, and not wanting to think about it didn't make it or her any less there.

"I might be a little bit late tonight," he said apologetically, pulling the blanket back up to her shoulder so she didn't get cold.

"Tonight?" she murmured sleepily.

"It's Friday."

"Oh. Well, you don't have to watch the bar while your family's here."

"Who will do it if I don't?"

Rose blew out a breath and looked away from him. "Maybe I'll call my brother-in-law or something. You should be spending the evening with your family, and I'm not sure how much longer I'll need your help. I think the problem resolved itself."

She wasn't looking at him, and he didn't think she was telling the truth.

"You don't have time to argue with me. Go home.

Hang out with your family. Text me the next time you want me to pretend or whatever." She waved a hand, dismissing him.

Pretend. That word he was beginning to hate. No matter how accurate it was. Whatever was between him and Rose wasn't the same thing they were pretending for his parents. Or, more specifically, to prove to Madison and Mike he was fine. But the more he got tangled up in Rose, the less he cared what anyone but the two of them thought. Let Madison pity him. What did he care? If Rose was in his bed, he didn't.

How long would he have Rose here, naked and vulnerable? What could they build if she wasn't even happy that there was something between them at all? Then again, wasn't that the point of a life that didn't have a road map? He didn't have any particular plans for the next year, let alone the next five. He could build whatever suited him. They could have something like nothing else he'd known or experienced, and that was okay. It would be whatever would work for both of their lives.

Except she wasn't meeting his gaze.

He pressed a kiss to her mouth. Soft, light. Finally, her brown eyes met his. He smiled. "I'll see you soon."

She rolled her eyes, but her mouth curved. And not that patented Rose smirk that meant she was about to eviscerate a guy. It was something sweet and soft, maybe even something she was trying to fight.

But his smile made her smile, and vice versa, and that had to be something. It had to be.

She gave his chest an ineffective shove. "Go and leave me alone. I'm exhausted." She looked it too. The crescent of faint purple under her eyes a clear sign she needed some rest. So he slid out of bed and grabbed his clothes.

She made a sound, and when he looked down at her, she was looking at his leg. It was the first time she'd seen all his scars in some semblance of light, and something painful shifted inside his chest.

"Told you it was bad."

She immediately sat up, moving across to his side of the bed. She brushed her palm up the particularly ugly web of scarring from his knee to his hip. Then she pressed a kiss to the middle of it.

He could only hold his clothes in his hands and watch her, fascinated by that response. Then she got on her knees on the mattress and wrapped her arm around his neck. "The only thing bad about it is I think about how much it must've hurt you, and it just about breaks my heart," she said firmly. "So it's not *bad* at all. It's brave and amazing." There were tears shimmering in her eyes, but then she pressed her mouth to his, and when she pulled back, the tears were gone.

"I have to go," he managed to scrape out.

"I know."

He cleared his throat, trying to convince himself family obligation was more important than erection obligation. "So that kiss was mean."

She grinned. "I know." She yawned and lay back down on the bed, snuggling under the blanket. "Bye, Jack."

"Bye," he returned, staring at her there in that grimy bed as if it were the nicest, warmest of places to sleep. Slowly, he got dressed and tried to work out any of what had just happened, but it was impossible. There were too

many competing things going on, too many raw emotions swirling around.

It was something like physical pain to leave the house
with Rose still in it, but she wanted it that way, and he
had things to do. He walked out to the front, grabbed the
keys she'd left on the half-broken table by the door, and
went to Rose's car.

He drove back to Revival in a dark, predawn world.
The earliest hint of pearly light was just a tinge behind
the mountains, but mostly he could still see the stars
and the moon in the sky. Night, but not. Promises all
along the horizon.

She'd called his scars brave, and he knew they
weren't. They were just bad luck of the draw, but he felt
proud somehow, that he'd done something to amaze her
even if he'd simply endured it.

He pulled up the ranch drive and winced. The RV's
outside light was on, and the figure of a woman holding
a baby stood in the bright center. He cursed under his
breath and pulled to a stop next to Becca and Alex's truck.

The last person he wanted to talk to right now was
Madison. He'd rather listen to Gabe give him crap about
disappearing with Rose. He turned off the ignition and
paused, but Madison was standing there, staring at him,
and he wouldn't give her the satisfaction of seeing him
slink away. *He* had nothing to cower about.

He stepped out of the car and offered a little wave.
"Morning," he muttered, hoping that would be that and
he could keep walking toward the bunkhouse.

"Jack. Wait," she said softly, taking a few steps after
him. Croy whimpered in her arms.

He stood trying to make eye contact without *feeling*

anything. The moment seemed to taint everything he'd had with Rose last night. He never wanted to feel as though *that* had been a reaction to *her*.

"I...I guess you've been out," she said, her pale eyebrows drawn together as she studied him.

He didn't respond to that. What was there to say? So he gestured at the kid. "Having trouble sleeping?"

Madison smiled. Grimaced might have been a more accurate description. "He's an early riser and still on East Coast time."

"Well. I've got chores," he offered, making a gesture toward the bunkhouse. "See you at breakfast." He started to head away again, but he could hear Madison's footsteps following him.

"Jack, wait. I just have to say this, because I know this is probably the only time we'll have alone together."

Jack decided to keep walking. "I'm going to have to pass."

"I never meant for it to happen," she called after him, her voice breaking. "We never meant for it to happen."

Jack stopped abruptly. Never *meant*... He turned to face her, old anger and new anger twining inside him like wildfire. "I should fu—" He glanced at Croy and stopped himself from swearing. From yelling. "I should hope you guys didn't *mean* for it to happen, considering we were engaged. You and *me*. So if you had *meant* for it to happen, that would be even shi—*crappier* than I already thought it was."

She sniffled. "I just don't want you to hate me, Jack."

He didn't know what to do with that teary statement. Because *hate* wasn't the right word. He didn't *hate* her, but he sure didn't like her. And he was furious with her.

Still. It had been two years, and that anger still burned in him. He'd tried to tell himself that things had turned out for the best after all. That he hadn't had to worry about being a burden to her when he'd been recovering.

But all he could think was that if he'd had someone at his side, someone who loved him, the tragedy, rehab, all of it—it wouldn't have felt so bleak.

"I did love you," she said in a squeaky voice.

He laughed, bitter and caustic. Ugly. How dare she throw out the word *love* like it hadn't been a lie? "You slept with my brother, you got pregnant by my brother while my ring was on your finger." Something niggled in the back of his brain about the last few hours, but he pushed it away, fueled by anger and outrage.

"It wasn't you. It was just, he was so nice, and we both missed you. Neither of us knew quite what to do without you."

"I don't want to do this with you. I don't care why you slept with Mike. I will never *care* why you slept with Mike. I will never be able to look at the fact that you two did that to me and thought it was okay or for the best or however you justified it to yourself. What you two did was wrong on every level. I get that we all do stupid things, but you chose to hurt me and couldn't even tell me yourself. *Dad* had to tell me. Neither of you had the balls to own up to your mistakes."

"Dad thought it would be best," she said weakly. "To hear it from a detached party. Since you were—"

"Deployed in Afghanistan. Risking my life every day for something I believed in."

"Something you believed in. Not me."

And the wildfire burned hotter, because he had not

been selfish. He had never been anything but *honest*, and how dare she throw that at him? "I gave you the chance. I told you what my plans were. When I asked you to *marry* me, I told you what I wanted to do. I gave you an out, and you didn't take it."

"Because I loved you! But it's hard to love someone who's not there."

"Then you should have told me that. You should have told me the second you thought, hey, maybe I'd rather have someone other than my fiancé touch me."

"You can't tell me you never touched another woman while you were gone. I don't believe for a second you never kissed another woman."

"Never," he said, and he didn't know if it was a shout or a whisper. "I never *looked* at another woman. I had a plan, all along, and it was *you*. I was never, ever going to deviate from it. I knew what was right and wrong, and I was going to always, *always* do the right thing."

Knew. Was. So much past tense.

Madison was crying now, and he felt a little bit like crying himself, but he wouldn't do that. He wouldn't give in to this horrible *thing* inside him. He was better than that. Maybe it was egotistical or something to think he was better than *them*. But he did. He *was*.

"You're my sister-in-law now. The mother of my nephew. You are married to my brother. You're in my life and in my family, and that is irrevocable. I will treat you with respect, but if you're looking for forgiveness or some way for me to ever look at your choices and not think they were anything but horribly wrong, you'll never get it from me. What both of you did *was* wrong."

He wanted to swallow down the rest of what he had

to say. It was the Armstrong way, to ignore the pain and hurt, to never let someone see your pain or too much of your happy.

Maybe the Armstrong way sucked.

"It hurt me," he said, the words raw and sharp against his throat. "And it's been a while, and I am healing from that hurt, but that doesn't mean I can ever think of you as anything but someone who betrayed me."

"That isn't fair," Madison cried, her face illuminated by the slowly raising dawn, blotchy and tear soaked. Croy looked around, wholly unperturbed by everything.

Fair? Hell if he knew what fair was. "I have work to do. Don't follow me."

He walked away. Limping. Feeling cracked open and a little bit ugly. Broken. He thought about what Monica had said at their session the other day though. About dealing with the fallout instead of pretending it didn't matter.

Maybe Monica was right. Maybe things could only heal once they had been completely broken.

Everything sure felt broken, so maybe healing was next.

—⁘—

When Rose woke up a few hours later, she did not call Delia. Or anyone. For good or for bad, she still didn't want anyone knowing about her little refuge.

Except Jack.

She wouldn't analyze that or anything about last night. It had been a moment of weakness, and it would be stupid and harmful to Jack to let it ever happen again. She had to erase last night from her mind.

No matter how he'd looked at her this morning, as though she were something special. No matter that he'd been embarrassed about that maze of scars that was his body's proof of how strong and brave he was, and she'd been desperate to wash that away. To show him how much he amazed her. How much he meant, but that only gave him the very wrong impression she meant something too.

Where had that ever gotten her? Delia loved her, and Rose had nearly cost Delia and Caleb their lives. Maybe that was all ancient history, and *maybe* Delia and Caleb had no idea she'd had something to do with it. She swallowed at the lump in her throat. She wasn't going to cry, and she wasn't going to mourn the loss of something she didn't even deserve.

She was going to walk over to the Lane property, have Summer give her a ride to the bar, and she was going to go on with her life, everything about last night forgotten.

Like the way Jack had whispered her name like a benediction, the way she'd woken up and naturally curled into him like he was a safe shelter.

She shook her head, as if she could make her brain listen from sheer force of movement. She left her house, walked by the pond, ignoring the memory of that night she and Jack had jumped in, ignoring the reminders she'd started this all—and she had to be the one strong enough to finish it.

It was a little less than two miles over to the Lane ranch and house, their driveway butting along the wooded edge of her property. She walked and walked, focusing on the way her limbs moved, focusing on the blue sky. The truth was, she didn't get out of her bar enough, she didn't *walk* enough, and this was good exercise and a timely reminder that life existed outside of sticky tables and grumpy, drunk patrons.

Rose focused on breathing and her destination and fought off the intrusive thoughts and memories with every kernel of strength she had built during her thirty years on this planet. She found the place in the barbed-wire fence that had sagged and fallen and stepped over it, walking up the winding drive to the Lane ranch.

A little over a year ago, her friend who was also Caleb's sister, Summer, had married Thack Lane and moved onto the property with his father and daughter. After a few months of married life, Summer had quit singing at Pioneer Spirit on the weekends to spend more time with her husband and stepdaughter. These days, Rose saw Summer mostly when she went to Shaw family gatherings. They seemed to have more and more of those as their families expanded.

Something clutched in Rose's chest, but like she did with every other conflicting feeling, she pushed it away.

She trudged up the porch stairs and knocked on the door. She glanced around, but Thack would probably be out working.

The door swung open, Summer's bright expression falling. "Oh, it's you."

"Ouch."

"Sorry," Summer said, reaching out and pulling Rose into a hug, something Summer did no matter how many times Rose threatened her. "I'm waiting on someone else." But the normally overly friendly Summer did not invite her in, despite the hug.

"I suppose you can't give me a ride into a town?"

"Oh, um." Summer looked inside before turning an

apologetic gaze to Rose. "I can't. I'm so sorry. I can call up to Shaw, but we have…"

"Someone mysterious coming."

Summer took a breath, darting a gaze inside and then at the stables. Then she grabbed Rose's arm and leaned forward, all cloak-and-dagger like.

"This is a huge secret, but I have to tell someone, and I know you'll keep a secret."

"Sure." Though Rose wasn't sure she wanted to be anyone's confidante right now when she was sucking so bad at just about everything.

"It's just, well, the whole pregnancy thing wasn't happening."

Something in those words hit Rose a little funny, but Summer was chattering on in a breathless, excited way.

"Which the doctor says is normal for the first year of trying, but you know, I started reading about other options, and…" Summer's smile spread across her face and she grabbed Rose's other arm, clutching both in an exuberantly tight grip. "We're going to try to become foster parents. Maybe adopt, or just help kids out who really need it."

"That's great." And would be perfect for Summer and Thack and whatever kids were lucky enough to come across their path.

"So, anyway, we're having our first home visit, and then they have to do a whole bunch of other stuff, but we all have to be here, and she's supposed to be here any minute, so I can't give you a ride. I can call over to Shaw though and—"

"I'll walk."

Summer didn't let Rose bolt, holding on tight. "No, don't walk."

"It's a beautiful day and not very far. I think I need a walk."

Summer's expression immediately softened. "Are you okay?"

"Yeah. I'm…" She blew out a breath. *Confused*. She felt confused for the very first time in she didn't know how long. Her whole life, she had been sure of what she was doing. Sometimes what she'd been doing had been wrong, but she'd been sure of it nevertheless.

Jack was somehow right and wrong all at the same time.

She forced herself to not smile, because that wasn't very Rose-like, and she smirked instead. "I'm fine, and I'll walk over to Shaw. You stay here and have your perfect home visit. I cannot think of a better thing for you and Thack. I really can't."

Summer pulled her into another hug, tears shimmering in her hazel eyes. "I'm going to call you later."

"Be sure that you do," Rose returned, stepping out of Summer's arms and heading back down the stairs, another walk ahead of her.

All in all, the way the Lane and Shaw houses were situated on their intersecting land, it was kind of funny to think how close her little house was to all of them. And she'd never told them.

Why that caused the lump in her throat to grow exponentially, she didn't know. When a tear slipped over, she figured to hell with it.

She climbed across the Lane/Shaw fence line and had herself a good cry. Once she got *that* out of her system, she could figure out how to get Jack out of it too.

Chapter 18

"So are we going to talk about the fact that you didn't sleep here last night?"

Jack had spent most of the day avoiding Gabe, but he'd had to come to the bunkhouse to shower off the manure he'd been hauling before he took his family to dinner. When he'd stepped out of said shower, there was Gabe, sprawled on his bed, pretending to read.

Jack decided to ignore him and walked over to his dresser to pick up his wallet and keys.

"What's going on, Jack?"

"On?" Jack repeated, looking as bland as possible.

Gabe frowned and tossed the magazine as he got out of his bed. "Did you sleep with Rose?"

"Wow, that's none of your business."

"Look. It's not that I don't like Rose."

Jack's jaw clenched tight and he had to purposefully relax it. "Be careful where you go with that line of thought, Gabe."

"I just want you to be careful. You're not Mr. Casual, and Rose Rogers doesn't strike me as Ms. Serious. I don't want you thinking there's something more serious going on."

"I'm not some stupid, lovelorn idiot who doesn't understand how the world works." He hated that Gabe's words made him question that. He was a grown man, and yes, he'd once been cast aside fairly easily, and no, he hadn't done much of anything in the interim, but that didn't mean he didn't know what he was doing.

Rose was special. One way or another.

"Look, I don't want to play big brother or—God forbid—Alex, but the fact of the matter is you're young and you've just had the one relationship. You never even had a drunken one-night stand when we were on furlough."

"I was engaged," Jack replied through gritted teeth.

"And good for you, but you're… The world doesn't always work like it did in Podunk, Indiana."

"Would you like to be a little more insulting?"

"Shit, I should have had Alex do this," Gabe muttered, shoving a hand through his hair. "I'm not trying to be insulting. I'm trying to protect you. I'm worried you're going to get yourself into the same position you were in not that long ago."

That awful tide of emotion from this morning's run-in with Madison was rising over him, hot and impossible to beat back. "Well, I'd have to propose to Rose first. Then she'd have to fuck my brother, and you know, I don't think he's her type."

"All I'm saying, as your friend, is to have a care, Jack. Rose is great. She's smart and she's funny, but she's all sharp edges, and you're…"

Jack raised an eyebrow. "What? A marshmallow?"

"Already wounded," Gabe said all too carefully.

Which was the last thing Jack wanted to hear or be reminded of. These past few weeks… Yeah, his leg still hurt, and his family crap was still crap, but he'd felt something close to whole for the first time in years. He didn't need anyone telling him it was a mirage. "Mind your own business, Gabe."

"Fine." Gabe grabbed his hat off the hook and pulled it onto his head. "Hope you were smart enough to have safe sex," Gabe muttered, striding out of the bunkhouse.

Jack stood stock-still at that parting shot, which hit like…well, like a grenade. Maybe not as painfully, but with that same loss of sound and the feeling that everything had stopped.

Because it suddenly dawned on him, far too late, that they had very much not had safe sex. At all. Not even a little bit.

"Jack?"

It was Vivian's voice, and Jack realized he'd been standing frozen for more than a few seconds, panic pumping through his veins—a real and very serious panic. Somehow, he had to focus. His family was here. He was taking them to dinner. All while knowing he'd forgotten to wear a condom during the first time he'd had sex in years. *Years*. There'd been a few times where he and Madison hadn't used one, but she'd been on the pill, and they'd been engaged.

Well, maybe Rose was on the pill and this was no big deal. No big deal.

"Jack?"

"Yeah, sorry." He shook his head and turned to face his sister with the best smile he could muster. "I'm ready." He stepped outside the bunkhouse to where his family had congregated.

"We're going to take the RV down, so we can all drive together," Mom said brightly.

"I need to drive separately," Jack blurted.

His family looked at him strangely, and he couldn't

say that he blamed them. He tried to act natural, but that only made him feel more uncomfortable. Still, he gestured toward Rose's car. "I have to return Rose's car. So, um, I'll drive down there separately, and you can drive me back."

Which sounded like hell on earth, but at least he had a reason to not do it both ways.

"I'm going to ride with Jack," Vivian announced.

"But...I have...an errand."

Vivian shrugged. "That's fine. I'll come with. I'm not taking no for an answer." She linked her arm with his and started tugging him toward Rose's car. "So much to catch up on," she said, patting his arm, grinning widely. He'd never trusted that grin when she'd been a little girl, and he really didn't trust it now that she was a grown woman.

They climbed into the car and Jack watched as the rest of his family piled into the RV. His heart was beating rapidly. How was he was going to have a chance to talk to Rose with all this going on? He'd have to find a way.

"Why are you acting nervous?"

"I'm not nervous," Jack replied, turning the key in the ignition.

"Good. I only cornered you into giving me a ride because Mike and Dad are driving me nuts, *and* I wanted to tell you how much I like Rose. She's so much better than Madison."

"Vivian, you shouldn't say things like that."

Vivian shrugged as he turned around and headed down the drive. "It's just the two of us, and it's true. You know, Rose actually asked questions about my business instead of getting huffy that we weren't always talking about her precious baby."

"Rose doesn't have a baby," Jack managed to choke out.

"And I can *tell* Rose likes *you*, not just the idea of you."

"What does that mean?"

"It means…" Vivian sighed, her gaze on the mountains outside her window. "I always got the impression Madison was more into the idea of our family and being a part of it than…well, you specifically."

"And you never thought to say anything?"

"Come on, Jack. We're not a family that *says* things. Even if we were, *you* loved her, and how am I going to tell my big brother who's joining the navy I don't think his girlfriend is quite as in love with him as he thinks she is?"

It would have been hard enough to process if he hadn't already been reeling from the whole *lack of a condom* thing, but now Vivian was sitting here telling him that it had been *obvious* Madison wasn't in love with him.

"I didn't say that to make you feel bad," Vivian said, touching his arm lightly, another thing their family wasn't big on—easy, affectionate touches. "I just know that I like Rose because she seems to really make you happy. And not only that, but when she looks at you, it's like she sees *you*. And when you look at her, it's like…everything you want out of two people who love each other."

Love. Christ. "Love takes time, Viv. To be in love is complicated. Rose and I…we haven't been together all that long."

"You could have fooled me."

"I like her a lot. But…"

"But what? You like each other a lot. She's great and funny. What else do you need?"

Jack parked Rose's car in the Pioneer Spirit lot. He stared at the bar and tried to work out any of this.

He glanced at his sister, who was an adult woman, talking to him about love and a family that didn't talk about their feelings.

"I love you, and I'm proud of you," he said out of nowhere.

Vivian startled and looked away for a second before she looked back at him. "Is that your way of throwing me off the scent?" she demanded, her voice scratchy.

"It's both that and the truth. Our family doesn't say things like that, and we don't talk. And I love you all, but I think maybe I need to talk. And say things."

Vivian nodded. "I know that feeling." She took a deep breath. "What did you say to Madison this morning?"

"I told her the truth. How'd you hear about that?"

Vivian sighed. "Mike was mad. He was telling Dad you'd upset her."

Jack scowled. "She wouldn't let it go and was trying to, I don't know, explain herself. Maybe she needed to do that, but I gave her the truth. I can't magically forgive her for what she did, even if I'm moving on. Quite honestly, that was more than generous."

"You always are," Vivian said quietly, squeezing his arm this time. "Maybe once in a while, you could be selfish. Like a mere mortal."

He looked at the bar again. "Maybe I'll try that out."

—◊◊◊—

Rose worked the bar with an odd sense of dread in her stomach. She shouldn't have felt any kind of dread right now, considering she'd talked to Delia about the private investigator this morning. Apparently, Dad barely left the house. Mom ran all the errands, and Dad seemed content to stay far away from all his daughters.

Of course, he could change his mind at any point. Rose didn't believe for a second that he'd actually changed, but considering all the sisters had restraining orders against him, if he did try to contact them, he'd be back in jail. So maybe that had given him enough reason to finally leave them alone.

It felt so anticlimactic though. It felt unfinished. It felt wrong.

And you're upset that it means Jack doesn't need to come and play security at the bar anymore.

God, she wished she could cut the *Jack* part out of her brain. She'd made a lot of mistakes in her life, so why couldn't she stop thinking about this one?

The door opened, and Rose watched it to make sure it wasn't her father. It was Jack instead. His blue gaze immediately met hers, everything in his expression grave. Her stomach swooped and she wanted to run away.

You want to run to *him.*

He strode through the room, not looking at anything else but her, his gaze completely and fully on Rose as if she was the most important thing there. As though she *was* that precious thing he'd tried to make her out to be last night.

She wasn't that. She couldn't be that. And she hated that she wanted to be.

"We need to talk."

"You're not supposed to be here," she managed, sounding weak and foolish.

"We need to talk. In private. Now."

She frowned. She wasn't used to bossy Jack, and she couldn't say she cared for it. It seemed important though, so maybe it was something to do with his family.

She signaled Tonya that she was going into the back for a few minutes, and Tonya nodded. Rose led Jack into the back hallway, but he didn't stop there and went right for her little disguised door.

"Can't we just talk here? I have a bar to run."

"Private, Rose."

Pulling her keys out of her pocket, she flipped the panel and unlocked the door and stepped inside. Jack followed, closing the door behind him. She forced herself to look at him, keeping it cool, in control. His grave expression shuttered into something she didn't recognize and couldn't read.

"We have to talk about last night."

"I don't want to talk about last night," she replied. She wanted to relive it. She wanted a million more last nights. Since that wasn't possible, she had to get a little mean. "As far as I'm concerned, last night didn't happen."

He stopped short at that. "Why?" There was that undercurrent of hurt she hated to put in his voice, but that's what she'd always bring him. Everyone she loved ended up hurt. She wasn't even sure she knew what love was or if that was the awful thing inside her. She only knew she had to save him instead of draw him deeper into her.

"Jack, everything we have is fake."

"I believe we covered that last night. It's not. You admitted that to me. You can't take it back now."

"I can do whatever the hell I want," she returned. Losing control wouldn't get her what she wanted, but trying to deny it? Push him away? It was too hard to do *and* stay in control at the same time.

"Rose. We didn't—"

"I don't want to hear it," she said, making a move for the door. He stopped her, both by standing in front of her and grabbing her by the shoulders. Her body shouldn't have reveled in that touch, in him getting in her way, but God, it did.

"Listen to me," he said, brooking no argument. "We didn't use a condom last night."

Everything inside her froze, hard and tight. That niggling thing that she'd been pushing away all day. Jack deep inside her. Jack. Only Jack.

Oh God. They hadn't used a condom, and she wasn't on anything, and...

She pressed a hand to her stomach, feeling nauseous, but then she immediately yanked her hand away. No stomach touching. No nausea. No... No.

No, this couldn't happen. So it wouldn't. "It's fine," she forced herself to say, and she almost sounded certain.

"It is?"

"Well, I've never..." She cleared her throat, trying to say it in a way he wouldn't read anything into. "I've never had that particular issue before, and you've only slept with the one woman, right?"

"Right."

"So, disease free. Lucky us."

"Rose."

"And as for…" She couldn't say it. She couldn't think it. "It's fine. You can't…from once."

"I'm pretty sure that's the opposite of every sex-ed talk ever."

Rose blew out a breath. If she refused the possibility, it couldn't happen. "It's just…you know I have a friend who's been married for a year and trying for months and she hasn't gotten…"

"Pregnant," Jack said firmly.

She wanted to shush him. To take that word out of the atmosphere. If it sat there in his military-sure voice, it would somehow come to fruition, and no.

No.

"Rose."

She hated that he kept saying her name in that calm, even tone. That he took her hand in his and squeezed. That he was so handsome and so *good*.

"Breathe," he instructed.

So she did. In and then out. She would have been fine with that, breathing and finding some center, some surety, but he reached out and touched her cheek, that gentle, undoing touch.

Why was she fighting him so hard? What was the worst thing that could happen if she let him take care of her? If she let him think she was something worth gentle touches and sweet words?

She thought of that night so many years ago. Dad with a gun to Delia's head. All Rose's fault.

That was what happened when she went after something for herself. When she believed she deserved something good.

"We're not a thing, Jack," she forced herself to say.

"We're not *not*," he said so much more firmly than anything she'd said. "Regardless of anything that results from last night, I do care about you, Rose. I like you. And maybe I'm not the best judge of return feelings, but I do think you feel *something* back."

She hated seeing a waver in his self-confidence. Last night he'd been so sure that they were *destined* for this, and now he doubted her feelings. She even knew why— Madison and his dick of a brother had planted the little seed that he might not be able to properly suss out when someone loved him or not. She should pounce on that. Exploit it. Make him think he'd read this all wrong. She could do it. If she cared at all about him, truly and self-lessly, she would. But selfless had never been her style.

"I do feel *something*, but, Jack—"

"We're in this together. Whatever happens. So if you want to…well, we could go to a doctor and talk about options."

"No. No." A doctor. Options. Firstly, it wasn't pos-sible. She was *not* going to be pregnant, and if there was that possibility… She thought about Summer trying and not getting pregnant, and yeah, life was about that unfair. *Options* seemed so wrong in the face of that.

"Rose, I'm on your team. Whatever this is. You have to know I'd be there for you and…" He swallowed. "You know me better than to think I'd walk away from you or anyone else."

She looked up at Jack, so determined and sure. So *cer-tain*. "You'd want…" She couldn't bring herself to say it. She just couldn't. She had to believe it wasn't possible.

He took her other hand in his and pulled her closer to

him. "A baby doesn't scare me, Rose. I mean, it does, but not in the grand, big scheme of things. I always figured I'd have kids. I always wanted to eventually."

Not like this. Not with me. She couldn't make herself say that, because this was all so premature. She wasn't going to be pregnant. It wasn't going to come to this.

"Look, I have to get back to my family. I left them at Georgia's, and you have work to do. I'll meet you at your house after the bar closes, and we can talk more about it."

"Jack."

He leaned forward and pressed a firm, certain kiss to her lips.

"Meet me," he said, and then he was opening her door and striding out of it.

She could chase after him and tell him no. Just no. She could not show up tonight. There were a million things she could do, but all she wanted was another night with Jack. What would be the harm with just one more?

You know the answer to that.

But she didn't want to, so she pretended she didn't.

Chapter 19

JACK HAD NEVER IN HIS LIFE CONSIDERED himself anything close to romantic. He was pragmatic, loyal to a fault, and stoic. But he thought Rose could use a little romance. A little finesse. Rose could use a lot of things, and for the first time in his life, he wanted to give someone those softer things.

It had felt good to tell his sister he loved her and was proud of her. It had felt good to tell Madison he would always be hurt by what she'd done. Cathartic.

The fact of the matter was, his family might not be the demonstrative, *I love you* type, but he'd always known they did love him and support him. They hadn't been thrilled about his plan to join the navy and devote ten years of his life to military service before coming home to the farm, but they had supported him. They had never, ever spoken a word against his choices.

Rose's father had beaten her when he'd lost a poker game. He'd beaten her and her sisters, period. Clearly, her childhood hadn't been idyllic. She had her sisters, and they were some piece of her source of strength, but he wanted to give her more. He wanted to stamp all that wariness out of her eyes, and if it took candlelight and flowers and nice blankets, he'd do it ten million times over. If it took more, he'd do his best to find it.

First, though, she had to get here. It was already thirty minutes after the bar closed. For some reason, he couldn't accept that she might stand him up. They were starting something here.

Maybe even a family.

He shoved that thought away. It was pointless to think about *that* until they knew for sure. Pointless to imagine, to let himself want things he probably wasn't really ready to want. God knew Rose wasn't, but he liked to think there was some possibility. He liked to believe they were inching toward digging out a space where a foundation could be poured.

It wasn't like what he'd felt with Madison years ago. That had been a concrete foundation of his life. An accepted tenant. He loved Madison and would marry her.

Rose wasn't concrete—she was all question marks and quicksand. He cared about her, but there were so many contributing factors, so many things that could twist and turn to make it all evaporate. He couldn't take anything with her for granted, including her arrival tonight.

He hated that uncertainty. His life had somehow become an exercise in never knowing, in never being certain what the next step should be when he'd always been so sure.

Somehow, if he had Rose as a partner in that uncertainty, he didn't hate the idea. Or even mistrust it. He'd follow it and her and these things that gave him hope wherever they led.

"If past Jack could see me now," he muttered into the flickering candlelight.

He heard the faint mechanical rumble of what he hoped to God would be Rose's car, because if he was hallucinating, then maybe he wasn't quite as close to moving forward as he thought he was. Then there were footsteps on the stairs, a door creaking open, and Rose's voice echoing through the crumbling hall.

"Jack?"

"In the bedroom," he returned, swallowing down the odd flutter of nerves jumping into his throat.

She stepped into the doorway and froze, her eyes darting around the room. He'd set up the candles in various containers he'd been able to cobble together from the ranch and what Felicity sold at the general store. He'd bought three bunches of flowers as well and some vases, and Vivian had enthusiastically put them together in something that resembled artistry. Along with all that, he'd brought over a quilt his mother had made him after he'd joined the navy and some softer sheets from the ranch, and he'd spread them all out on the bed.

"What's all this?" Wariness edged her voice, her gaze, her posture. As if she didn't know how to trust a gesture or anything good. Maybe she didn't, when it came to that. He'd seen civilians in war-torn countries have that same kind of look. When he'd been young and naive, he'd wondered what was wrong with them that they couldn't see they were being helped.

Then he'd seen the gray moral complexities of real war. He'd learned that horrible things could happen, no matter how good or upstanding or brave you were.

He thought maybe now, in the shadow of all that, he could understand how Rose would only see a shoe waiting to drop. A grenade ready to explode.

The problem was, of course, he didn't know how to fix it.

"Jack?" She still hadn't entered past the doorframe.

"Sorry. Right, all this. Well." He made an ineffectual

gesture at the surroundings, watching the light flickering against her face, reflecting in those dark eyes. "Felicity's had more candles than camping lamps, and I figured more light couldn't hurt."

"What about the flowers?"

He shrugged. "Thought the room could use some sprucing up."

"The blankets?"

"I was cold last night." He forced himself to smile past the nerves, because she never managed to keep up that closed-off facade when he smiled at her.

She stepped into the room. "Well, that's a lot of work for a roll in the hay."

"Then it's a good thing I didn't do any of this for a *roll in the hay*," he replied, some irritation creeping into his voice. His instinct was to smooth the irritation away and ignore it. That's what he'd always done with Madison, with his family—suffocate any *irritation*. But he hadn't been doing much hiding of his negative emotions over the past two years, and he'd grown out of practice.

Maybe that wasn't such a bad thing, as long as he started letting out the good too. Like telling Vivian he loved her and telling Madison how badly he'd been hurt. Maybe they were two balancing sides of the coin. Both necessary.

He stepped toward her, never letting his gaze waver from those wary, dark eyes. "I don't like it when you diminish this," he said, letting that feeling seep into his voice, his expression.

She raised her chin, defiant, even as he thought he saw a shimmer of tears in her eyes. "Maybe I don't like it when you exaggerate it," she retorted.

He reached out and cupped her face with his palms. Soft and warm, even as she aimed that sharp chin at him like a dagger. "Like it? Maybe not." He swept his thumbs up and down her cheekbones. "But you feel it."

Her lips trembled for only a second before she firmed them. In that wariness, he saw fear. True fear. His heart squeezed painfully, because he wanted to wipe it all out, take away all her hurts and fears, and he knew he couldn't.

"If this is all because you think you accidentally knocked me up—"

"It's not," he said firmly.

"I don't know how to believe that," she said, and he didn't know if it was an honest admission or a way to fight him off, but either way, he wasn't cowed.

"Then don't. Don't believe it. Question it till the last, but I'm not going anywhere. I care about you, Rose. Knocked up or not knocked up. Whatever happens, I'm riding this out, seeing where it takes us."

She closed her eyes, and a tear trickled over and down her cheek.

He lowered his mouth to it, kissing it away. "Why are you crying?"

She didn't answer him. She stood stock-still, her eyes closed, and if he had to guess, he'd say she was willing away all those tears. So he kept his hands on her face and waited, watched and waited and *willed* for her to give. Just a little.

When she finally opened her eyes, they were free of tears, but she didn't say anything. She rose to her tiptoes and pressed her mouth to his, sliding her arm around his neck and pulling him closer. She kissed him soft and sweet. Slow. It *felt* like she was giving him more than a kiss—herself or her heart.

"You win, Jack," she murmured against his mouth as she met his gaze. "For tonight, you win."

He didn't have a clue what he'd won, but she kissed him again, that honeyed sweetness feeling new and hopeful, full of limitless possibility. So he lost himself in that, in her, and in claiming whatever it was he'd won.

—∾—

Rose dozed curled up with Jack, in her crappy bed, in her falling-down house. Funny how the blankets Jack had brought over made it feel very close to cozy, even with most of the candles burnt out.

Funny how so very many things felt different with Jack around.

Okay, not funny. Downright petrifying.

Yet she didn't wriggle out of his grasp or bolt from the bed. She was naked, warm, and far too happy for any kind of good.

This was a fantasy, a break with reality. Dawn—and real life—would be here soon enough. But she'd made a decision the night before. She'd take what she could from Jack, and when she was sure she wasn't actually pregnant, she'd cut it off.

She'd be hard and cruel and certain. If she was lucky, Jack would see the truth of her soul before she had to do it. Even if he somehow missed it, she'd be strong enough to walk away. She'd always been selfish— why not embrace it? As long as it was temporary, Jack wouldn't be collateral damage. He'd walk away with the chance to find someone better.

And if it turned out she was, by some horrible twist of fate, pregnant after one foolish night, well, she had a plan for that too.

One she wasn't too interested in contemplating here in bed with him, where thoughts might turn to realities.

She hadn't thought he was awake, but his fingertips had begun to trace the tattoo between her breasts. His scarred hands traveled gently over each card that had won her freedom. Given her power. And now he was a threat to both. Her freedom. Her power. *Your heart.*

She wasn't going to worry about that. She would enjoy the moment, then start a new phase of her life without him. Maybe she'd even sell this place. Rip him out of her life completely.

She swallowed at the heavy lump in her throat. It'd give her a reason to hate him, anyway, having to give up this sanctuary because she'd let him into it.

"The bar isn't your heart, you know," he murmured into her ear, his eyes still closed, everything about him sleepy and relaxed.

The comment rankled, that easy way he declared things about her to be true. "You seem to be under the very false assumption that you know me, Jack," she replied as haughtily as she could manage.

"I do know you. Not everything, no, but plenty."

Which was the biggest problem with Jack. His certainty. The way he embraced the truths whether she wanted him to or not.

"If the bar was your heart, you wouldn't need this place." He opened his eyes, that cool blue so familiar to her now. It didn't matter how often she lost herself in the depths of that pure, breathtaking color, everything inside her shivered to verdant, sparkling life each time.

She forgot, whenever she was away from him, that she didn't seem to have control of much of anything when she was in his orbit. How had she ever thought she could handle him? How did she keep fooling herself into thinking she could do this and then walk away?

Because you are Rose Rogers, and you are stronger than this. There'd been some mantra Delia had chanted to herself when they were little girls. Something about a heart of steel. Rose had memorized it, whispered it to herself when she was alone and had something hard to face, but in the pull of Jack's gaze, she couldn't remember a word.

"Are you ever going to tell me what the feather tattoo means?"

She was actually glad he'd asked that, because it snapped the spell. "No," she replied with a conviction even *he* couldn't break. That was *her* reminder, *her* mark, and no one, not one other human being, would understand it.

He made a considering noise, but he didn't let her wiggle away. He wrapped his arms around her instead and held her close. He didn't cop a feel, didn't even rub himself against her, though the stiff length of his erection was evident against her thigh.

No man had ever held her close like this. Like you just *held* a person because you woke up together. And okay, maybe she'd never really spent the night with a guy. The few times she'd allowed herself to be charmed into sex, she'd always vamoosed either once the act was done or once the guy dozed off.

She didn't *stay*. She didn't *do it again*. And she did not, God forbid, *cuddle*. Someone holding her was supposed to be stifling. It was supposed to feel awkward. She was supposed to want to make fun of an act as soft and pointless as this.

Mostly she wanted to cry again and stay here forever. What was this man doing to her? And why him? Was it the scars—internal and external? The sob story? Or just those eyes?

"Do you have nightmares?" he asked out of nowhere.

She shifted in his arms. "Why would I have nightmares?"

He kissed her bare shoulder. "PTSD."

"Hate to break it to you, sailor, but I never went to war."

"You survived your own hell," he said so matter-of-factly, she couldn't even think up a response. "War isn't the only thing that stamps itself on you, and death isn't either. You know, when I was in the rehabilitation center, someone told me foster kids suffer from PTSD at a higher rate than military veterans."

"What asshole said that to *you* while you were in a rehabilitation center?"

He shrugged. "Mike."

"I'd like to wring that little fucker's neck."

Jack's mouth curved into a smile. "I'd rather you didn't. My mother likes you, but she wouldn't approve of that."

"Your sister likes me too." Which she shouldn't have said or even thought. What did it matter what his family thought? It was a fake like, for a fake her…but she liked them in return.

Except Dick Bag Mike.

"My sister worships you and might not care if you wring Mike's neck."

She laughed. Oh, damn him for having half a charming family. Vivian was adorable, and his parents were…

Well, she didn't want to think about how lovely they were.

"You had your own trauma, Rose. I just wondered if it still bothered you. Nightmares. Panic attacks. I've done it all, so…"

Trauma. As though she were a victim. She had been, in a sense, but not like her sisters. They'd all looked after each other. *They* had put each other first at great risk to themselves. Only Rose had ever taken their father's teachings to heart.

Always look out for number one.

"Just tell me the truth," he said, and it was all gentle and impossible to fight him off.

The truth. She didn't want to acknowledge the truth, but lying to Jack seemed so impossible. "S-sometimes. I've had nightmares. Rarely, but sometimes."

"Mine have gotten fewer ever since I started talking. I told my sister I loved her last night." He paused, rubbing his lightly stubbled chin against her temple. "I don't think I've ever done that. And it was something. Telling Madison how much she hurt me changed something. I've still got scars, Geiger is still dead, Madison is still married to my brother, but…"

"But what?"

"See, that's the thing. There didn't used to be a *but*. It was a list of horrible, dark things, and it ended there. Everything was awful. Now? I still feel beat down by those things, by those hurts and scars, but…there's a *but*. There's *more*."

She wanted to cry. For him. Because of him. She knew what it was like to have a *but*. Her sisters had always been that. It was so strange to realize that, over the past year as her sisters had been building their lives, she'd lost that *but* for herself.

She had her bar, her power, and her freedom. It should have been enough, but the list of bleak was holding her down, and she didn't know how to be as brave as Jack and believe in a *but*.

"I'm not your happy ending, Jack," she rasped.

"I don't believe in happy endings anymore, Rose. Maybe I never did. I do know we don't get what we deserve, and hard work doesn't always pay off. That doesn't change the beauty and hope of having a *but*." He smiled then, so open and perfect and *beautiful*. "I care about you, Rose." A gesture she didn't deserve.

"I wish you wouldn't," she whispered.

"I know." He sighed and brushed his lips across hers, light and quick. "I have to go do my chores before the family wakes up. Why don't you come with me?"

"Come with?"

"Yeah, you can watch me do manly chores, we can eat breakfast with my family, and then you can head home and get some rest before you have to open the bar."

She should refuse, stop diving deeper into this thing that was going to end so very badly if she let him get more attached.

If you let yourself get more attached.

"Say yes," he murmured against her neck, nuzzling there.

And she was a very, very stupid woman, because that's exactly what she said.

Chapter 20

JACK FELT A LITTLE LIKE HE'D CONQUERED THE world. Maybe he shouldn't have been quite so pleased with himself for convincing Rose to follow him back to Revival, but he couldn't help it. She might not think of herself as his happy ending, but he was starting to think of her as an important part of his new beginning.

He pulled his truck next to Becca's, Rose parking behind him. It was almost the exact same time as he'd arrived yesterday morning, and he stiffened as he looked toward the RV. Madison wasn't standing there with the kid this time. The world was pinkish gold, and the only things that seemed to be awake were the cattle in the distance.

Thank God.

He left the truck and watched Rose get out of her car. The world behind her was still dusky dark where the sun hadn't touched. Watching her walk toward him with the mountains in the distance was perhaps all he needed to know for sure that everything he'd done since leaving that rehab center had been the right choice. What possible other future could match up with this one?

"These chores better be super manly if I got out of bed for the show," she grumbled, coming up next to him.

He took her hand in his. Though she tensed for a second, it was only another second before she relaxed into it. "Oh, they will be. And you can join me in the shower after."

She snorted. "Don't you share that bunkhouse with Gabe?"

"I'll put up a no trespassing sign."

"Yeah, he'll *love* that."

"He'll deal," Jack replied, tugging her close and brushing a kiss to her temple.

He thought maybe she tried to scowl, but she didn't pull away. She leaned into him. Rose. Leaning. And he held her up. That was what he needed, what *she* needed. To just keep stepping forward, holding out a hand, being there.

They walked across the yard, but most of that solid *happy* feeling that had been taking up all the space in his body this morning leaked straight out.

"Mike."

His brother was standing outside the bunkhouse, and Jack might have laughed at how *familiar* Mike's expression was. He hadn't been around his brother for years, and he still remembered that belligerent, agitated pose.

Rose muttered something under her breath, but Jack couldn't make it out. Which was probably for the best.

"We need to talk." Mike glared at Rose, who glared right back.

Jack shouldn't find that amusing. "Okay, talk."

"You can go," Mike said pointedly at Rose.

Jack crossed his arms over his chest, torn between the desire to keep her beside him to prove a point and the urge to shelter her from whatever this was going to be. Rose kept her defiant gaze on Mike and crossed her own arms over her chest, so he figured he'd go with that.

"She'll stay," Jack said firmly.

"You sure you want her to hear about how you've been harassing my wife?"

"How I've been doing *what*?"

"Leave Madison alone."

Jack could only stare. He and his brother had always been more rivals than friends, and he'd always known Mike harbored a certain amount of resentment toward him. That had never bothered Jack too much. He'd been happy with his life and figured all Mike's behavior stemmed from him being unhappy with his.

Why was Mike unhappy now? He'd gotten everything that had been Jack's.

"I don't know what crap Madison's feeding you, but I haven't been talking to either of you more than I have to."

"Bullshit," Mike spat.

Jack tried to keep a leash on his temper. After all, what was the point in getting worked up over lies? Except Mike had essentially stolen his life. Jack didn't want it *now*, but that didn't mean he wasn't owed an apology—or at the very least, some respect.

"Don't come at me like this, Mike. Do yourself a favor and head back to your wife and kid."

"Never were my boss, Jack, so stop trying to tell me what to do."

"What are you trying to prove?" Jack demanded, losing what little patience he had left.

"Oh, I know," Rose said, raising her hand as if they were answering questions in a classroom. "He thinks wifey-poo is still in love with you. And instead of being a man and dealing with Madison directly, he's coming after you." She smiled all sharp-edged, faux sweetness at Mike. "Do I have it about right?"

"Fuck you."

Jack took a step toward him, fingers curled, muscles bunching for impact, but Rose rested her hand on his shoulder.

"He's not worth it, Jack. Sad, really." Rose tsked and shook her head. "To be that insecure in your relationship."

Jack glanced down at Rose and the self-satisfied smirk on her face, then at his brother, still spluttering and fuming.

It was so disorienting. No one ever provoked Mike. Mike was the one with the temper, so everyone ignored him or placated him or whatever. No one ever *fought* with Mike. The few times Jack had, he'd been tasked to be better. Because he was the even-tempered one. The calm one. The oldest.

"I came here this morning to talk to you, but like always, you're hiding behind someone," Mike said, sounding almost rational. So rational that Jack had to pause. *Did* he—No. No. *No*.

Mike gestured toward Rose. "Jack the Perfect, having a woman do his dirty work for him. You think you're so great? Pretty sure you wouldn't have gotten your dumb ass blown up if you knew a damn thing."

The only thing that kept him from punching his brother right in the nose was the fact that Rose stepped forward and...

Did it for him.

Mike's howl of outrage barely got through Jack's utter shock. It happened so fast, he could only blink at Mike holding his nose and Rose shaking out her fist.

He wasn't proud of it, but Jack started to laugh. And laugh. Until he could barely catch a breath.

Mike swore and threatened up a storm as he stalked away toward the main house.

"I probably shouldn't have done that," Rose muttered.

"Oh, but I am so, so, so glad you did," Jack managed between laughs. He pulled her to him and kissed her hard on the mouth. Her fingers curled into his shirt, and he would have been happy to sink into that kiss for approximately forever, but a clearing throat interrupted them.

"Do you mind?" Gabe asked when Jack pulled away from Rose. Gabe gestured at the door they were blocking. Then he frowned. "I thought I heard someone yelling."

"That was Mike," Jack said, laughing again. "Rose punched my brother." Jack couldn't keep the sheer *awe* out of his tone. "You protected me," he realized aloud.

"I wasn't protecting you," Rose retorted, wiggling out of his grasp. "I was giving that dick bag what he deserved is all." She hugged her arms around herself, looking from Jack to Gabe and then back again with an expression he couldn't read.

"Because he said something nasty about me."

"I should have let you punch him. That would have been better."

"No, no. Me punching him would have given him a little bit of what he wanted. He could have been the victim, which is where he prefers to be. But you? A *woman*? Oh, that's going to eat him alive."

"Your mom's going to hate me."

"If you're faking, what do you care if his mom hates you?" Gabe asked.

Rose blinked, a pretty pink staining her cheeks. "I-I don't want his m-mom to hate his fake girlfriend," she stammered.

"And it isn't all that fake," Jack added.

Rose scowled at him, but he wasn't about to pretend in front of Gabe. His family was one thing, but Gabe was a permanent in his world now.

Rose was going to be one too.

Rose looked back and forth from Gabe to Jack and back again, some weird thing fluttering around inside her. It wasn't even panic. It was something she didn't recognize at all.

It wasn't as though she'd never punched a guy before. It was usually a drunk patron trying to cop a feel, not her fake boyfriend's obnoxious brother. Occasionally, she'd get a smattering of applause in the bar if the guy was really annoying people, but no one ever looked at her with awe or pride over it.

There was nothing to be *proud* of, or in *awe* of. That little weasel had been insulting the most decent, brave, *good* man she'd ever met, and she just hadn't been able to stand another moment.

"Well." She took a breath in and out, trying to calm herself. There was nothing to get worked up about, other than the fact that she'd stepped her foot in Jack's family drama. Other than the fact that she'd forever be the girl who'd punched Jack's brother. Not just some random footnote everyone forgot about—she was a part of their history now. She couldn't just *disappear*.

She wanted to bolt. She wanted Jack to wrap her up

in those big, strong arms and tell her everything was going to be fine.

Which was so stupid. She had never in her life relied on anyone for that. Delia had tried, but even when Rose had been a little girl, she hadn't wanted anyone protecting her, comforting her.

"Should I apologize? I don't want to apologize. He's a Grade A jackass."

"You don't need to apologize," Jack said with that bedrock conviction that always made her feel calmer against her will. "You don't need to do anything. Whatever happens with this, I will handle my crazy family."

"How on earth can he think he has any right to criticize you for not coming out of a *war zone* unscathed? How dare—"

"That little fucker said what?" Gabe demanded.

"Right?" Rose said, waving her arms in the air, feeling that fluttery worry perk up again. Maybe it was panic.

"That's just Mike."

"That's bullshit. You are a million times the man he is."

"Seconded," Gabe added.

"Thank you. Both."

And Jack seemed so touched. Why should he be touched? He *was* good. He was fantastic. He was damn near perfect, and she had punched his brother and complicated his life. "I need to go." Somewhere safe. Somewhere far away from Jack and all the ways he changed her into someone and something else.

Or is this just a sign of the person you are under the armor? Oh God. She made a move to bolt, but Jack's hand curled around her arm. Gently. So gently.

"Don't go."

She opened her mouth to argue, but Gabe interrupted.

"Uh-oh. Angry mom, twelve o'clock," he said, nodding toward the ranch house.

"Did that little asshole go tell on you to Mommy?" Rose all but shrieked. "I'm going to punch him again."

Jack and Gabe both chuckled, but Rose couldn't manage any lighthearted response. Not just because she was enraged at Mike's tattling, but because Mrs. Armstrong was striding toward them in a robe. And slippers. She looked like every family-sitcom mother ever—perfectly coiffed though it wasn't even six in the morning and just...mom-ish. Maternal.

Rose had never known anyone like that. Delia was a great mom, and so was Delia's sister-in-law, Mel, but they tended to look more like frazzled ranchers than anything else. Her own mother had looked like...well, like anyone might expect an impoverished, chain-smoking, abused woman who'd had five kids to look like.

Rose swallowed. She would never be like Delia or Mel. Not like this amazing, put-together force advancing on them. Rose took another step backward, but Jack's hand squeezed on her arm.

"You're not a coward," he said in that even, *I'm in charge*, soldier voice. "I'm sure she just wants to hear our side of things. Everyone knows Mike has a temper and—"

"And I punched him in the nose. Which is not the first time I've punched a guy. That was no lightweight, pulled punch."

"It isn't like you to panic," he murmured, stoically watching his mother's approach.

"It isn't like me to have to deal with the mothers of decent, upstanding guys," she muttered back, but he linked his fingers with hers, and oh, she was weak, because it steadied her immeasurably.

"Jack. Rose." Mrs. Armstrong stood before them, and Rose could see where Jack got that blank-faced, *what the fuck are they thinking* expression. "Come inside the main house, please."

"You're in trouble," Gabe singsonged quietly from behind Rose.

Which earned him a sharp look from Mrs. Armstrong.

Gabe cleared his throat. "Well, I've got chores to do. I'll see you around." He patted Rose on the shoulder. "Good work, barkeep," he said low enough that only she could hear before he hurried away from Mrs. Armstrong's unreadable gaze.

This was awful. Disastrous. Stepping into his family drama was bad enough, but now she'd impressed his friends. Everyone was going to expect things of her. Of them. Things she'd never be able to give.

How many years had she kept her distance from her sisters for fear they'd see she wasn't all she made herself out to be? For fear they'd find out she was made in Dad's image. The only reason she still hung around was to keep them safe.

Or so you tell yourself.

Jack squeezed her hand, and she forced herself to focus on the present. Yeah, things were getting a little too real with Jack, with his family, but she'd still survived a hell of a lot worse than an awkward family confrontation. Why should a somewhat functional family and a woman in a robe frighten her? She took a deep breath in and then out and straightened her shoulders as Mrs. Armstrong marched them to the main house.

As they stepped into the cozy living room of the ranch house, Mike was sitting in an armchair looking like a petulant child with a baggie of ice pressed to his nose.

"Have a seat," Mrs. Armstrong said, pointing to the couch. Mr. Armstrong was standing quietly in the corner. Vivian must have still been asleep. With any luck, Alex and Becca were out doing chores or something, because this was bound to be a little embarrassing for all involved. "Now, clearly we have some things to discuss."

"Yeah, like why this bitch thinks she has any right to hit me."

"Michael David Armstrong, you will watch your language," Mr. Armstrong said gruffly, an odd kind of fury in his voice. Rose had never seen parental fury that didn't turn into violence, and she tensed. Mr. Armstrong merely stood there, still and stoic, the only hint of that anger in his voice, not his face or fists.

"She sucker-punched me! I think I can use some foul language."

"But you won't, because it's unnecessary and inappropriate," Mrs. Armstrong replied, and Rose supposed most people would mistake her for calm, but there was a vibrating *something* under that demeanor.

Which made Rose stand and say the last thing she'd thought she'd say. "I want to apologize."

"Rose," Jack said, clearly not wanting her to, but he didn't get it. He didn't get that his poor mother was clearly upset—not just about the violence, but at the way everything was going. She was a woman who clearly prided herself on having it all together, or at least looking like she did.

And to Rose, she looked like she was about to break.

"I can't apologize for punching Mike, because he deserved it." Rose kept talking over his outraged splutter. "I can't sit back and listen to someone say awful, untrue things about someone I…" Oh shit, she'd almost said *love*. "…care about. It wasn't right, especially from a brother, and maybe punching isn't the answer, but it was the only one I had. So I'm sorry that my action upset you, Mrs. Armstrong. I lost my temper at the way he was talking about Jack."

Mrs. Armstrong held herself very still for a moment and betrayed nothing, not one flicker of emotion. Rose couldn't help but think of Jack talking about the marvel of telling his sister he loved her. Rose had grown up in despair, but her sisters had always told her they loved her. In whispers, late at night, when no one could hear except one another, but it had been something.

Distracted by her own thoughts and memories, Rose didn't have a chance to fight off Mrs. Armstrong's next move. It came in the shape of a warm, fierce hug, whatever perfume she wore potent and pretty. Rose almost smiled at the image of Mrs. Armstrong throwing *perfume* on when she donned her robe.

"How are you hugging her?" Mike demanded, jumping to his feet.

Mrs. Armstrong gave one last squeeze and then released Rose, who had barely registered Mike's outrage. Mrs. Armstrong had hugged her twice now, and Rose couldn't remember her own mother *ever* hugging her.

"Sit down, Michael," Mrs. Armstrong said quietly.

"You're hugging the woman who punched me in the nose, and I'm supposed to sit down?"

"Yes," Mrs. Armstrong snapped, and it was that snap that had Rose sinking into the couch herself, that snap that had her leaning into Jack when he slid his arm around her shoulders.

"What did you say about your brother?" Mrs. Armstrong asked, her voice shaking.

"Mom."

"I allowed you and Madison to come on this trip because I thought you would make amends. I thought you would at least try." Her voice broke on the last word, but she pulled herself together. "I did not expect *this* of you, but maybe I should have. Now, what did you say to your brother?"

"He's been harassing Madison. He has!"

"Answer your mother's question," Mr. Armstrong bit out. He moved to stand behind Mrs. Armstrong, putting his hand on his wife's shoulder.

"He said it was Jack's fault he was in that grenade blast. That it must be his own *dumb* fault for getting hurt," Rose supplied, because she wasn't letting Mike weasel out of anything.

Though she immediately felt bad when Jack's arm withdrew from her shoulders, when both Mr. and Mrs. Armstrong's faces paled.

"He provoked me! He—"

"Stop," Mrs. Armstrong rasped.

"Mom!"

"You are not the victim here, Michael. My God, what on earth is wrong with you?"

"What?" Mike blustered.

"You've gotten everything you ever said you wanted. The farm. A family. It all came to you, whether you deserved it or not, and you sit here so certain *you're* the victim. I don't know where I went so wrong."

There were tears on Mrs. Armstrong's cheeks now, and Rose felt a little like crying herself. She didn't know why. She'd witnessed the way families could be so much worse than this, but the clear pain on Mrs. Armstrong's face was too much to bear.

Jack stood and stepped toward his mother. "Mom, it's just words. It's just…" He touched her shoulder, clearly struggling with seeing her upset. "You didn't go wrong. We were just bickering."

Rose understood he wanted to soothe his mother, understood in a way she hadn't before that Jack would always do that—soothe and save the people he cared about at the expense of himself.

He loved his family. He still wanted to make things all right for them, but it wouldn't fix this.

"Jack."

He glanced down at her, mostly blank, just a hint of the hurt lingering in his eyes. "Remember what we talked about this morning? About talking?"

There was something a little haunted in that blue gaze then, and she knew this was hard for him. He could forge ahead with his new determination all he liked, but going back and fixing old hurts wasn't quite so easy.

Jack took a deep breath, never taking his gaze from her, and she wanted to believe he was drawing something from her—strength. Certainty. Anything. So she stayed. If she could know that she'd given him something valuable before she had to blow all this up, then maybe it wouldn't kill her to have to walk away.

Chapter 21

JACK STARED DOWN AT ROSE. SHE HAD HER HANDS clasped together as though she were begging him for something. He knew she wasn't, but her dark eyes were imploring and…

He'd been the one to talk about talking making things better. His life *had* gotten immeasurably better in these past few weeks, but he didn't know how to talk to his brother. They'd been at odds so long, always in competition. Always keeping score and protecting their softest parts from each other.

Rose was right though. Nothing healed if you didn't acknowledge the wound existed. Maybe he and Mike would never be best buddies, maybe Mike would never change, but this wasn't for Mike.

It was for himself. "Okay, it isn't just bickering," Jack said, his voice feeling like a raw scrape against his throat.

"Jack—" Mom reached out to him, but Jack turned to face his brother.

"You slept with my fiancée and got her pregnant— while I was deployed, and then you dare come here, to the place I've built a new home, and claim that my injuries were my own fault." He bit back the rest of what he wanted to say *while you sat at home like a coward and fucked my fiancée*.

But this wasn't about Mike. It was about Jack.

"Clearly you have no respect for me. No brotherly love."

"Or a conscience or a heart," Rose muttered under her breath. When Jack slid her a glance, she shrugged. "Sorry."

"The point is, I don't get too worked up about the things you say to me. I think they stem from your own insecurities. They're not about me."

Mike scoffed, but Jack kept talking.

"I don't know that I'll ever forgive you for what you and Madison did, but you're still my brother. As I told Madison when *she* insisted on talking, I'll treat you with respect because of that. I hope you can find it within yourself to do the same. For our parents' sake, if nothing else."

Mike's gaze darted from Mom and Dad to Jack, to Rose, and then at the floor. "Fine. Whatever." He stood, straightening his shoulders and fixing a glare on his face.

"With one caveat," Jack added. Because this couldn't be just a bunch of bluster before they fell back into the same old pattern of lashing out. "If you ever talk to Rose again the way you did this morning, you'll crawl away with a lot more than a sore nose."

"Oh," Rose added. "And the same goes for if you ever say anything remotely like what you said to Jack. I'll target something a lot more painful than your nose."

Mike rolled his eyes. "Just keep your girlfriend away from me, and stay away from my wife." Then he stalked out, baggie of ice still on his face.

Jack let out a long sigh. He doubted that would satisfy Mom, and he wasn't sure it *satisfied* him. He'd said what he needed to say though.

"I don't condone violence," Mom said carefully. "I'll trust that you've all come to an agreement of sorts and it won't happen again. Now, sit down, Jack. We have a few more things to discuss."

Which did not bode well, but Jack moved back into his seat next to Rose on the couch. She laced her fingers with his without looking at him, and it felt like they were a team. He realized that wasn't something he'd ever felt with Madison. It wasn't that he hadn't loved her at the time. It had just been different. Young and naive. What he was building with Rose wasn't that. It was the chance for something deeper, stronger.

"I was going to discuss this with you later, but since we have you alone, it might be good to do it now."

"That sounds ominous," Jack muttered.

"I talked with Monica."

Jack stilled. Well, he hadn't expected *that*. "What were you talking to Monica about?"

Mom took a deep breath, coming to sit in the chair next to the couch. Dad moved behind her.

They were a unit. Always had been. Jack couldn't remember ever seeing them be overly affectionate with one another, but they had always been each other's helping hand and support.

"It wasn't to try and figure out what you'd talked about with her. I know therapists can't do that, but I wanted to… Since you said she had experience with military families, I wanted to talk to her for me."

Jack couldn't work up a response to that. He'd only told his mother about Monica because she'd asked. They were not a family prone to trusting *therapy*, but his mother had gone of her own volition to talk for *her*.

"I was worried I had failed you. I wanted to get Monica's advice on the best role of a mother in this situation."

"Mom, how could you have failed me?"

"I let you have your space, and I should've pushed. I should've demanded you come home. I shouldn't have let you waste away in that rehabilitation center with only a few sporadic visits." She glanced around the room and smiled. "Except, coming here, seeing you here, I'm glad I didn't demand you come back. I just wanted to know I was being the mother you needed."

"You've always been the mother I needed."

Mom looked like she was going to cry again, and he hated this. Even knowing it was good and healing, he hated watching his mother deal with pain.

"I asked Monica what I could do for you, and she said the first step is to ask. Not everyone is in a place to ask for what they need, but she thought you were. And that I should ask. So I'm asking. Both of you. Because I see how much Rose has helped you."

Jack pushed off the couch and kneeled in front of Mom. A tear was slipping down her cheek, but he couldn't let that stop him. Talk—the thing that hurt like hell and made him feel vulnerable when so much of the past ten years of his life had been about becoming invulnerable.

Now, on the other side, it strengthened him. It made things better. It *healed*.

"I think space was exactly what I needed. And this place is exactly what I need. And though she'll undoubtedly argue with me later, Rose was exactly what I needed. I'm incredibly grateful for..." He winced, the kneeling not good for his leg, and shifted onto his butt, his shoulder against his mother's knee, like a kid—and he supposed, in his mother's eyes, that's what he'd always be.

"The fact of the matter is I was in a dark, ugly place after the accident and finding out about Mike and Madison." He stared at his hands—odd to realize he'd come out of it, really and truly, when not that long ago, he'd been wallowing in it. "I'd lost hope in pretty much everything, but there was nothing you or Dad or anyone could've done about that. It was something time and mountains had to heal."

He glanced at Rose, who was staring wide eyed at her feet, and he knew she was feeling out of her depth, wishing she wasn't here, but she didn't get up to leave. She might not *like* that she was getting involved in his world, but she wasn't running away, and that made him smile.

"I think the reason I could survive that dark place and come to this point is because I knew—even with everything that happened with Mike and Madison—I knew you and Dad were there. I knew I had a home to go to if I needed it. I didn't want to, not then and not now, but when you know that safety net is there, I think you can be in a really bad place and survive it."

Mom made a little sobbing sound, and he reached out for her hand, giving it a squeeze. "I need this. This place and the foundation we're building. It's important to me to have a chance to help other guys in that same dark place. To give them a home, especially if they don't have one." He glanced over at Rose, who was looking a little teary herself. "And Rose is important to me," he said, not missing the way she flicked her gaze to his, her panic as clear as day.

He'd stamp it out. He would.

"Well," Mom said, her voice a squeaky, watery thing. "My goodness, it's awfully late for me not to be dressed. I should head back up and get ready for the day." She squeezed his hand before releasing it and getting to her feet.

He stood too, and Mom looked up at him, so many things on her face that she'd never allowed to show before—pain, hurt, love.

"I love you, Mom."

She pressed her lips together and nodded. "I love you too, Jack." She pulled him into a tight, fierce hug. She released him, smiling a wobbly smile before she and Dad left the room.

Hand in hand.

Once they were gone, Jack glanced at Rose's very still form. There were things he could say, things he wanted to say, and talking could heal, but you had to be ready.

Rose wasn't ready.

"Do you really think Madison is still in love with me?" he asked instead.

She frowned at him, and he was maybe a little validated by the spark of jealousy that he saw there. "No, actually."

He raised his eyebrows at her and she sighed. "I think *Mike* thinks she still has feelings for you, or at least he's insecure enough to worry that she does. I don't think a woman would marry a guy that she doesn't at least *like* if she's still in love with his brother. Even if she is knocked up."

Rose let that sit there, something like a challenge in

her gaze, making it clear that wouldn't be a reason for her to stay with him either.

It grated, he wouldn't lie, but that wouldn't change his course of action. "When will we know?"

"I should get my period next week. If it's late, I take a test," she said, not even pretending she didn't know what he meant.

He nodded as she got to her feet, but he didn't let her say anything else, didn't let her make any excuses to leave. He pulled her close and pressed his mouth to hers.

She was a little stiff when he'd pulled her close, but she relaxed into the kiss, leaning against him, kissing him back, cupping his jaw with her hand.

Christ, he was in love with this woman. In a way that very nearly hurt. Because he didn't know how to trust himself to love someone when he'd mistaken love so spectacularly before.

With Rose, he didn't know how *not* to love her. He pulled away, and Rose frowned at him.

"What was that for?" she asked, weariness *and* wariness in those dark eyes.

"It wasn't *for* anything, Rose. I just wanted to kiss you." Someday she'd get it.

He hoped.

Rose had to get her ass off Revival Ranch and back to her bar, but every time she tried to sneak away, some Armstrong grabbed her and thrust her back into the fold. This time it was Vivian, and Rose didn't bother to hide her irritation.

"I have a bar to run, and I've barely slept." What was

the point in fake Rose now that she'd punched Mike in the nose?

Vivian's eyes widened, a beautiful blue just like Jack. "You have a *bar*?"

"Crap," Rose muttered. "Jack didn't tell you guys what I do?"

"I don't know that it ever came up. Although now that I think about it, I think he just always changed the subject when it did."

Rose rolled her eyes. Not that she could blame him. The Armstrong family didn't strike her as the bar type. The other night at dinner, Gabe had grabbed a beer, and Rose was pretty sure she'd seen Mrs. Armstrong level a glare at him so strong that he'd actually put it back.

"Are you going to tell your mother?"

"My mom, who's literally never had a sip of alcohol in my presence or probably her entire life? No, I think I'll keep that to myself." Vivian's mouth curved into a lethal smile. "On one condition."

Rose winced. "What condition is that?"

"Take me with you."

"With me?"

"Let me come along. Let me see your bar. Oh my gosh, you have a *bar*. That is beyond cool."

"Don't you want to stay here and hang out with your family?"

"I see my family all the time," Vivian said, already pulling Rose toward the cars. "I mean, not Jack, but you know. I've never met *you*. I'd like to spend time with you. One-on-one. Get to know you in a way I can't with my mother lurking." She winked. "Please, please, please, please."

Rose knew she should say no. She shouldn't keep twining herself into Jack's family, into their memories here. But much like she was powerless against Jack when he was all sweet and earnest, she was powerless against Vivian's effervescent enthusiasm.

"Okay. You're coming up with your own excuses though, because I'm not lying to your mother."

Vivian squealed happily and then bounded off toward Mrs. Armstrong.

Jack approached. "What was that about?"

Vivian was talking animatedly to Mrs. Armstrong, waving her arms.

"She wants to come to the bar."

"Christ."

"Don't worry, she's not going to tell your mother what I do."

Jack studied her. "I don't care if she does."

"Yes, you do. Vivian told me your mother's never had a drink in her entire life. I can't imagine her approving of a bar, and you want your mother's approval." *I want your mother's approval, moron that I am.*

"Oh, I don't know about that," Jack said contemplatively before he flashed her a grin. "She might have had some champagne at her wedding."

Rose laughed in spite of herself.

"We'll have to tell her about Pioneer Spirit eventually," Jack said, watching her with those patient, assessing eyes. He was waiting for her to argue with him. He was looking for some sort of reaction, and though she had one, she wasn't going to give it to him.

If he thought she didn't know he was waiting her out, wearing her down, then he didn't know Rose Rogers.

She was going to do the exact same—wait him out. Run him down. If he didn't catch on soon that she was not the woman for him, then, well…

Well, that was something to figure out once she knew whether or not she was pregnant. Because no matter how much she told herself she wasn't, couldn't be, the possibility sat there in her brain like a tumor.

"Anyway," Rose said, breaking eye contact. "I'll take her to the bar, give her a tour, maybe a little job to do. Just have someone come get her before the bar opens, so I don't have to explain to your mother why some grizzly rancher was hitting on her."

"I'll collect her before four."

"Thank you."

Vivian bounded back. "Did Rose tell you she's going to take me to her bar and let me poke around?"

"Yes. Be a good little girl and don't get in her way."

Vivian rolled her eyes.

"I'll come pick you up in an hour or so."

"No rush!"

"You're out before the bar opens, kid," Rose said.

"What?" Vivian fisted her hands on her hips. "You realize I am twenty-four years old."

"And you won't be hanging out in a townie bar tonight, Vivian Armstrong. I'll pick you up at four."

Vivian huffed over that, but she followed Rose to her car. And the whole way down to Blue Valley, she *chattered*. About everything. About how much she loved the mountains and how hot she thought Gabe was and a million other things, and Rose's heart ached a little bit, because she missed her sisters.

She saw Delia pretty frequently, but Delia wasn't a

chatterer. Get Billie, Elsie, and Steph together though, and they could chatter on about anything, just like Vivian. Vivian would fit right in with the younger Rogers girls, the two families clicking together.

Which will literally never happen.

Rose pulled into the parking lot behind the bar and gauged Vivian's expression.

"It's a glorified shack," Rose supplied, because Vivian was looking at the rough-hewn boards like they were magic.

"It's amazing," Vivian breathed. "It's like the Wild West. A saloon! So authentic."

"Yeah, authentic," Rose muttered. She got out of the car and led Vivian to the back entrance. Vivian exclaimed happily at everything, so much so that Rose didn't even show her the hidden apartment, because she was afraid Vivian would come unglued at the *authenticity* of it all. And still Rose smiled, because it was sweet, this enthusiasm. She hadn't felt it for a while, that simple joy in something kind of cool.

"And here's the bar."

Vivian squealed. "How do you stand how perfect this all is?"

"I guess cleaning vomit off the floor will do that to a girl."

Vivian rolled her eyes. "There are always downfalls to a job you love, but you love this, don't you?"

Rose looked around her bar. She did love it. She loved watching people and even serving people. She loved everything to do with Pioneer Spirit. She'd always thought loving this junk hole was just more proof she wasn't quite right. How could anyone else love it too?

But Vivian was so impressed, and Rose didn't know what to do with that.

She gave Vivian the job of putting all the chairs down. Rose checked the liquor stock and started filling dishes of peanuts. Tonya would arrive in about half an hour, and Rose hated the idea of explaining Vivian to her, but she'd deal.

"Rose?"

Rose froze as Delia stepped in from the back hallway. Oh crap, what was her sister doing here when she had Vivian underfoot?

"Delia, what are you doing here?" she asked, trying to sound casual.

Delia stood in the doorway staring confusedly at Vivian. "Did you hire a new bartender?"

Vivian perked up and came over to the bar, leaning over it. "Oh my gosh, do you need a bartender? I could so sell my store and move here and become a bartender! Wouldn't that be amazing?"

"You cannot do any of those things. I do not need a bartender," Rose said sternly. She was not going to be the woman who punched Jack's brother *and* ruined his sister's future.

Rose looked uncomfortably from Delia to Vivian. How was she going to explain this? Well, maybe she could work her way around it without actually—

"I'm Delia. Rose's sister," Delia said, holding out her hand.

Vivian grinned and took her hand. "Oh, I should have known, you guys look so much alike! Rose, you never said you had a sister." Vivian tsked. "I'm Jack's sister Vivian."

Delia released Vivian's hand and looked at Rose questioningly. "Who's Jack? The kissing guy?"

"Shouldn't you be sitting down?" Rose asked, trying and failing to lead Delia away. "She's pregnant and very, very sick," Rose explained to Vivian.

"I'm feeling much better. The doctor gave me this medicine pump thing to wear, but that's beside the point. Are you going to explain this?"

"Later."

"I'm sorry. Did I say something wrong?" Vivian asked, looking suspicious and maybe hurt.

"Vivian, you're fine. I just—"

"Hadn't told your sister about your boyfriend?" Vivian supplied for her, accusation in her tone.

Rose closed her eyes, because she recognized that look on Vivian's face. She'd seen it on Jack's face often enough, a kind of protective determination. Vivian was going to stand up for Jack's honor, and no amount of liking Rose was going to change that.

"Look—"

"Don't blame Rose," Delia interrupted. "She's a very private person, and we can be very overbearing when it comes to guys. I'm sure she was just trying to keep Jack safe from our interrogation. Right, Sissy?"

"Something like that," Rose muttered, feeling beyond shitty. Now *Delia* was lying for her.

"Oh. Well. I'm sorry I ruined it," Vivian said uncertainly.

"No, don't be." Rose forced a smile. "It's long past time I told them I was dating Jack." She turned to Delia. "Jack's family is visiting from Indiana, and Vivian wanted to see the bar."

Delia nodded. "Well, um, if you have a minute and you don't mind, Vivian, I have something kind of private to talk to Rose about."

"I can go walk around town and—"

"Stay here and put down all the chairs. I'll talk to Delia in the back and be right back."

"Okay," Vivian said.

Rose took Delia into the back hallway, feeling a headache brewing. How…how was she going to untangle all this?

"Look, it's just pretend—"

"Don't lie to me. We will be having a very long discussion about what the heck is going on with your *boyfriend* later but…" Delia sighed heavily. "I don't have much time. Caleb's trying to wrangle both chores and Sunny, and Summer had some mysterious appointment, and anyway, Aunt Beth called me last night."

"Why?"

"I guess Mom wanted me to know, without having to contact *me*. Dad is…really sick. Like dying."

Rose had to reach out to steady herself. She tried to grab for the wall, but in the end, it was just Delia. Clutching her hand in hers.

"Aunt Beth didn't know any details. She only knew that it was bad and he's refusing to get any sort of help, obviously."

"So he really isn't a threat."

"No. And I called the sisters. You won't like it, but I think we all need to go see him."

"What? Why would we do that?"

"Closure. Good riddance. Not our last respects—he doesn't deserve that. A chance to tell him, to really tell him, what shit he is. To show him that he didn't win and he deserves whatever's coming to him. Maybe it won't make us feel better, but I don't know. I have to do it. I have to have that kind of closure. And I think the other girls feel the same. Do you?"

Rose couldn't meet Delia's gaze. She couldn't process all this. Dad was dying. Dad wasn't a threat. And Delia wanted them to all go talk to him. All of them.

"You don't have to decide right now. I just wanted to tell you in person. This isn't phone news, and you've been scarce."

"I haven't been scarce," Rose replied automatically.

"Are you going to tell me what's going on with this guy?"

Rose opened her mouth to lie, to minimize, to blow it off, but Delia was staring at her with those furrowed, big-sister eyebrows. "Honestly? I don't know. It was supposed to be pretend. A favor. And now he…"

"He what?"

"He likes me. God knows why, but he seems to think we could…" Rose swallowed. Too much. All of it. "I don't know. I just don't. On all fronts."

"You like him," Delia said quietly.

Rose didn't know what to say to that, especially when it hadn't been phrased as a question.

"It's hard," Delia said. "It's a hard thing to trust in someone else, but you're not a coward, Rose. Never have been."

Rose managed a smile. Funny how Delia should echo Jack's statement from this morning, but unfortunately, Delia didn't get it. Delia had been afraid to trust Caleb, because there'd been no one to trust in their

lives. Especially men. Rose didn't have any compunction trusting Jack. He was infinitely trustworthy. It was
herself she didn't trust.

She'd failed her own sister so spectacularly, how
could she not fail a guy like Jack?

"Think about the Dad thing. The sisters are working
on a few days they can all get off work."

"If I need to chip in to get Steph home, let me know.
She's not going to miss class over this, is she?"

"We'll figure something out so she doesn't have to."
Delia frowned, studying Rose's face. "You okay? Really?"

"I'm fine." Rose knew this was the time to let it all
out. That there was a possibility she was pregnant. A
very large probability she was falling in love with a guy
she could never be with. She should take a page out of
Jack's book and talk, and maybe things would stop feeling so horrible.

All she could think about was Delia's family though.
She had a daughter waiting on her and a medicine pump
keeping her from puking her guts out so she could have
another kid. Rose thought about Caleb and Sunny's first
steps and all those things that just…

They weren't in the cards for her, and talking wasn't
going to change that.

"Go home to your girl. Let me know what day the
sisters decide."

"So you'll come?"

Dad was dying. *Dying*. Rose didn't know that she
wanted any come-to-Jesus moments with him, but if her
sisters needed her, she'd do it.

"I'll come. I better get back to Vivian. I can't imagine
we were very smooth in our lying."

"Very unlike us." Delia pulled her into a quick hug. "I'm checking on you in a few days, fair warning. If you're still this mopey, I will be forcing you to tell me what's actually up."

"I'm not mopey." But Delia wasn't listening. She was striding down the hall, and Rose scoffed into the empty hallway.

Now she had to brace herself for Vivian's million questions. When Rose stepped back into the bar, Vivian was sitting on a stool, toying with a glass of something she'd poured for herself.

"That'll be five bucks."

Vivian offered a smile, but it was faint, not one of her excited, vivacious grins. "Hope that includes tip." She frowned down at it. "Rose, I'm only going to ask once, so please, don't lie to me. What's really going on? Why hadn't you told your sister about Jack?"

Rose knew she should lie. This was all Jack's idea anyway, and it should be his job to tell her.

"Rose. Please. The truth."

"I was just pretending to be Jack's girlfriend," Rose said, exhaling slowly. "Your mom said something about Madison not thinking he was over her, and I happened to need a favor. So we decided to trade favors. It was all pretend."

Vivian frowned. "*Was* pretend, right? I mean Jack's a pretty smart guy, but he's a crappy actor. If he didn't have feelings for you, it wouldn't be written all over his face like they very clearly are."

"I'm not saying we don't have a certain amount of chemistry," Rose said carefully. "And whatever else there is."

"Love?"

Rose winced. God, she hated the word *love*. It was a weapon or armor more than anything worthy of poetry.

"He's already been hurt. You can't hurt him like this."

"Vivian, I have tried to be up-front with the guy, but you have to understand. I own and run a *bar*. I have tattoos everywhere and grew up in really shitty circumstances. I am not Armstrong material."

"That sounds a lot like Mike's excuses for his life, Rose."

"Hey. That isn't fair."

"Isn't it? Are you implying that because you had a rough life, you live a rough life, you're not good enough for Jack?"

"Exactly. Actually."

"Except Jack is so clearly in love with you. And look, I was around when he was with Madison, and I'm around right now. I can tell that—"

"What? He never loved her, but I'm some miracle?"

"No. He loved Madison, but he was also a teenager and so very Jack. I know when he loves someone, because he looks at them like they matter, and no matter how stoic our family is, he's never been able to hide that. With you, it's different. You grab his hand when you can tell he's upset, which is no easy feat. He wraps his arms around you when you're about to bolt. You two fit like puzzle pieces, instead of the same puzzle piece stacked on top of each other."

"That's a great analogy, but I'm not…I am very much not good enough for your brother. Okay? He's going to realize that soon, and nobody will get hurt."

"If he doesn't?"

There had to be an answer to that question. An answer that wasn't "blow it all up and disappear."

"Maybe instead of being convinced you're not good enough for him, you could find a way to *be* good enough for him."

Rose stared at her bar, that fluttering panic taking up the entire expanse of her chest. It was a really tempting thought, this idea she could suddenly change the way she'd always been. That, much like she'd decided to win this bar or to put her father behind bars, she could just *decide* to be good enough for Jack—that from here on out, she could be what he needed.

But her father was dying, and she would have to face him. She'd have to stand in that old nightmare and remember, no matter how much she loved her sisters, she'd failed all of them.

She forced herself to smile at Vivian, just like she'd forced herself to smile at Delia and Elsie and Billie and Steph a million times over in their childhood. "I'll think about it."

Vivian grinned and reached over the bar, pulling Rose into a perfume-scented hug so much like Mrs. Armstrong's. "I know you can do it, Rose. You two are so good together."

Rose pulled away from Vivian's embrace, fake smile plastered on her face. "Thanks," she said firmly, even though gratitude was the absolute last thing she felt.

Chapter 22

JACK STOOD BY THE RV, HIS FAMILY GATHERED around, and didn't know how the two weeks had passed in the blink of an eye. Mom, Dad, and Vivian felt like part of the landscape now, and it would be hard not to have them here anymore.

Vivian was openly crying, and Mom was trying very hard not to. Jack kept scanning the horizon for Rose. She'd texted that she was running late but had given no explanation, and Dad was eager to get on the road.

"I want to beg you to come home, but that just wouldn't work, would it?" Vivian asked with a sniffle.

"No, it wouldn't. I'm glad you came, Viv. And you know you can always come back whenever you get another break from the store."

She flung herself at him as she'd done when she'd arrived, as she'd done when he'd left for the navy and deployment all those years ago. Vivian had always been the brightest of all of them, the most effervescent. She wasn't a paragon of unveiled emotions, but she'd always been sweet. She always hugged him when he went away, tighter and longer than everyone else.

"I'll miss you, kid."

She sniffled into his shoulder. "I love you, Big Brother. Tell Rose bye for me?"

"I'm sorry she didn't make it. I don't know what could have happened to her."

Vivian released him with a sad smile, which meant he had to address Mike and Madison and little Croy.

Jack offered Mike a hand. They'd never be buddies, but they were still brothers, and as much is it brought Jack a little joy to still see the mark of Rose's punch around Mike's nose, Jack didn't want to leave the resentment to simmer after they'd gone. "I wish you the best of luck, Mike."

For a second, Mike acted as though he wouldn't acknowledge the gesture or his words. Madison gave him a nudge, and he finally took Jack's hand. "I'm..." He cleared his throat. "I'm glad you found a place here."

Mike quickly turned and headed into the RV, and Jack was going to pretend like his brother meant it.

Madison was next, and Jack didn't want to hug her, but it seemed weird to shake hands. All of this was weird still, and probably always would be. Maybe that was just something to accept as the new Armstrong normal.

"It was good to see you," Jack offered a little stiffly. "Thank you for bringing Croy. I hope you'll send pictures and keep me up-to-date with how he's doing. I do want to be part of his life."

"I want that too." She hugged him then, wriggling Croy between them. "I'm glad you're happy," she whispered, giving him a squeeze before letting him go. Madison climbed into the RV.

Jack scanned the horizon again, but there was still no sign of Rose. He was starting to get a little worried. Rose didn't love all the family stuff, but she also didn't promise something and then not follow through. So something had to have happened.

"When she does pop up, let me know so I don't worry about her," Mom said.

"I will."

"She's a nice girl."

"She's something else," Jack returned with a smile.

Mom pulled him into a tight hug. "I love you, and I'm so proud of you. I miss you so much. I expect you home for a visit one of these days. You understand me?" She pulled away.

"Yes, ma'am," Jack said, giving her a little salute.

He shook his father's hand and mainly kept it together as they piled into the RV and turned down the gravel drive.

Jack watched the RV move away. There'd be something nice about getting back to real life and not having to worry about everyone entertaining his family. He'd always miss them when they weren't around, and yet this life he'd built here at Revival Ranch in Blue Valley was everything he never could have dreamed of in that rehabilitation center.

The RV came to a halt before it disappeared down the hill, and that was when Jack realized Rose's car had appeared. He stood where he was by the house, watching as Mom, Dad, and Vivian each stepped out of the RV and gave Rose a hug before getting back in and rolling away.

Rose got back in her car, and for a second, he thought she was just going to drive behind them and head out of his life. It was a silly worry though, because she drove the rest of the way to park next to his truck and got out of her car.

He walked toward her as she walked toward him. She was holding a bag and looking incredibly grave. "Sorry I'm late. I ran into a llama jam."

Jack opened his mouth to tell her it was all right, but those words penetrated his automatic response. "I'm sorry, did you say *llama*?"

"Yeah. I ran into Bozeman this morning, and the road coming back was completely blocked by llamas."

"Am I supposed to believe that story?"

"Have you not heard of Dan Sharpe's llama ranch?"

Jack shook his head. "I think I've heard Becca talk about llamas. I'm almost certain I pushed it completely out of my mind."

"My sister's brother-in-law runs a llama ranch. There was a fence breach, and they were all out there on the road blocking traffic. So yes, I am late due to llamas, and that is not something I ever thought I'd say." She took a breath, that graveness never leaving her expression. "I bought a test."

Which was when her nervous llama babbling suddenly made sense. "Did you take it?"

"No! The llamas got in my way, and then I didn't want to miss saying goodbye to your family. So." She blew out a long breath. "I'm not usually late."

"It's okay. You made it in time."

She rolled her eyes. "Not time late. Late late. Period late. Pregnant late."

"Oh. Um, well, Gabe is out working with Alex, so we have an empty bunkhouse and bathroom to ourselves."

"Okay."

They walked over in silence, and Jack knew he should say something. Something profound and important. He should somehow explain to her that she meant a lot to him no matter what the result was.

Words failed him. He opened his mouth, but nothing

came out. They stepped into the bunkhouse and he closed and locked the door. He pointed to the bathroom door. "You, uh, can do it in there."

Rose nodded and strode for the door. She went in and closed it, and suddenly he was alone in the bunkhouse. Rose was in the bathroom peeing on a stick to determine if she was pregnant or not. With his baby.

Jack felt a little bit like hyperventilating. A lot like hyperventilating, actually. He felt a million things, and none of them made any sense.

"Rose makes sense," he muttered aloud to himself. Then he did it again. Because she did. *They did.* He went over to the bathroom door and tried the handle.

"Rose."

She opened the door and opened her mouth, but he steamrolled over her. "Wait. I have to say something first. You know I care about you. Regardless of anything that happens in this bathroom, this thing between us matters. You know that."

She took a deep breath. "I'm pregnant." She pointed to the little stick thing on the sink.

Jack brushed by her. There was a little digital window, and there in actual letters, it said *pregnant.* Pregnant.

"Okay," he breathed.

"What do you mean *okay*?" she demanded, panic sneaking into her tone.

"I mean, okay, you're pregnant. You're pregnant, and now we work out how we're going to deal with that."

"I don't want to," she said in a rush.

"You don't want to what? Work out how to deal with it or be pregnant or…?"

"I don't want to deal with it!" she shouted. "I want

to pretend like I don't know that I'm pregnant. I want to fake the next I don't know how many weeks. I don't want to figure out what's going to happen. I don't want to work out how I'm going to shove a child out of me. I don't want any of it. I want it to go away."

"Right. Okay."

She smacked him on the chest. "I can't actually do that!"

"Well, I know, but I wasn't about to point it out."

"Jack, you cannot want to have a baby with me."

"I can't want to have a baby with you?" he returned.

"That is what I said. You don't want this. You want picket fences and T-ball and…I run a bar!"

She was clearly panicking. Which surprised him and warmed him, oddly. Because he'd figured she'd take the test far away from him and hide her panic. She was here instead, talking to him, and he wanted to smile—but he also didn't want to be punched in the nose, so he kept his expression stoic.

"I admit I'm a traditional guy. I would prefer to, you know, have been married before this sort of thing happened, but we're not. I'd also prefer not to have had a chunk blasted out of my leg, but things happen. I'm learning how to roll with the punches, and this one is a lot softer than others I've been dealt lately. Quite frankly, I can't think of anyone I'd rather have a baby with than you."

"I'll be a terrible mother," she breathed.

"You will not be a terrible mother. You are amazing. You are strong and forceful and—"

"Selfish. I am so utterly selfish, Jack. Good moms are not selfish."

"You are not selfish. A selfish woman wouldn't pretend to be a man's girlfriend to keep his family off his back. A selfish woman wouldn't give all the tips to one of her bartenders because her husband can't work. There is not a selfish bone in your body, Rose."

She looked up at him, dark eyes filled with tears and that awful certainty he couldn't seem to overcome. "You don't know me. You don't know anything about my life before the past few months."

He took her by the hand, rubbing a thumb over her knuckles. "So I'll learn. I would suggest we get married—"

She screeched.

"Except," he continued before she could protest more loudly. "I know that's not what you want. So instead of jumping to the next step, we'll focus on this one. You didn't want options, so you're going to have this baby?"

She shook her head, but her words were the opposite of that negative movement. "Yes," she breathed.

"Which means *we're* going to have this baby. We care about each other. You cannot deny that we care about each other. We'll get to know each other better, and if, at the end of this whole pregnancy thing, you don't want to be with me, then we'll work out some sort of joint custody thing or whatever people do. We'll do whatever it takes."

"Whatever it takes for what?" she asked, sounding tired.

He led her over to his bed and nudged her into a sitting position. "Whatever it takes to give our kid a good life. Maybe I didn't picture it quite like this, but I always assumed I'd have kids. I'll be a good father, and if I suck, I'll learn how to be better. And so will you. We made a baby, so we give that baby the best life we can."

She looked up at him and something in her expression changed. He wasn't sure he liked or trusted it. She took a deep breath and straightened her shoulders. "You're right. The most important thing is giving the kid the best possible life." She kept staring at him, and he had no idea what she was thinking, but they had time now. She agreed with him. So he had something like nine months to do whatever it took to win her over.

He had no doubt he would.

Rose took a week to perfect her plan. It was risky, and it would require striking just the right balance. Spending a week with Jack without his family around was killing her slowly. He was sweet and attentive and all the things she'd known he'd be. She couldn't count how many times she'd opened her mouth to tell him what was going on with her family, with the impending visit to Dad. There was some stupid part of her that occasionally got fooled into thinking this was real life.

Everything with Jack had been built on something fake. Including her. Whatever he saw in her had to be a figment of his imagination, and she had to save him from her.

Because the worst part of this week was knowing he was trying to wear her down, convince her that they belonged together, that a baby would be great.

Rose knew what was coming. He was in love with her. He hadn't said it, but she wasn't dumb. He was waiting her out, making sure she wouldn't bolt when he said the words.

Which meant she had to get her plan off the ground before he convinced her she didn't have to run.

What Jack had said as they were staring at that damned pregnancy test made everything crystal clear. She knew what was best for this child beyond a shadow of a doubt. And that was Jack. Jack wanted to be a father, and the thing he'd said about trying to be better if he wasn't… He believed in right and good, and he had his parents' example to guide him. There was no way he wasn't what was best for this child.

All Rose had to do was figure out how to disappear. She'd done it before. She'd escaped Dad and that hell house. She had disappeared and only kept tabs on her sisters to make sure they were okay. Doing what she could to get them out.

So now, she'd do it again. No matter that the past two years had been the best years of her life, and she loved her life and her bar and actually having contact with her sisters.

She wouldn't be selfish this time though. She was going to put everyone else first. Jack was so good, she had no doubt he'd let her sisters be a part of the baby's life. He'd give the baby everything he'd talked about that morning she'd punched Mike—a home, a safety net, and enough love to get through whatever shit life threw at it.

She couldn't let this thing between them go on any longer, but she also wasn't strong enough to stay around him after she cut it off. So she had to leave. If she could get Dan to help her out without telling the Shaws, she could get out, have the baby, and then make sure she got the baby back to Jack while she stayed far away.

Everyone—*everyone*—would have a better life if her plan worked.

Except you.

She shoved that thought away, along with the idea that Vivian had tried to implant in her, because it was all crap. She had never been a better person and couldn't become one. The only way she knew how to be good was to stay far, far away.

She knocked on the screen door of the Sharpes' ranch house. There was a chance Mel, Caleb's sister, would answer. There was every chance this could blow up in her face, but then she'd just find another way to disappear. With or without Dan's help, she could disappear. This was worth a shot though, and if it didn't work out, she had a backup plan.

The first person to come into view through the screen wasn't Mel or Dan, but their two-year-old, Lissa.

"Dee," Lissa called out because she always confused Rose and Delia.

Dan came around the corner next. "Not Delia, sweetie. That's Rose." He scooped up the little girl easily as he walked toward the door.

A few years ago, Rose would never have believed a man could be a good father. She'd never seen any until the past two years. Now she was surrounded by them—Caleb, Dan, Thack. Good men. Truly good. And Jack was just like them, if not better. He would be the best father.

"Hi, Dan," Rose offered as he opened the screen door.

"Hey, Rose. Come in. You didn't come to yell at me

about the llama incident, did you? Because trust me, the residents of Blue Valley have made their irritation clear."

She managed a smile. "No complaints," she said, stepping into the kitchen. "I came to ask you a favor."

He set Lissa down next to a bunch of toys. All llama related. Weird.

"If it has to do with money, I'd be happy to help. No need to be embarrassed," he said, gesturing her to a seat at the kitchen table.

"How did you know it was about money?"

"Well, we're not exactly best friends. If you needed help with anything personal, I'm sure you'd go to Delia or Summer first. What I do have that most people around here don't is disposable income. And llamas. But I don't think you're here for llamas."

"No. No llamas. My favor isn't just about money though. It's more of an investment." Or so she'd tell herself.

"Like I said, I'd be happy to help. You don't have to sell me on anything."

"No. It really is. I need you to buy my bar."

"Buy your bar?"

"That's it. All you have to do is buy it, keep the staff on. Tonya will do the day-to-day work and run it. You don't have to do anything. I just need the capital."

"Why are you selling the bar? You love your bar."

She felt more than panicked at the question, so she ignored it. "It's a great investment. It doesn't do gangbusters, but it does well. You wouldn't lose any money. You won't gain much either, but Tonya is amazing and so well trained. And if she ever leaves, you can sell it. Straight out."

"And you've discussed this with anyone?"

"No. No one will approve of this. But I need this. It's really, really important, and it's for the good of my family. I know you can understand how important that is. I know how much you love Mel and Lissa, and I know you would do anything for your family. Well, this is me doing anything for mine. I would just really appreciate it if you could do this for me without telling anyone."

Dan glanced at Lissa before returning his gaze back to Rose. "I do understand how important family is," he said carefully. "I also spent a lot of time in my life running away before they came along."

"I'm not running away. I'm making something right."

"If I give you this money, are you going to disappear?"

Rose opened her mouth to lie, but for some reason, she couldn't get it to come out. "I-If you're not going to give me the money, that's fine, but I need you to not tell anyone that I came here."

"Are you in trouble, Rose? Because I can help. We can all help."

"No. It isn't that. I just have to make something right. That's all."

Dan scratched a hand through his hair. "All right. I'll buy your bar."

"You will?" She practically sagged with relief. She had been steeling herself for disappointment, but he… he was going to do it.

"I'll have to talk to my finance guys and move some money around. They'll bitch and moan about taxes and whatnot, so it might take some time, but I'll do it."

"And you won't tell anyone?" she whispered, too afraid to believe this was really happening.

"I'm going to strongly encourage you to tell someone."

"But you won't?" she insisted.

Dan frowned at his daughter, and Rose wished she knew him better, so she could read that face.

"I can't promise not to tell Mel. She's my wife, and she's involved in all our financial decisions, and I can't promise *she* won't tell."

Rose wilted.

"I can ask her if she's okay with it though. And if she's not, if she's going to go tell someone, I can give you a warning. How's that?"

It was risky. It was incredibly risky. Mel was not the kind to keep secrets, but maybe she'd understand. Maybe…maybe…

"And if you change your mind, I will happily never tell anyone this meeting ever happened."

Rose forced herself to smile. "I like the plan where you ask Mel and warn me if she's going to squeal to Delia."

"Fair enough."

"Thank you, Dan." She stood, because there was so much to do now. "Really. I owe you."

"Let's see what Mel has to say before you owe me anything."

"Make sure you tell her that it's for the best for everyone. I know I'm making the right choice."

"Leaving?"

"Let me know what she says," Rose said, ignoring Dan's question. She left the house, brimming with possibility. Mel was a gamble, but it was also a chance. Maybe a slim one, but no matter what happened, she'd either have the money or a head start before her family came after her.

Now she just had to make it through tomorrow's visit to Dad and a few more days of Jack, and then she would be free.

She climbed into her car, that word bouncing around in her head. *Free. Free.* She'd chased freedom before and suffered the guilt of the hell it had wrought ever since.

It was different now. Everything was different. She was doing the selfless thing now, and it would all work out.

Chapter 23

JACK HAD NO IDEA WHY HE WAS *NERVOUS*. HE should save nerves for when he'd have to break the news to his family. Telling his friends was like a practice run, a training exercise. Nothing major at stake.

It might have helped if Rose were there. She could have given one of her patented razor-sharp grins, and everything would be fine. Except there had been nothing razor sharp about her the past few days. She'd been quiet. Dazed. And every time he'd tried to reach her, the real Rose under all this muffled whatever, she'd smiled at him. Just a sad, paltry smile.

So he'd given her some space. Pushing at her had been driving her deeper into the odd cocoon she'd wrapped around herself. Maybe this was how she dealt with a change in plans. He'd have to learn how to gauge those moods.

He wanted her to be happy, and if she needed a few days to withdraw inside herself and wrap her head around this brave new world, then he would give them to her—even if it drove him insane.

But it didn't mean *he* had to sit still and silent. He was going to have dinner with his friends and tell them the news. He needed someone besides Rose to know, to understand, to…something. He needed to say it and acknowledge it. Rose could burrow; he would act. Maybe that contrast made them an even better team.

He walked into the ranch house to the smell of something delicious but frowned a little when he stepped into the kitchen. The table was set, the nice glasses were out, and Becca was fluttering around the kitchen humming while Alex and Gabe sat at the table sipping beers.

"There you are! The bearer of big news," Becca greeted, all grinning excitement.

"I didn't say it was big exactly. You didn't have to go through so much trouble, Bec." Jack had the sudden and uncomfortable feeling that he was very much in the spotlight.

"You said you had news, big or not," Becca said all too brightly. "I wanted to set the stage."

Jack narrowed his eyes. "What news do you think I have?"

"Oh, I don't know. You and Rose seemed awfully happy together, and she did punch your brother for you. I thought maybe…"

"Maybe what?" he replied, sliding into his seat.

"Well, obviously something real is going on. I thought maybe something permanent was happening."

"Oh, Christ. She thinks you're getting married," Gabe said in disgust. "You have weddings on the brain, Bec. Poor guy has been fake dating for a few weeks. Chill."

"I thought you liked Rose," Jack said to Gabe, a little offended at Gabe's tone.

"I like Rose. I don't like weddings." Gabe groaned in disgust. "Oh no. You can't be serious. You're not going to—"

"There's not going to be a wedding yet," Jack replied before Gabe could go on a rant to end all rants.

"Yet!" Becca shouted.

"Bec," Alex muttered under his breath.

"He said 'yet,' which means he's *considered* a wedding."

"He hasn't considered shit," Gabe argued, making Becca frown.

"Oh, you're in his brain, determining what he can and can't consider? What's crawled up your butt lately, Gabe?"

"Rose is pregnant," Jack blurted. Oh, it was going to be so much worse when he inevitably blurted that news to his mother. She might like Rose quite a bit, but she wasn't going to like a baby with no wedding.

The silence was deafening.

"Someone say anything. Please. Anything," Jack said, looking around the table at his friends' shocked faces.

"Is it yours?"

He glared at Gabe.

Gabe flinched. "Sorry. Saying a nasty thing in an awkward situation is a bad habit. In all fairness, I got it from you."

"Yeah, well, don't say anything like that around her. We didn't exactly plan it, and she's a little shell-shocked."

Gabe snorted, and Becca slapped his shoulder.

"But it happened," Jack continued. "We're a little surprised, but we're figuring out a way to make it all work." Except that she wasn't talking, and he was giving her space.

"So you're not getting married?" Becca asked, poking at the lasagna on her plate.

"Rose isn't quite ready for that."

"But you are," Becca said with a grin, pointing her fork at him.

"Maybe we could focus on our wedding first, huh?" Alex said, giving Becca's arm a squeeze. Jack had known Alex long enough to know he was stepping in to give Jack a little breathing room.

"A baby is great news, wedding or no wedding," Becca said, beaming at him. "I just want you to be happy. I'm not trying to be the wedding harpy."

"You don't have to be married to be happy," Gabe muttered.

"No, but you're not happy and you're unmarried, so you have no right to add to this conversation," Becca retorted.

"I'm happy enough."

"Ha!"

"I believe the point here tonight, guys, is that Jack is going to be a dad," Alex said in his *brook no argument or further ridiculous conversation* tone.

Jack felt his heart stop. It was the way Alex said *dad*. A dad. Like his dad. To the kid. Like an actual baby.

"Went a little pale there, buddy," Gabe said, nudging a beer toward Jack.

"I'm feeling a little pale," Jack returned, taking the beer and a very long sip.

"You know no matter what happens, we're here for you," Becca said, their little mother hen. "To help and do whatever. And Rose too. I like her a lot. I hope she knows that."

Jack looked around the table at the family he'd made here. He missed his own family. He did, but these people…there was no weird history. There was no minefield of betrayals to step through.

He'd been through hell with Alex and Gabe at his

side, and they'd all come out of that hell here, together, with Becca. It was kind of amazing to think of how far they'd all come.

"Thank you," Jack said. "Not just for that, but for the past few months. The past few years. It was an incredible stroke of luck that I was assigned to the same team as the two of you, and that it brought us all here to you, Bec."

Becca sniffled, and Jack felt a little misty himself, but Gabe and Alex had their stoic Navy SEAL faces on, and that made Jack smile.

"How about a toast?" Alex said, raising his beer bottle. "To many future incredible strokes of luck."

"Hear, hear."

Rose sat in the driver's seat of her car, wondering if it was possible for a heart to beat out of a person's chest.

Delia was in the passenger seat, looking pale and drawn. Steph, Billie, and Elsie were crammed together in the back, arms linked as if their solidarity could ward off what they were about to do.

Rose had stopped at the beginning of the driveway that would lead them beyond the tree line and to their childhood home. She wasn't sure why she'd stopped, why she couldn't seem to push the gas pedal. They'd come this far, piled into the car that would lead them to a final confrontation with their dying father.

Back to the hell they'd grown up in.

"If anyone doesn't want to do this, they don't have to," Delia said, sounding as calm and in charge as she always did. She was so clearly the strongest out of all of them. The oldest sister. Always looking out for them.

"No. We do this together. You were right, Delia. This is going to be great closure for all of us," Elsie said firmly.

Steph and Billie echoed Elsie's words, and Rose could only sit in the driver's seat, clutching the steering wheel.

"Rose? You can still turn around. You don't have to do this." Delia rested her hand on Rose's arm.

That was exactly what Rose wanted. She wanted to turn around and run away. She wanted to do something— anything—that didn't involve putting her foot to the accelerator and facing her father. Not with her sisters in tow. She wanted to be out of this so badly, it hurt.

But her sisters were here thinking it would be good. That it would be closure. Nothing good would come of this. There was no closure to be found.

"Rose?"

"I'm pregnant."

Her sisters all gasped, and it echoed around the interior of the car. Rose could only sit frozen. She'd been the one to say it, had felt her lips move and the words escape her mouth, and yet she couldn't quite believe what had come out.

Why here? Why now?

"Jack?" Delia asked carefully.

Rose nodded, her hands starting to hurt, and yet she couldn't loosen her death grip on the wheel.

"Who's Jack?" Elsie demanded.

"The guy Rose has been seeing," Delia supplied when Rose said nothing.

Rose wanted to correct Delia. Not seeing. Ruining. Ruining him from the inside out. He'd been giving her space even though he didn't want to, and the fact that he was acting against what he wanted was all she needed to know she was no good for him. She would never give him space. She would never give someone what they wanted at the expense of something she wanted. She wasn't wired that way. Dad said so. Mom said so. Every man she'd ever let into her orbit had told her she was hard or selfish or mean.

Except Jack.

She couldn't think about Jack. She had to think about the future. Her sisters knowing she was pregnant would help them understand when she disappeared. Dan was talking to Mel about the money this evening, and then Rose would have an answer. This was going to be her last hurrah with all of her sisters for a very long time. So it was good she'd told them.

"You really don't have to do this," Delia said gently.

"I want to," Rose lied.

"I wasn't talking about visiting Dad. I was talking about going through with the pregnancy."

Rose turned to actually look at Delia, who was clearly so worried about her. Rose swallowed at the lump in her throat. "I know. I want to." Jack would be a great father, and the baby she had would be so lucky to have him. So very lucky.

It was that reminder that had Rose's foot hitting the gas pedal. She had things to do, and so did her sisters. They all had to make their choices and live their lives, and maybe once they put this man in the ground, they really could move on for good.

She drove up the drive, an oppressive silence filling the car—the silence was full of memories and horrors, the kind no one wanted to relive.

The last time she'd been here, she'd come with the intention of provoking her father into beating her up so she could send him to jail. It had worked. Finally, they'd all been free.

Rose couldn't hold on to that feeling of success. All she could remember, even as the falling-down shack came into view on this bright summer afternoon, was the day she'd escaped. The day she'd sacrificed Delia, the one person who'd cared about her more than anything.

The car came to a stop, and the girls got out. Rose felt numb and cold even though it was warm and sunny. She trudged after her sisters, a coward in the back.

"What are you girls doing here?" Rose heard Mom's voice demand, though Rose kept her gaze on the ground. She focused on the cracked ground, the dirt where no grass grew.

"Aunt Beth called about Dad," Delia said, always so strong and defiant.

"Yeah, so?"

"We'd like to say goodbye."

"Why should I let you girls do that? All you ever did was cause us pain and suffering. All you ever did was disappoint us and degrade us and—"

"Mom. Move."

Rose didn't know what their mother's response to that was, but the girls started shuffling inside, and Rose could only follow. She kept her gaze on the back of Steph's bright-red tennis shoes, so incongruous to the dark atmosphere inside the house.

The house smelled. It always had. It was as cramped and dark as it had ever been. Nothing had changed except the decay was worse, the darkness heavier, the smell potent.

When Steph stopped, Rose stopped. Only then did she look up.

Dad sat in a chair in the corner of the living room, his eyes closed. His skin looked almost yellow, and he was at least a third of the size he'd once been. He had withered down to nothing but sagging skin over bones. Rose was almost convinced he was dead sitting right there.

Slowly, his dark eyes opened. *Your eyes, Rose.* He scanned the room, and when he finally decided on somewhere to look, he chose her. *Always.*

He just stared. All the hate in the world aimed at her. *Just like me, aren't you, Rosie girl?*

"I'd beat every last one of you if I could," he rasped, his gaze never leaving Rose's.

"I suppose it's a very good thing you can't, because we would kill you," Delia said in the same tone someone might use to ask how he was feeling. "You're a miserable human being," she continued. "I have never been so glad to hear the news of someone's impending death. I hope you rot in hell. While you do, I hope you know that each of us has built a happy, amazing life. Full of love and forgiveness and everything you never had in you."

He spit at Delia, but she jumped back. He rasped out a laugh.

"You tried to ruin our lives," Billie said, her voice wavering but loud. "But you didn't."

"Every time I succeed, I toss a middle finger your way," Elsie added.

"The only thing I have to thank you for, you worthless, cruel, useless excuse for a human being, is that you created five strong women who will make sure to change the world for the better despite you," Steph said, sounding so grown-up and sure, Rose wanted to cry.

All her sisters had spoken, but she couldn't find the words. She didn't know what to say to this man who'd promised her ponies and broken her bones. The man who'd taught her how to play poker and used her. She didn't know what to say to a man she'd saved, a man she'd had thrown in jail, a man who'd made so many women's lives hell.

"Don't you have anything to say, Rosie girl?" Dad rasped, glaring at her.

Rose was paralyzed. She felt weighted down by how being here tainted her all over again, by how his nickname for her made her feel dirty and worthless. This was the last time she'd see him. She was sure of it. This was the last time she would see her father alive.

She wasn't like her sisters, so strong and brave, with practiced speeches to ensure he knew that they had won. That they'd overcome everything he'd tried to use to tie them down.

Instead, Rose was running away. From her life. From the man she loved. Even from a child.

That was exactly what he should have done—he should have abandoned them. Rose was going to fix his mistakes.

"We should go. Unless you want to say something?" Delia asked.

Rose didn't have the words. The man was dying. He'd been to jail. He'd spent his life beating up women. There was nothing to say.

She could punch him like she'd punched Mike and

suddenly feel better about herself. She could tell him she was the one who'd called the ambulance the night he'd almost died. She could tell him he had tried to mold her in his image and that he'd succeeded. She could tell him a million and one things, but nothing would come out of her mouth.

"Leave?" Billie asked gently.

Rose managed a nod, and they started filing out. Rose could feel Mom's gaze on her. She looked back, just once, after all her sisters had stepped out the door.

"You didn't have anything to say because you're just like him. You always have been," Mom hissed.

Rose stared for a very long time at her mother. She was old and bedraggled, and even though her father was sitting there looking like death himself, she had a bruise under her eye.

"But I won't be. I won't be," Rose whispered in return.

Chapter 24

JACK WALKED OUT OF THE STABLES AT THE END OF A long day. His leg ached, and he was more than a little exhausted, but he couldn't wipe the smile off his face. Aching muscles and exhaustion paled in the anticipation of seeing Rose tonight. Though she'd been withdrawn the past few days, each night, he had hope he'd find some crack to sneak through. She wasn't letting him in yet, but she wasn't pushing him away. With Rose, that was still a step in the right direction.

He was going to bypass the barn and head for the showers, but he frowned at the angry voices wafting out of the barn. Before he could figure out what Gabe and Monica were arguing about so vehemently, he heard the unmistakable grind and putter of Rose's car. Which was odd—usually they met at her house after she'd closed the bar.

He shaded his eyes against the fading sun as she stepped out of the car and slowly walked over to him.

"Hey, everything all right?" he asked.

She smiled thinly, sunglasses shielding her eyes from him. "Yeah."

"You're not at the bar."

"No, I decided to take the night off."

Jack couldn't hide his surprise. "You feeling okay?"

She peered into the open barn door. Gabe and Monica's argument ended with a yelled insult and

Monica storming away, brushing past them without a greeting. Gabe stomped out of the barn in the opposite direction.

"Is Monica Gabe's therapist as well?" Rose asked, watching Monica get in her car and slam her door shut before driving away.

"Gabe hasn't quite made that step yet."

Rose cocked her head, and still those sunglasses hid whatever she was dealing with today. "What step?" she asked.

"The *agree to therapy* step."

Rose smirked, some flash of her normal self in it. "How surprising. He's always so cheerful and well adjusted."

The sarcasm in her voice gave him pause for a moment, because that was exactly how most people would describe Gabe. It went to show just how much had obviously changed in the past few months, changes Jack hadn't completely absorbed, because he'd been wrapped up in his own. "You know, I actually think that's a good thing," he murmured.

"Guys being assholes is rarely a good thing, Jack. I mean, I know he's your friend, and I'm not saying he's an asshole. He just..."

"Has been a bit of an asshole lately, but when we first got here, Gabe was all fake jokes and empty smiles, pretending like everything was great. The fact that he's letting some of that not-great show is a good first step, I think."

Rose blew out a breath and offered him one of those small, forced smiles that made a hard weight settle in his gut. He had a bad feeling, but that was silly. She was still uncertain about everything and trying to brave her way through it like she always did.

It was nice to see her brave it with something softer than all her usual sharp edge. Or so he was trying to convince himself, but part of him couldn't help but wish she'd fight—hard and mean.

"Why aren't you at the bar tonight? I thought it would take a team of wild horses and possibly a blizzard-hurricane-earthquake combo to make that happen."

She didn't laugh at his joke, and that made the hard weight heavier. He reached out and nudged the sunglasses off her face, because he needed to see her eyes. See *her*.

She flinched a little. Without the glasses on, she looked pale and exhausted. He frowned at the puffiness in her eyes, as though she'd been crying. She was running herself too hard, and he doubted the emotional upheaval was helping any.

Irritation clawed at him that she was off crying when he wanted to be the one to hold her while she did. That she wasn't any closer to letting him in.

She swallowed as if she was working through some emotion, some deep feeling that she wasn't going to show him. "I'm just so tired, and I don't know why."

That deflated some of his irritation, replaced with concern for her. "Come lie down. I'll clean up, and you can take a little nap, and then we can have dinner with everybody." She needed some normalcy, some company.

Rose studied the house warily, and he ignored that too. The only weapon he had against her mistrust was time. No words would take it away, no combination of actions. Just time. Much like Gabe, Rose had to be ready to take this step. Just like when they'd first arrived at the ranch and Jack and Alex themselves hadn't wanted a therapist on the grounds, period. They hadn't been ready, and no amount of pushing had made them ready. They'd both reached their *talk to a therapist* moment in their own time.

It took time and consistency and support and *love* to give someone the foundation that allowed them to reach out. He'd give her all that.

He forced himself to smile and slide his arm around her shoulders. "And if you just want to sleep, you can just sleep."

"I don't know why I'm so tired," she said, and he was gratified when she let him lead her.

"Well—"

"Don't say it."

Because she wasn't ready to think about the whole pregnancy thing yet. Which was her right and her choice. No matter how impatient it made him on the inside. He didn't want to talk about anything else, no matter how much it freaked him out. He wanted to talk, because talking had been working, but on the other hand, he didn't want to force her into talking. He didn't want to fight with her or…

Well, he supposed the main thing he didn't want to do was run her off, and he was afraid that's what pushing would do—send her running, make her realize that she didn't care about him.

Isn't that what you did with Madison? Gave her space when she didn't want to get married? Let her have the time she wanted? Never pushed. Never demanded.

It was an uncomfortable realization that he was

falling into old habits. Wasn't that how it went though? Weren't you supposed to give the people you loved what they wanted? The things they said they needed?

He led her to the bunkhouse, confused and wishing he could find the right words, wishing he knew how to break down all those walls. Wishing he had the courage to fight her.

They were having a kid. There were plans to make. Things to learn about each other. Fears and hopes to share. He'd talked a little bit about it with Monica at his last session, but it felt so wrong to discuss his future with her without first discussing it with Rose.

Rose, who he doubted was confiding in anyone. She was so damned determined to handle things on her own.

Monica's words about self-worth haunted his thoughts every night these days. Maybe he couldn't make Rose believe in herself, but it was starting to feel like she was going to slip through his fingers no matter how he tried to do the right thing.

He shook that thought away. He was being a love-lorn idiot and overreacting about every little thing. She wasn't Madison. This wasn't the past. She said she needed time and space, and he'd give her both. Plus a bed to nap in, a shoulder to cry on—he'd be anything and everything.

He took her inside and led her to his bed. "Lie down. Rest. Once I'm out of the shower, you can decide if you want to go eat dinner at the big house, or I can go get you something."

"You don't have to wait on me," she mumbled miserably.

"I don't recall believing I had to. I *want* to wait on you."

"Because I'm pregnant," she said flatly.

"Because a lot of things, Rose. Only one of them is you being pregnant. The other reason is one I don't think you're ready to hear."

She slid into his bed, avoiding his gaze, but before he could step into the bathroom, she said his name. "Jack?"

"Yeah?"

"Can you lie with me for a few minutes?"

She had her back to him so he couldn't see her face, and her tone was something different and foreign he couldn't read. She was reaching out though, and no matter that he was dirty and sweaty from a hard day's work, he slid into his bed, pressing his front to her back and pulling her into the circle of his arms.

Rose nestled in, quiet but tense.

"What's wrong, baby?" Because if she was taking nights off the bar and asking to lie with him, then something was definitely wrong. And he wanted to be the bearer of all her wrongs and all her hurts. Maybe this was the start of that—her coming to him, lying with him.

"Nothing. Everything's going to be all right."

She sounded so convinced, he could only hold her close and believe her.

————

Rose awoke to her phone going off in a dark room. She didn't remember actually dozing off in Jack's tiny bed in the bunkhouse, but apparently she had.

He was still there, holding her close, snoring lightly in her ear. It was in the moments like this, waking up with him, that she wished things could be different.

But they couldn't. She shifted and pulled out her phone. A text from Dan. She swallowed and shakily brought it up on the screen.

Got the okay. Meet to talk details tonight?

Rose glanced at Jack's still sleeping form, then at the time. It was only eight o'clock. Which meant she could make up an excuse to leave that Jack wouldn't suspect. But she couldn't meet Dan at Pioneer Spirit or anywhere in town where someone might see them and ask questions, or worse, overhear. Dan's place was out as well. Mel might know some things, but Rose didn't want her overhearing details or asking questions Dan might not think of.

There was only one place she could have the conversation she needed.

Meet me at the old, falling-down house at the end of Reece Road around eight thirty?

Jack stirred, his arms tightening around her in a light squeeze. "Time is it?" he murmured sleepily.

"Eight."

"You want me to go round up some food for us?" he asked with a yawn.

"No, actually, I have to go. Um, my sister. She isn't feeling well. I'm going to go bring her some food."

"Want me to come with?"

He would offer that. Why had she fallen for this good guy? *How* on earth had he fallen for her? "No. No. She's all pregnant and puking. Trust me. It's ugly."

He looked at her then, the sleepiness fading away. "Your sister is local. Pregnant and local?"

"Um. Oh. I hadn't told you that?"

"Not to my recollection."

Rose stared hard at her phone screen, quickly hiding Dan's Sure text. "Yeah, she's a couple of months along. She gets really sick. This is her second."

Jack sat up a little. "Your sister already has a kid and another on the way and lives in Blue Valley?"

Rose shrugged. "Yeah. Well, outskirts of Blue Valley."

"So our kid is going to have cousins around their age here? In Blue Valley? And you didn't think to mention it?" he demanded. His voice was still sleepy, and she knew he was trying to sound curious instead of pissed, but he was so obviously mad that she'd kept things from him.

She hadn't even meant to. Except maybe she had subconsciously. She'd already told him things about her childhood she'd never told anyone, but she'd needed to keep him separate from the good things.

If things went well tonight, then she would be gone soon. This baby would have cousins and an aunt and uncle local, and Jack should know that. He should absolutely know that, so when she was gone and the baby was here with him, they could be a proper family.

"I…"

"Rose, I know you don't want to talk about baby stuff yet, but shouldn't I meet your family? Shouldn't we all know each other and spend time together? Regardless of everything else, we're all connected now."

Which made the lump in her throat fizzle painfully. "Yes," she croaked. "You're right. The baby will have cousins and aunts and uncles and…yes, you should know them."

"So I'll come with?"

"Not tonight." She forced herself to look him in the eye and lie with everything she had. He'd meet them once she was gone. She couldn't stand the thought of introducing them to him, watching their interactions. She couldn't bear the thought of watching him interact with Sunny and knowing it would be the way he'd act with their child someday.

"Delia won't want to meet anyone right now, feeling like she's feeling," Rose managed to croak. "And Sunny's already sleeping. I'll talk to her about a good time to meet though."

Without Rose. Because if Dan was quick enough with the money, she could be gone tomorrow. This might even be the last time she saw Jack. That filled her with a horrible, painful pang, but she shoved it ruthlessly aside.

She was doing what was best. She was proving she was nothing like either of her parents. Her child would have the best, and that wasn't her. She would save Jack and her baby from the pain she could inflict.

This might be goodbye, and she couldn't tell him goodbye, but she wanted to give him something. *Something*.

"My tattoo. The one you're always asking about?" It was a stupid parting gift, but maybe if she explained it in vague enough terms, he'd understand why she was doing what she was about to do.

"The bloody feather."

"I got it after I…" She had to clear her throat and make it sound unimportant. Casual. "I tried to escape my parents' house once, and I did some crappy things in order to do it. I hurt some people, so it's a reminder that freedom isn't free. Not for me."

"You're free now."

Except she wasn't. She was bound by all those old hurts, all the things she knew inside her to be true. Selfishness. Meanness. Cruelty. She wouldn't inflict them on Jack, and she wouldn't inflict them on this child. So she put on her best fake smile and brushed a kiss across his cheek. "I have to go."

"Are you sure I can't drive you?"

"Not tonight." She slid out of bed, and he did the same. She looked up at him for a few seconds, wanting both to memorize his face and to pretend she'd never seen it.

She rose to her tiptoes, hoping he couldn't see the tears in her eyes in the dark. "Goodbye, Jack," she whispered, leaving as quickly as she could.

She would meet Dan, get the money, and then she'd leave. Leave Blue Valley and her sisters and a wonderful man.

The fact that it hurt so badly only meant she was finally, *finally* doing something right.

Chapter 25

JACK COULDN'T SLEEP AFTER THAT, NOT EVEN AFTER he'd showered and gone and gotten himself dinner. Now he sat on the porch of Alex and Becca's house on a pretty star-dappled night, and he worried.

Something was off. Rose was not acting right, even given the circumstances, and no matter how he tried to explain it away, that gnawing, *wrong* feeling ate at him. Maybe he should go to the bar or find out where her sister lived and show up there.

Maybe he needed to fight for her. Like she always did. Maybe, just maybe, he needed to channel some of Rose's strength and go after what he wanted, fight a little dirty till he got it.

Gabe appeared and slid a beer bottle into Jack's hand. "Here. You need a beer if you're going to be brooding all night."

"I'm not brooding," Jack muttered, even though that's exactly what he was doing. He accepted the beer and took a long sip.

"Baby mama drama?"

Jack sent Gabe a scathing look. "No drama, baby mama or otherwise."

Gabe settled into the chair next to Jack. Alex and Becca would likely join them at some point if they heard voices and weren't otherwise occupied.

"And yet, you look very, very dramatic."

Jack let out a hefty sigh. "Something's not right."

"What?"

"That's the problem. I don't know." He glanced at the stars, questioning himself over and over again. "I feel it in my gut," he said, his voice low and serious. "Like that day." Jack didn't need to explain—Gabe knew. They'd all felt that odd sense of unease around them the day of the grenade blast. Everyone except Geiger, who was dead.

And Jack was alive and worried about, well, baby mama drama, and he supposed that was enough to be thankful for.

"Then you should do something about it."

"I don't know *what* to do," Jack replied. "What do you do when you know something is wrong but you don't know how to fix it?"

Gabe was quiet a long while. "I wish I knew the answer to that," he finally said.

Which was when Jack remembered what his mother had said. That Monica had told her that being good for someone started with asking how you could help. He didn't think Rose would ever tell him, but maybe it wasn't so much about the answer as it was that someone cared enough to ask the question.

"Are you okay, Gabe? Really okay."

Gabe took a long pull of his beer. He squinted out into the night around them as he considered the weight of that question. "Yes and no. How's that for an answer?" He took another long sip. "I'm not struggling. I like it here. I like what we're doing."

"But?"

He heaved out a breath, resettling himself in his chair.

"But it feels like something's missing, and I don't know what, and that pisses me the hell off."

Jack took a thoughtful sip of beer. "What were you and Monica arguing about?"

Gabe shifted in his chair again. "That woman drives me crazy."

"Uh-oh."

"No 'uh-oh.' I was just giving her advice is all, and she had to get on her high horse."

"Because you love it when people give you advice?" Jack replied sarcastically.

Gabe grunted. "What am I supposed to do when Colin begs me to ask her to lighten up?"

"Not step in between mother and child would be my first suggestion."

"She keeps too tight a rein on that kid," Gabe muttered irritably. "And she's way too defensive when I bring it up."

"So don't."

"I was just trying to help. I don't see what the big deal is or why she had to bite my head off."

"She moved her kid to another state, the kid she's been raising on her own since the kid's dad died. Give her a break, Gabe."

"Fine. Whatever," Gabe grumbled.

Jack studied his friend. "You've taken quite a shine to that kid."

"Yeah, well, at least I didn't knock anyone up like an idiot, no matter how fine a dad you'll be."

Which Jack supposed was a compliment, all in all. It brought him back to *his* problems. Baby. Rose. Going after her. Before he could finish that thought,

Becca pushed the door open and held out the landline phone receiver.

"Jack, it's for you. She said you wouldn't know her, but it's important."

Jack stood and took the phone, that note of unease burrowing deeper. "Hello?"

"Hi, um, is this Jack?"

"Yes. Who is this?"

"This is Summer Lane. We haven't met, but I'm friends with Rose."

His heart dropped, everything inside him turning to ice. "What's wrong?"

"I'm not totally sure. Rose is fine, I think."

"You *think*?" he yelled.

"Crap. I'm messing this all up. Something is going on with Rose. She and her sisters went to see their father this afternoon, but then... We're not sure what's going on. She's been making some plans that point to her leaving town. And I'm totally overstepping my place here, but we all kind of are."

"Where is she?" Jack demanded, holding the phone so tight, he thought it might break.

"She's at a house. It's off Reece Road, way in the back?"

"I know it," Jack growled. "I'll be there in ten."

"Okay, I—"

Jack hung up, already in motion. She'd had a meeting with her dad. A psychopath who had *beat* her. She'd *met* with him. She was planning to leave town? And she'd told him none of this.

She'd come here this evening looking sad and tired and slept with him and... Christ, she'd told him what her tattoo meant. He'd taken that as some step, some movement forward.

It had been a goodbye.

"Jack!"

He finally realized everyone was yelling at him and following him. "I have to go." He absently shoved the phone toward Becca and realized he didn't have keys. He started striding for the bunkhouse.

"Where?" Alex demanded.

"Is everything okay?" Becca added. Everyone was trailing after him.

"I don't really know. I just know that something is wrong, and I have to get to Rose."

"Here. Take our truck," Alex said, pulling his keys out of his pocket. "Or I can drive you?"

He took Alex's keys. "No. No, I can handle it myself."

"You don't have to," Gabe said firmly.

Jack stared blankly at Gabe, because that hit like a ringing gong. Or maybe a grenade blast. Something big and loud and continual.

He didn't have to do anything alone. He always had people there ready to have his back. Give him keys. Offer to go with him to do something hard.

Rose didn't. She thought she had to get through everything on her own. No matter how hard he tried to prove that he was good and could be there for her and they could be right together, she just thought she had to do everything alone.

That wasn't going to change. No matter how hard he tried or worked or gave her space or didn't. He'd changed himself, but that was all he could do. He couldn't change any other damn thing.

"Jack?"

He glanced up at Alex.

"One mission at a time."

Jack nodded. Alex was right. Make sure Rose was safe first.

Then he could figure out the rest.

———

Rose paced the yard of her house. She hated being here without Jack. Hated it. This had once been her sanctuary, but now it was theirs.

Only there wasn't a *theirs*, because she was getting her tainted self out of here.

When the rumble of a truck reached her, she stood up. She knew immediately this was not going to be what she had hoped it would be.

Because it wasn't just one truck. Two eventually crested the hill. It did not take a genius to figure out who they might belong to.

Dan and Summer and two of her sisters stepped out of the first, Caleb, Delia, and Steph the second. They must have left the kids with Mel and Thack and were here to corner her.

"I can't believe you did this to me," she threw at Dan, feeling far too close to tears. She'd known he might tell, but she'd never expected him to gang up on her, to leave her with no choice and no out. He'd promised to give her a head start.

"I apologize. I do. But—"

"Rose Kimberly Rogers, what the *fuck* do you think you're doing?" Delia yelled as she advanced.

"Thanks for getting my pregnant sister worked up, you asshole," Rose muttered.

"I am sorry," Dan repeated.

"You don't sound sorry."

"Have you lost your mind?" Summer said, right on Delia's heels.

"I can't believe you would try to skip town without telling us. Without coming to us," Billie continued. "Is he hurting you?"

"Is he hurting…" Rose could barely make sense of the words, and only their meeting with Dad earlier made it possible to connect. "God no. Jack is perfect."

"Then why are you skipping town while you're *pregnant* with his *kid*?" Steph demanded. "Why would you hide the baby from him?"

"I wasn't going to hide the baby." At the disapproving, disbelieving looks she got, defensiveness got the better of her. Because she was doing the right thing. They might try to gang up on her and change her mind, but she knew she was doing the right thing. They couldn't stop her from finally making things right. "I'm going to give him the kid."

"What?" the entire female legion screeched at her.

And if she'd been anticipating this or had time to think, maybe she could have worked through it all. Maybe she could have planned and strategized, but all she could do with them surrounding her was yell right back.

"I was going to leave, send the kid to him once it's here, and…" Why was her voice cracking? She wasn't cut out to be a mother—she knew that. Why would she get emotional over giving her kid the best shot it could possibly have in life? "I am getting out of the way of everyone else's happy ending, okay? There's no need for dramatics. I'm doing the right thing." She knew that. She did. Down to her soul.

"You owe all of us an explanation before you go anywhere or sell anything," Summer said sternly. "Why didn't you talk this over with us?"

Rose didn't know what to say to that or the hurt on all her sisters' faces. Why should they be hurt? She was doing them all a favor. "I—"

"She wanted to sneak out of town, because she knew we'd stop her," Delia said firmly as if she just knew everything.

"Don't stop me. Don't," Rose pleaded, losing the battle to be strong. She needed to get away. So very far away. "What good could possibly come out of you stopping me, Delia?"

"My sister in my life," Delia replied as if Rose weren't a stain…because Delia didn't know the truth. "You know how hard I worked to make that happen, and now you're throwing it all away?"

Rose didn't know how to absorb that sharp pain of truth or the sound of another truck coming up the road.

"Who on earth is that?" Rose demanded, frowning.

"Well," Summer said, twisting her fingers together. "I may have made a call."

"To who?" Rose saw the answer then, recognizing Alex and Becca's truck. She somehow doubted they were behind the wheel.

Jack hopped out of the truck, slamming the door behind him. "What the hell is going on here?" Jack demanded in that military commanding voice that seemed to make everyone stand a little straighter.

"Is that the guy?" Steph whispered.

Rose managed a nod, and Jack shoved his hands into his pockets as he surveyed the crowd.

"Jack, meet my family. Who have overstepped every boundary pretty much ever. I have no idea what they told you—"

"I haven't been told much of anything," he said, his voice so cold, she shivered. "So if you could fill me in, that'd be great."

"She's selling the bar and leaving town," Delia said, no compunction about throwing it all out there.

Rose watched each word land on Jack's face like a blow, and those blue eyes went a degree colder than just *cold*.

"It's not what you're thinking, Jack," she managed weakly. He couldn't think she'd take the baby away from him. She couldn't let him think that, no matter how well that would work to burn his faith in her down to the ground.

"I don't know what to think," he said. It was that horrible blank tone he'd used all those months ago when he'd been just a stranger in her bar. At the first dinner with his family, when he'd been so clearly numb to every horrible thing. Even then it had made her heart hurt a little—now it felt like she was cracking.

Why was she always bringing pain down on people? Why wouldn't they let her go?

"I wasn't going to keep the baby from you. Yes, I was selling the bar, and yes, I was planning on disappearing, but you were always going to have the baby, okay? You'll be a great dad. I'd be a shitty mom. I wasn't cutting you out or anything. I was cutting our losses. Making everything right."

"You were cutting *you* out. What about *you*?" He asked it so incredulously, like it didn't make all the sense in the world.

"Why can't you get it through your thick skull? There is nothing about me worth keeping," she said, panic throwing all the words out. "I am cutting *me* out for your own damn good. All of you!"

There were outraged protests from her sisters, and Summer stared at her in frozen horror.

Then Rose finally understood what she had to do to make this work. She had to show the people she loved all the horrible, ugly pieces of herself that she'd kept hidden for so long. Because the reason they loved her was simple: they didn't know.

They didn't know all the things she'd done to them, all the ways she'd failed them. She'd never wanted them to know, but it was the only way. The only way to save them.

She was made up of all the horrible pieces of her parents, but she wouldn't inflict them on the people she loved. That's how she'd be different from them. If she had to show everyone that horror inside her in order to make them understand, well, here went nothing.

"All right," Rose said, trying to pull herself together. "I need you all to listen really closely and think with your brains instead of your hearts."

"Hard pass," Delia said coldly.

"Ditto," Summer echoed.

"Whatever. Just listen. Please listen." She looked at Jack, and her lips trembled, but she couldn't let her weakness for him win. "Please listen. I know you all think I'm the good sister who swept in and got Dad thrown in jail, but I only did that because of all the things I did before that. I hurt all of you. Immeasurably."

"Rose, we were all there. We all survived the same thing," Billie said.

There were a hundred little stories she could tell, but she figured going with big guns would be the better route to take. Quicker. Deadlier.

"Delia. Do you remember the night when we were teenagers and you tried to escape, and Dad found you? Then he held a gun to your head?" She turned to Caleb, who was standing with Dan in the back of the little group. "Do you remember, Caleb?"

It was dark, but she could see the way shock slackened their features.

"How did you know about that?" Delia whispered.

"I'm the reason Dad was even going after you that night. I'm the reason the ambulance came and he lived."

Her sisters started chattering questions, one over the other, because no one had ever heard this story. No one knew anything about that night except Caleb and Delia.

And her.

Rose stood in the middle of her sanctuary, the place where Jack had somehow wormed his way into her heart. She was standing on this ground that had called to her, telling her deepest, darkest secret. Blowing up her life in the process. While a baby grew inside her, too tiny to feel.

Maybe it was poetic justice.

"How old were you, Delia. Eighteen? Nineteen?"

The sister she resembled the most closely nodded wordlessly.

"Delia was nineteen, and she was planning on getting

us all out, always trying to get us out without hurting anyone. Always big sister protecting us. Saving us. Dad had lost quite a few poker games in a row and things were getting scarier. I just wanted out. So bad. I knew all I had to do was win one game, steal the winnings, create a diversion, and I'd be gone."

She was shaking so hard, she could barely stand, but when Delia reached out, Rose stepped away. "That's what I did. We won a game. I told Dad Delia was trying to escape. She was going to the old Paulle house to run away. I had the cash in my pocket, and I sent him after Delia so I could leave without him finding me."

The tears started to fall, too hard to fight. Why was she was crying? She wanted to be strong as she retold it, so they understood how callous she'd been, how horrible and selfish.

"You were home that night, the night Dad was found at the Paulle place. You didn't go. I remember because we were all so worried about Delia not being there, and you comforted us," Steph said with such certainty.

"You couldn't have gotten out of town if you were there. At the Paulle house," Delia added so rationally, so calmly. Why couldn't Rose find that kind of calm?

"I was halfway to Bozeman, and I started worrying. I started worrying he'd do more than just hit Delia. So I came back. I came back to check and make sure, and he was holding a gun to your head."

Rose saw it over and over again in her nightmares. Because if her conscience had kicked in even two minutes later, what might've happened?

"Jesus, you were the one who called me," Caleb said.

Rose glanced at him, now standing next to Delia, his

hand on her back. "I didn't know anyone who would help, but I-I knew you two ran in the same circles, and you'd been nice. I thought maybe even if you couldn't help, you'd distract him."

"What is he talking about?" Elsie demanded.

Caleb stepped forward, but Delia stopped him from whatever he was about to say.

"You came back to make sure Dad didn't kill me, and you called Caleb to step in, and you somehow think Dad's actions were your fault?" Delia asked.

"You could've died because of me! And Dad lived because of me. He would've died there, and we would've been free all that much sooner. He was bleeding so badly, and I just couldn't leave him. So I called the ambulance before I went home, and you guys suffered for how many more years?"

"If Dad had died, my husband would have been a murderer, Rose. It's not… It wasn't such a terrible thing that you called the ambulance."

"He wasn't your husband then," Rose returned. "He was just some guy who hadn't been a dick. Even so, even *so*, I saved Dad because I couldn't let him die. I thought if I saved him, he'd owe me something. He very clearly didn't feel that way, and I caused so much more pain. You all went through it for nothing. Nothing." She'd saved him and gotten nothing for it—not leverage and certainly not his love.

"No, you didn't cause it. He did," Steph insisted as though she hadn't heard the story. She clearly didn't understand.

"I was willing to sacrifice Delia to escape. Don't overlook that."

"We all sacrificed each other over the years," Elsie said quietly. "I can't count the times I would hide in the closet and block anyone from getting in with me so he'd beat one of you next instead of me."

"The amount of times I blamed something Dad was mad about on someone else," Billie added with a little sob. "I couldn't even begin to remember."

"We were little girls being beaten and starved, and no one would help us. We all made awful choices because we had to *survive*. Because we were babies. How can you blame yourself? They did that to us. Them," Delia said, the same vehemence from earlier in her tone.

Rose could only stare at her sisters. How could they not see? But they were standing there saying they'd all made the same choices. It wasn't the same.

Was it?

"Why do you think you have to leave us?" Delia implored, tears pooling in her eyes. "We don't want to lose you. We love you. No matter what, Sissy. No matter *what*."

Rose glanced at Jack. She didn't know how to say that she had to leave because he loved her. Because he wanted to make this thing between them real. Because he believed she'd be a good mother. And that was her greatest wish, but the idea that it could never come true was her deepest fear.

There was nothing good inside her, no matter how much she wanted there to be.

Jack cleared his throat and stepped forward. "I might have an answer for that."

Everyone looked at him, and Rose could only look away. He was always so brave. So strong. His fingers brushed her wet cheeks, and he tilted her chin up, so she had to look at him. If the light wasn't totally tricking her, there were tears in his own eyes, and that made her cry harder.

"She thinks she has to leave because she doesn't think she's worth it," Jack said quietly.

"Worth what?" Summer demanded.

"Love," Jack said, brushing his fingers across her cheek again.

"Stability," Billie said.

"Hope," Steph added.

Rose didn't hear the rest of it, because she was sobbing. It hurt—all of it. Too much. Because it was all the truth, and she didn't know how to make it the lie she needed it to be.

Chapter 26

JACK COULD PINPOINT EXACTLY THE LAST TIME he'd felt the stabbing hopelessness he felt listening to Rose describe her horrible past.

He'd been in the rehab center, alone. There had been a horrible space of a few weeks where he'd had to deal with the true extent of his injuries, his brother's betrayal, and the loss of every hope and dream he'd had for his future.

Until Alex had visited and told him about his move-to-Montana plan.

This was so much more than that. Any other time in his life, Jack might have felt somewhat ashamed or weak for losing a little bit of his emotional control, but Rose's sisters naming off all the things Rose didn't think she deserved—it broke something in him.

Luckily, everyone else was crying too.

Rose was sobbing. He stepped closer, and she leaned into his chest. She kept saying she was sorry, over and over again, and he couldn't seem to get through that chant of hers.

Her sisters gathered around her, and Jack slowly stepped out of the way to give them the moment they obviously needed.

"Thank you for coming," a brunette said, sniffling. The voice was faintly familiar, and he assumed it was the woman who'd called him.

"Thank you for calling me, considering I don't have the first clue who you are."

She laughed a watery laugh. "Summer Lane. Rose was my very first friend when I moved here. My brother is married to her sister." The woman hugged herself against the cool evening. "We didn't have much to go on, but the sisters told me about you and… She's always… She's always been so strong. I never would've guessed she didn't see that in herself." The woman started crying in earnest.

Jack used the back of his sleeve to wipe away the remnants of his own tears. He'd known. Known and not been able to get through that armor of strength.

She'd broken down now though, and he could only hope, pray with everything he had, that this was her turning point. Her chance to heal.

The man next to him cleared his throat. Jack had met him maybe once before, since Monica lived on the Shaw property, but he hadn't quite put together the knowledge that Caleb Shaw was Rose's sister's husband. Maybe he should have, but Rose had kept him very separate from all this. She had very purposefully kept him far away from her family and her life.

He wished he could work up anger right now, but all he felt was a horrible sadness at all the pain Rose had endured.

"Rose told Delia about you," Caleb said.

"And yet I don't even know who Delia is."

"My wife. The oldest Rogers sister. They've been through hell," Caleb said, his voice raw.

"That I did know."

"Delia told me Rose had mentioned a guy, and Delia thought it would be permanent maybe. Possibly."

"Well, she is carrying my baby," Jack muttered.

"I think the question of whether you love her or not is more important at the moment."

"She doesn't want me to say that." Didn't want love. Was it because she didn't think she deserved love, or because she didn't want it from *him*?

"Yeah, it's not always easy to hear. When you don't think very much of yourself, you don't really want the people you love to love you back," Caleb said gruffly.

Jack thought about the way she'd leaned into him before her sisters had surrounded her. The way she hadn't ever just cut him off or even told him to back off. The *fear* in her eyes when she'd told him over and over it was just pretend.

Why would she be afraid of love unless she thought she didn't deserve it—not that she didn't want it. "I'm not going anywhere," Jack finally responded.

Maybe he could never get through to Rose. Maybe she would never believe the depth of his feelings or how much he believed in her, but he would make that his new mission in life. Rose and loving Rose was his new goal, his new everything. He would pour all he had into it, because love wasn't like being a Navy SEAL or even building a foundation. He could keep failing at it until he decided to stop trying or until he died. No bomb or lack of money could eradicate what he felt.

And he wasn't alone. *She* wasn't alone. There was a small army of people here tonight ready to fight to make sure she stayed, to make sure she understood.

He'd never had to worry if he was loved, if he *deserved* to be loved, and he would do anything and everything to make sure Rose and their baby felt the same from here on out.

—◦◦◦—

Rose didn't know what she felt except emptied out. Her sisters were here. They'd all fallen to their knees, but they were holding her in this little heap on the ground, and somehow it started to fill up that empty feeling, smooth out all those jagged edges that had always existed inside her.

"Don't let him win, Rose," Billie whispered.

"That's my mantra," Elsie said. "Whenever I'm down on myself. When I feel like a failure or nothing is going right, I tell myself he doesn't get to win. I won't let him win."

"Mom always said I was like him," Rose whispered. Hell, if it was confession day, she might as well get them all out. "He'd say it too."

"We are nothing like them. You're ready to sell your bar that you love, leave town, and give your kid the best life you could imagine. You were so very wrong to think that was the answer, but that's not them. They kept us there in that hell and made sure no one could help. You are trying to do all the right things," Delia said.

"I wanted to protect everyone from me. From what I am."

"We know who and what you are, Rose Rogers," Steph said. "You kept us going after Dad kicked Delia out."

"And you were the one who came up with plan to get Dad in jail without risking the rest of us," Elsie added.

"You helped Caleb get me out of jail," Delia said. "You've always been the bravest out of all of us."

Rose started sobbing anew with that one. She didn't know how to believe or accept what her sisters were telling her. It was the opposite of everything she'd told herself for so long, and yet it was their truth. How they'd seen things.

"If you hate yourself, he wins. Mom wins. If you don't believe you can overcome the little they gave us in order to be an amazing mother, they win. Now, if it's that you don't want to be a mother, that's one thing." Delia squeezed her arm. "If you think you *can't*, I know you're wrong. I've seen you with Sunny and Lissa and Kate. Those girls all adore you, and you're good and kind and patient with them. You are capable of so much more than you're giving yourself credit for. You're letting them warp you, but I won't let them. I won't let you. You are good and brave and strong. No one's supposed to be perfect, Rose. Not a one of us is. We get to choose who we want to be though. We make choices every day, good and bad, right and wrong."

"And if you don't believe you are one of the best sisters in the world, then they've won too. When I think work is too hard, I think about all you've built. All you did," Billie said.

"I want to be just like you," Steph added. "The way you and Delia have chosen to stay here in Blue Valley and face our past every day. That's true strength."

Rose looked around at all her sisters, and as much as that horrible voice inside her head whispered she was just like Dad and Mom, she remembered Vivian sitting in her bar saying Rose could be better if she simply chose it.

With her sisters surrounding her, reminding her, she thought maybe…maybe she could. They thought she was strong, but Delia was all heart and grit, and Elsie was so smart, Billie good and kind, and Steph was so vibrant. They all had these wonderful things about themselves, and mostly she wanted to be like all of them. Bundle it up and find a way to be good. For them.

"I started seeing a psychiatrist," Elsie said, looking at the ground. "I was having nightmares. I couldn't sleep, and I have these panic attacks. I was about to lose my job, and my boss suggested I see a professional. It helped. It really did."

"I got in a fight with my roommate, and we had to go meet with a counselor," Steph muttered. "Somehow it turned into talking about Dad. I'm going to keep talking to her. I still feel jumbled up, but it feels like a good step."

Rose thought about Jack and his talking—not just to a therapist, but to everyone. He was this strong, proud former Navy SEAL, and he went and saw a therapist without embarrassment, without worrying that it would somehow make him less.

There was nothing less about Jack Armstrong. She looked over at him standing next to Caleb, looking determined. Oh so very determined.

"He's hot," Steph said, earning her a laugh from a couple of the sisters.

"Agreed," Billie added. "Super hot."

"He was a Navy SEAL," Rose managed to croak out. "Get out!"

"No, he really was. Scars and everything."

"I'm in love," Steph breathed.

"I think the question is, is *Rose* in love?" Delia murmured.

Rose nodded. "Yeah, I am. He's so good," she whispered. "Upstanding and decent, and he comes from this totally normal family." She swallowed against all the *you are not good enough for him* feelings. "Well, aside from his brother sleeping with his fiancée when Jack was deployed."

That comment earned a lot of screeching indignation from her sisters, and even more of that empty feeling inside Rose filled up.

"Believe it or not, love isn't only giving the best of yourself to someone," Delia said, her eyes on her husband. "It's trusting them with your whole self. It's being a team. Sometimes it's really hard, and you don't put your best foot forward, and they don't put theirs forward either, but you're a unit.

"You love each other, and you love your kids, and you want what's best for everyone, and sometimes you fail spectacularly, but you help each other up and dust each other off and try again. The only thing running away does is hurt everyone. You. Us. Him. Everyone. It's not the great sacrifice you've made it in your head. It's just wrong."

"I just… I'm afraid." Which was very hard to admit for a girl who'd learned to hide her fears since she could remember. "I don't want him to love me if I don't deserve it. I don't want to mess up our kid."

"We all worry we'll mess up our kids," Delia said gently. "And I think we all worry at times that we're not enough for the people we love. But…you know when Sunny was born, I was convinced I'd do it all wrong. I think Caleb and I were both convinced of that. But we held each other's hands, and we talked. To each other. To Dan and Mel. To Summer and Thack. We had all these people who wanted us to succeed. And you have so many people who want that for you."

"But—"

"No, you don't get any buts right now," Delia said firmly. "You're part of this. This family stitched together from all these disparate pieces. You don't have a choice. You're ours. Everyone here loves you, including that Navy SEAL over there, and love makes us better. Makes us stronger. We'll never be perfect, but when you're willing to open up and give and receive it, you get to the hard times, and someone holds your hand. And you get to celebrate the good times with all this *love*. That's the point of love—it's the point of family. Get each other through. Celebrate when you can. Hold each other up, and then let us hold you up when you're falling."

"Don't run away from us, Rose. Please. We're finally getting to the good stuff," Steph said, leaning her head against Rose's shoulder.

Maybe Rose was weak or maybe she was just very well loved, because she didn't want to run away anymore. She wanted all those things Delia had described. She wanted to be stronger and more whole. She wanted her sisters around her when things were awful, and she wanted Jack holding her hand. She wanted to celebrate with all of them, over and over again.

"I won't go anywhere," she said on a shaky exhale. "Not without talking to all of you first. I promise," she said more firmly.

"Thank God," Delia said. "Now can we stand? I think I'm about to hurl."

They all got to their feet, a tangle of arms and tears.

"For the record," Delia said, glancing at Jack, "Summer made the phone call to Jack, not any of us."

"Well, as Summer didn't know Jack existed, you had *something* to do with it."

"I may have spilled the Jack beans. I may have thought her plan to call him was a good one." Delia smiled and pulled her into a hug. "If you thought I was nosy before, I am going to be such a hard-ass on you now. Anytime I think you're even a little bit mopey, I'm camping myself out at your door or sending someone to do it for me."

"Okay," Rose said, holding on tight.

Delia pulled away and looked her in the eye. "I expect the same from you. Deal?"

"Deal." Rose tried to blink back even more tears, but apparently it was just a night for uninterrupted crying. "I'm sorry."

"For what?"

"All of this. All of before. I feel like you've been cleaning up after me through a million bad decisions."

"Think about the good decisions, because you've made a hell of a lot of good ones." Delia smiled, looking back at Caleb, Jack, Summer, and Dan. "I'll get everyone out of here, and you patch things up with your Navy SEAL."

Rose bit her lip and looked at Jack. "I don't know how."

"Start with love." Delia gave her one last squeeze, and then everyone was dispersing, climbing into trucks and driving away.

Then it was just her and Jack, and she had to somehow make up for all this.

"Well, I didn't punch any of your brothers-in-law, so I'm still a step ahead of you in the family drama department," he said in some faraway voice she couldn't read.

"I think you'll probably always win that." Somehow they were standing in front of this house that, in her brain, had become theirs, the pond where she'd maybe fallen a little bit in love with him. This place that had been so important from the start.

And she didn't know what to say, but she should have known Jack would.

He reached out and touched her cheek. "I love you, Rose. I'm pissed you were planning on leaving without telling me, but my God, I love you so much. I was trying to give you space and not tell you, but that's over now. Every day, every second, I want you to know how much I love you."

"I'm probably going to need the reminder," she managed to whisper.

"Your sisters convince you to stay?"

She took a deep breath and stepped into him, let herself lean against him, rely on him to hold her up. "All of you convinced me to stay."

His arms wrapped around her, strong and sure. And he loved her, this wonderful man.

"I am afraid of you, because I don't think I deserve this."

"I know a really great therapist you can talk to about that."

She managed a watery laugh. "I'm going to need one, I think." She looked up at him. Her sisters thought she was strong. Brave. She knew he thought she was too, so maybe she could be.

"I don't need one for this though. I love you, Jack. I love you so much, and that scares me. I am not promising that this is going to be easy in any way, shape, or form, because I have a lot of work to do. But I love you, and I want to raise this baby *with* you."

"Are you proposing?"

"No. Not yet. I need to put some time in on myself, but…we're in this together, right? You and me. A team."

"I like the sound of that," he said, cupping her face with his big, rough hands. He glanced at the house behind her. "We should live here, don't you think?"

She looked back at the dilapidated house bathed in moonlight. "It's a shit hole, Jack."

"We'll fix that right up. We've got, what? Almost nine months?"

"I think it'll take a miracle."

Jack looked down at her. "I think I believe in miracles now. What about you?"

She swallowed. "Maybe I do," she whispered. Jack Armstrong was a miracle. This baby was a miracle. And the fact that Rose Rogers had survived and come out on the other side to be here, right here, with the man she loved?

Yeah, that was definitely a miracle.

Epilogue

Three Months Later

JACK FROWNED AT THE CLOUDS ABOVE THE HOUSE. Snow was threatening, and once the snow started, getting the house done was going to be more and more of a challenge.

He wanted it livable for him and Rose by Christmas, livable for Baby by the time he or she made an appearance in the spring. Gabe and Alex seemed dubious, but they'd been working as much as they could on it. Becca had even suggested they push back taking veteran applications and formally opening Revival until next year, so she and Alex could have their Christmas wedding, and Jack and Rose could have their Christmas move-in.

Everyone had agreed. It seemed right somehow to get settled in their own lives, so that, when Revival officially opened, all their focus could be poured into the foundation.

Gabe stomped out of the house, grumbling about something. Rose followed, grinning.

"Your woman is driving me crazy, Jack," Gabe yelled.

"Good," Jack called back. "You work extra hard when you're driven crazy."

Gabe muttered something, probably swearing. "I'm going to the ranch to grab lunch and check on the horses.

Alex is coming out this afternoon to see if he can fix the plumbing issue, because I can't figure the thing out. You may have to pay a plumber."

Jack nodded as Gabe climbed in his truck. "Thanks."

Gabe flipped him off and drove away as Rose came to stand next to Jack.

He placed his hand over the slight rounding of Rose's stomach. No one could tell yet, not with her heavy coat on, but he saw it every morning. It wasn't much, but actually starting to see the change in her was amazing, made it feel more real somehow that they'd created a life together.

"I know what I want for Christmas," she said, surveying the house and the snowflakes that were beginning to fall.

"Christmas is two months away," Jack returned, pulling the hood on her coat up over her head.

"Do you want to know what it is or not?"

"Okay."

She kept her eyes on the house, but her mouth curved in that sharp smile he'd never have enough of. "An engagement ring."

He glanced down at her smug face. "You're telling me when to propose?"

"Yes. I'll let you pick out the ring though."

"How generous of you," he replied dryly even as he smiled. *Finally*. Two months seemed like an eternity, but a little less of an eternity than he'd been certain he'd have to wait.

"We don't want to steal any of Alex and Becca's wedding thunder, but Delia's due in February, so I can't steal baby thunder. I want a ring on my finger before our baby comes. So Christmas seems like a good in-between time."

"I'll mark it in my calendar, Queen Rose. And when, pray tell, will we be actually getting married?"

"Summer," she said firmly. "Right in front of the pond. Maybe at night."

He slid his arm around her shoulder, pulling her close. "Hard to argue with that. No naked swimming though."

"Hey, we weren't totally naked."

"Fully clothed weddings only," he said firmly.

When she tipped her head up to look at him, she was grinning. This beautiful woman, a partner in life, impending parenthood, love.

"I love you," he murmured, because he had kept his word. He said it to her multiple times a day. Over and over again, and even though she'd settled into it, he *liked* saying it.

"I know," she returned smugly, but she reached out a gloved hand and rubbed it over his beard. "I love you too."

"You're not talking to the beard, are you?"

"Not in this particular moment," she replied faux seriously.

He leaned down to kiss her, but she pushed her hand to his chest. "Gabe should meet somebody before we get engaged," she said, frowning. "I don't want him to feel lonely or left out."

"Finding Gabe anyone is going to take a Christmas miracle."

Rose smiled up at him. "We believe in those, remember?"

"Yes, we do," he murmured, and he pressed his mouth to hers as the snow fell down around them.

Maybe there were more miracles ahead.

Please enjoy this sneak peek of
Caught Up in a Cowboy *by Jennie Marts*

THIS COWBOY PLAYS TO WIN

Rockford James was raised as a tried-and-true cowboy in a town crazy about ice hockey. Rock is as hot on the ice as he is on a horse, and the NHL snapped him up. Now, injuries have temporarily benched him. Body and pride wounded, he returns to his hometown ranch to find that a lot has changed. The one thing that hasn't? His feelings for Quinn, his high school sweetheart and girl next door.

Quinn Rivers had no choice but to get over Rock after he left. Teenaged and heartbroken, she had a rebound one-night stand that ended in single motherhood. Now that Rock's back—and clamoring for a second chance—Quinn will do anything to avoid getting caught up in this oh-so-tempting cowboy...

Chapter 1

BITS OF GRAVEL FLEW BEHIND THE TIRES OF THE convertible, and Rockford James swore as he turned onto the dirt road leading to the Triple J Ranch. Normally, he enjoyed coming home for a visit, especially in the late spring when everything was turning green and the wildflowers were in bloom, but not this spring—not when he was coming home with both his pride and his body badly injured.

His spirits lifted and the corners of his mouth tugged up in a grin as he drew even with what appeared to be a pirate riding a child's bicycle along the shoulder of the road. A gorgeous female pirate—one with long blond hair and great legs.

Legs he recognized.

Legs that belonged to the only woman who had ever stolen his heart.

Nine years ago, Quinn Rivers had given him her heart as well. Too bad he'd broken it. Not exactly broken— more like smashed, crushed, and shattered it into a million tiny pieces. According to her anyway.

He slowed the car, calling out as he drew alongside her. Her outfit consisted of a flimsy little top that bared her shoulders under a snug corset vest and a short, frilly striped skirt. She wore some kind of sheer white knee socks, and one of them had fallen and pooled loosely around her ankle. "Ahoy there, matey. You lose your ship?"

Keeping her eyes focused on the road, she stuck out her hand and offered him a gesture unbecoming of a lady—pirate or otherwise. Then her feet stilled on the pedals as she must have registered his voice. "Ho-ly crap. You have got to be freaking kidding me."

Bracing her feet on the ground, she turned her head, brown eyes flashing with anger. "And here I thought my day couldn't get any worse. What the hell are you doing here, Rock?"

He stopped the car next to her, then draped his arm over the steering wheel, trying to appear cool. Even though his heart pounded against his chest from the fact that he was seeing her again. She had this way of getting under his skin; she was just so damn beautiful. Even wearing a pirate outfit. "Hey, now. Is that any way to speak to an old friend?"

"I don't know. I'll let you know when I run into one."

Ouch. He'd hoped she wasn't still that bitter about their breakup. They'd been kids, barely out of high school. But they'd been together since they were fourteen, his conscience reminded him, and they'd made plans to spend their future together.

But that was before he got the full-ride scholarship and the NHL started scouting him.

And he had tried.

Yeah, keep telling yourself that, buddy.

Okay, he probably hadn't tried hard enough. But he'd been young and dumb and swept up in the fever and glory of finally having his dreams of pursuing a professional hockey career coming true.

With that glory came attention and fame and lots of

travel with the team where cute puck bunnies were ready and willing to show their favorite players a good time.

He hadn't cheated on Quinn, but he came home less often and didn't make the time for texts and calls. He'd gone to college first while she finished her senior year, and by the time he did come home the next summer, he'd felt like he'd outgrown their relationship, and her, and had suggested they take a mini break.

Which turned into an *actual* break, of both their relationship and Quinn's heart.

But it had been almost nine years since he'd left; they'd been kids, and that kind of stuff happened all the time. Since then, he hadn't made it home a lot and had run into her only a handful of times. In fact, he probably hadn't seen her in over a year.

But he'd thought of her. Often. And repeatedly wondered if he'd made the right choice by picking the fame and celebrity of his career and letting go of her.

Sometimes, those summer days spent with Quinn seemed like yesterday, but really, so much had happened—in both of their lives—that it felt like a lifetime ago.

Surely she'd softened a little toward him in all that time. "Let me offer you a lift." The dirt road they were on led to both of their families' neighboring ranches.

"No thanks. I'd rather pedal this bike until the moon comes up than take a ride from you."

Yep. Still mad, all right.

Nothing he could do if she wanted to keep the grudge fest going. Except he was tired of the grudge. Tired of them being enemies. She'd been the best friend he'd ever had. And right now, he felt like he could use a friend.

His pride had already been wounded; what was one more hit? At least he could say he tried.

Although he didn't want it to seem like he was trying too hard. He did still have a *little* pride left, damn it.

"Okay. Suit yourself. It's not *that* hot out here." He squinted up at the bright Colorado sun, then eased off the brake, letting the car coast forward.

"Wait." She shifted from one booted foot to the other, the plastic pirate sword bouncing against her curvy hip. "Fine. I'll take a ride. But only because I'm desperate."

"You? Desperate? I doubt it," he said with a chuckle. Putting the car in Park, he left the engine running and made his way around the back of the car. He reached for the bike, but she was already fitting it into the back seat of the convertible.

"I've got it." Her gaze traveled along the length of his body, coming to rest on his face, and her expression softened for the first time. "I heard about the fight and your injury."

He froze, heat rushing to his cheeks and anger building in his gut. Of course she'd heard about the fight. It had made the nightly news, for Pete's sake. He was sure the whole town of Creedence had heard about it.

Nothing flowed faster than a good piece of gossip in a small town. Especially when it's bad news—or news about the fall of the hometown hero. Or the guy who thought he was better than everyone else and bigger than his small-town roots, depending on who you talked to and which camp they fell into. Or what day of the week it was.

You could always count on a small town to be loyal. Until you let them down.

"I'm fine," he said, probably a little too sternly, as he opened the car door, giving her room to pass him and slide into the passenger seat. He sucked in a breath as the scent of her perfume swept over him.

She smelled the same—a mix of vanilla, honeysuckle, and home.

He didn't let himself wonder if she felt the same. No, he'd blown his chances of that ever happening again a long time ago. Still, he couldn't help but drop his gaze to her long, tanned legs or notice the way her breasts spilled over the snug, corseted vest of the pirate costume.

"So, what's with the outfit?" he asked as he slid into the driver's seat and put the car in gear.

She blew out her breath in an exaggerated sigh. A loose tendril of hair clung to her damp forehead, and he was tempted to reach across the seat to brush it back.

"It's Max's birthday today," she said, as if that explained everything.

He didn't say anything—didn't know what to say.

The subject of Max always was a bit of an awkward one between them. After he'd left, he'd heard the rumors of how Quinn had hooked up with a hick loser named Monty Hill who'd lived one town over. She'd met him at a party and it had been a rebound one-night stand, designed to make him pay for breaking things off with her, if the gossip was true.

But she'd been the one to pay. Her impulse retaliation had ended in an unplanned pregnancy with another jerk who couldn't be counted on to stick around for her. Hill had taken off, and Quinn had ended up staying at her family's ranch.

"He's eight now." Her voice held the steely tone of anger, but he heard the hint of pride that also crept in.

"I know," he mumbled, more to himself than to her. "So, you decided to dress up like a pirate for his birthday?"

She snorted. "No. Of course not. One of Max's favorite books is *Treasure Island*, and he wanted a pirate-themed party, so I *hired* a party company to send out a couple of actors to dress up like pirates. The outfits showed up this morning, but the actors didn't. Evidently, there was a mix-up in the office, and the couple had been double-booked and were already en route to Denver when I called."

"So you decided to fill in." He tried to hold back his grin.

She shrugged. "What else was I going to do?"

"That doesn't explain the bike."

"The bike is his main gift. I ordered it from the hardware store in town, but it was late and we weren't expecting it to come in today. They called about an hour ago and said it had shown up, but they didn't have anyone to deliver it. I was already in the pirate getup, so I ran into town to get it."

"And decided to ride it home?"

"Yes, smart-ass. I thought it would be fun to squeeze onto a tiny bike dressed in a cheap Halloween costume and enjoy the bright, sunny day by riding home." She blew out another exasperated breath. "My stupid car broke down on the main road."

"Why didn't you call Ham or Logan to come pick you up?" he asked, referring to her dad and her older brother.

"Because in my flustered state of panic about having to fill in as the pirate princess and the fear that the party would be ruined, I left my phone on the dresser when I ran out of the house. I was carrying the dang bike, but it got so heavy, then I tried pushing it, and that was killing my back, so I thought it would be easier and faster if I just tried to ride it the last mile back to the ranch."

"Makes sense to me." He slowed the car, turning into the long driveway of Rivers Gulch. White fences lined the drive, and several head of cattle grazed on the fresh green grass of the pastures along either side of the road.

The scent of recently mown hay skimmed the air, mixed with the familiar smells of plowed earth and cattle.

Seeing the sprawling ranch house and the long, white barn settled something inside of him, and he let out a slow breath, helping to ease the tension in his neck. He'd practically grown up here, running around this place with Quinn and her brother, Logan.

Their families' ranches were within spitting distance of each other; in fact, he could see the farmhouse of the Triple J across the pasture to his left. They were separated only by prime grazing land and the pond that he'd learned to swim in during the summer and skate on in the winter.

The two families had an ongoing feud—although he wasn't sure any of them really knew what they were fighting about anymore, and the kids had never cared much about it anyway.

The adults liked to bring it up, but they were the only kids around for miles, and they'd become fast friends—he and his brothers sneaking over to Rivers Gulch as often as they could.

This place felt just as much like home as his own did.

He'd missed it. In the years since he'd left, he'd been back only a handful of times.

His life had become so busy, his hockey career taking up most of his time. And after what happened with Quinn, neither Ham nor Logan was ever too excited to see him. Her mom had died when she was in grade school, and both men had always been overprotective of her.

He snuck a glance at her as he drove past the barn. Her wavy hair was pulled back in a ponytail, but wisps of it had come loose and fallen across her neck in little curls. She looked good—really good. A thick chunk of regret settled in his gut, and he knew letting her go had been the biggest mistake of his life.

It wasn't the first time he'd thought it. Images of Quinn haunted his dreams, and he often wondered what it would be like now if only he'd brought her with him instead of leaving her behind. If he had her to wave to in the stands at his games or to come home to at night instead of an empty house. But he'd screwed that up, and he felt the remorse every time he returned to Rivers Gulch.

He'd been young and arrogant—thought he had the world by the tail. Scouts had come sniffing around when he was in high school, inflating his head and his own self-importance. And once he started playing in the big leagues, everything about this small town—including Quinn—had just seemed...well...small. Too small for a big shot like him.

He was just a kid—and an idiot. But by the time he'd realized his mistake and come back for her, it was too late.

Hindsight was a mother.

And so was Quinn.

Easing the car in front of the house, he took in the

festive balloons and streamers tied to the railings along the porch. So much of the house looked the same—the long porch that ran the length of the house, the wooden rocking chairs, and the swing hanging from the end.

They'd spent a lot of time on that swing, talking and laughing, his arm around her as his foot slowly pushed them back and forth.

She opened the car door, but he put a hand on her arm and offered her one of his most charming smiles. "It's good to see you, Quinn. You look great. Even in a pirate outfit."

Her eyes widened, and she blinked at him, for once not having a sarcastic reply. He watched her throat shift as she swallowed, and he yearned to reach out to run his fingers along her slender neck.

"Well, thanks for the lift." She turned away and stepped out of the car.

Pushing open his door, he got out and reached for the bicycle, lifting it out of the back seat before she had a chance. He carried it around and set it on the ground in front of her. "I'd like to meet him. You know, Max. If that's okay."

"You would?" Her voice was soft, almost hopeful, but still held a note of suspicion. "Why?"

He ran a hand through his hair and let out a sigh. He'd been rehearsing what he was going to say as they drove up to the ranch, but now his mouth had gone dry. The collar of his cotton T-shirt clung to his neck, and he didn't know what to do with his hands.

Dang. He hadn't had sweaty palms since he was in high school. He wiped them on his jeans. He was known for his charm and usually had a way with women, but not this woman. This one had him tongue-tied and nervous as a teenager.

He shoved his hands in his pockets. "Listen, Quinn. I know I screwed up. I was young and stupid and a damn fool. And I'm sorrier than I could ever say. But I can't go back and fix it. All I can do is move forward. I miss this place. I miss having you in my life. I'd like to at least be your friend."

She opened her mouth, and he steeled himself for her to tell him to go jump in the lake. Or worse. But she didn't. She looked up at him, her eyes searching his face, as if trying to decide if he was serious. "Why now? After all these years?"

He shrugged, his gaze drifting as he stared off at the distant green pastures. He'd let this go on too long, let the hurt fester. It was time to make amends—to at least try. He looked back at her, trying to express his sincerity. "Why not? Isn't it about time?"

She swallowed again and gave a small nod of her head.

A tiny flicker of hope lit in his gut as he waited for her response. He could practically *see* her thinking—watch the emotions cross her face in the furrow of her brow and the way she chewed on her bottom lip. Oh man, he loved it when she did that; the way she sucked her bottom lip under her front teeth always did crazy things to his insides.

"Okay. We can *try* being friends." She gave him a sidelong glance, the hint of a smile tugging at the corner of her mouth. "On one condition."

Uh-oh. Conditions are never good. Although he would do just about anything to prove to her that he was serious about being in her life again.

"What's that?"

"I need someone to be the other pirate for the party. I already asked Logan if he would wear the other costume, and he refused. I was planning to ask Dad, but I have a feeling I'll get the same response."

He tried to imagine Hamilton Rivers in a pirate outfit and couldn't. Ham was old-school cowboy, tough as nails and loyal to the land. He wore his boots from sunup to sundown and had more grit than a sheet of sandpaper. The only soft spot he had was for his daughter. And Rock had broken her heart.

If there hadn't been enough animosity between the two families over their land before, Rock had sealed the feud by walking away from Quinn.

And now he had a chance to try to make it up to her. And to keep an eight-year-old kid from being disappointed. Even if it meant making a fool of himself.

He squinted one eye closed and tilted his head. If he was going to do it, might as well do it right.

Go big or go home.

"Aye, lass," he said in his best gruff pirate impression. "I'll be a pirate for ye, but don't cross me, or I'll make ye walk the plank."

Her eyes widened, and she laughed before she could stop herself. An actual laugh. Well, more like a small chuckle, but it was worth it. He'd talk in a pirate accent all afternoon if it meant he could hear her laugh again.

She took a step forward, reached out her hand as if to touch his arm, then let it drop to her side. "All right, Captain Jack, you don't have to go that far." She might not have touched him, but she offered him a grin—a true grin.

Yeah, he could be a pirate. He could be whatever she needed. Or he could dang well try.

The front door slammed open with a bang, and Quinn jumped. As if on cue, her brother stepped out on the front porch.

Anger sparked in Logan's eyes as he glared at Rock. "What the hell are you doing here?"

Acknowledgments

Writing a book is an internal, solitary thing, but surviving writing a book comes through external supports. Maisey and Megan, I'm so lucky to have you in my corner, listening to my complaints, reading my words, and supporting my voice and vision every step of the way. My husband, who is forever thrusting my books upon every innocent bystander while being listener of rants extraordinaire, who always knows right when to land a joke and remind me to laugh. My mom and especially my in-laws, who are always ready to swoop in and take the kids to give me a working weekend. It would be impossible without all of you. To the Sourcebooks team, who does the work of turning my words into a tangible *book* and creating these gorgeous covers. Thank you.

About the Author

Nicole Helm is the bestselling author of down-to-earth Western romance and fast-paced romantic suspense. She lives with her husband and two sons in Missouri and spends her free time dreaming about someday owning a barn. You can find more information about her books on her website: nicolehelm.com.

Navy SEAL Cowboys

Three former Navy SEALs, injured in the line of duty, desperate for a new beginning... searching for a place to call their own.

By Nicole Helm

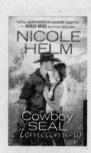

Cowboy SEAL Homecoming

When a tragic accident sends Alex Maguire home, he's not sure what to make of the innocently beguiling woman who lives there. He'll need to keep his distance, but something in Becca Denton's big green eyes makes Alex want to set aside the mantle of the perfect soldier and discover the man he could have been...

Cowboy SEAL Redemption

Jack Armstrong figured he'd never recover the pieces of his shattered life, but when he and local bad girl Rose Rogers pretend to be in love to throw his meddling family off his trail, he discovers hope in the most unlikely of places...

Cowboy SEAL Christmas

Gabe Cortez doesn't need to talk about his feelings, thank you very much. But when the ranch's therapist, Monica Finley, tempts him with all the holiday charm she can muster, it's hard to resist cozying up to her for Christmas.

For more Nicole Helm, visit:

sourcebooks.com

Also by Nicole Helm